DEATH
WISHING

DEATH WISHING

LAURA ELLEN SCOTT

PUBLISHING

BROOKLYN, NEW YORK

Printed in the United States of America
10 9 8 7 6 5 4 3 2 1

Ig Publishing
392 Clinton Avenue
Brooklyn, NY 11238
www.igpub.com

Library of Congress Cataloging-in-Publication Data

Scott, Laura Ellen.
 Death wishing / by Laura Ellen Scott.
    p. cm.
 ISBN 978-1-935439-39-4
 1. Wishes--Fiction. 2. New Orleans (La.)--Fiction. I. Title.
 PS3619.C675D43 2011
 813'.6--dc23
                          2011030932

For Dean, Mom, and anyone who ever missed New Orleans.

CATS

1.

The night that cats were wished away was a hard one full of wine, tears, and spectacle. Even those of us who were indifferent to feline companionship felt heartbroken for those who weren't, and together our humid, grieving silence was more tangible than the awe-filled silence that followed the disappearance of cancer. We were united by that particular loss. Despite the media promise that Japanese scientists were hard at work trying to re-engineer the common house cat, my beautiful neighbor Pebbles had lost her faith, burning all of her leopard spotted, tiger striped panties and bras in a small, neat fire out on the banquette in front of our building on Esplanade.

The flame-crumpled rayon impressed me enough that I drained a bottle of cabernet in tribute. We lived in a jazz/pot community on the fringe of the French Quarter called Faubourg Marigny where I worked in my son's vintage clothing shop as a cape and corset cleaner. Thus, my interest in her underthings was mostly professional.

Miss Pebbles stood over the ashes of her underwear and cried, and my respect for the phenomenon of Death Wishing deepened. They say Wishing started when some Army PR flak declared on his deathbed that there were alien bodies at Roswell back in '47. "Hunnerds of them," he swore. There weren't any aliens, of course. But the man said his piece and expired, and then all of a sudden there were. Rows and rows of the dusty bastards, stacked up on shelves in a shed in the desert. This occurred a couple of years ago.

Pebbles' panty fire had melted already. She deserved better—antique lace, satin, velvet trim. Especially if she was going to burn the stuff. She made me crazy with her red hair and baby fat, and the way she smelled like *Lisa*, the hand soap they put in Quarter hotels. But I was far too old and fat for her. Hell, my son was too old for her too, but I held the minority opinion on that.

She sniffled in my direction. I maintained a respectful distance. "Is Val coming out?" she asked.

It's two for flinching, so I didn't. "I think he has a date."

It no longer burned me that she had a thing for my son Val. I was quite comfortable dividing my fantasy from reality, and to a certain degree I preferred my love life to be all my own, compartmentalized, unrequited, and unspoiled. I had been married long enough, then divorced long enough, to appreciate the benefits of a purely invented reality. But human invention has its limits.

Upon dissection, we learned that every detail of alien physiognomy had already been imagined by scientists, artists, writers, etc. It was all very exciting, but ultimately there was nothing to be learned from hundreds of copies of an all too generalized ideal. The aliens didn't come from anywhere, and they couldn't tell us anything we didn't already know. They were the perfect ambassadors of our limits.

"There he is," said Pebbles, sounding brighter, breaking my heart again. My son had rounded the corner, deepening his lazy stride once he spotted us. All Pebbles could see was the swinging black hair, scuffed boots, stained T-shirt and jeans— he went for that semi-retired rock star look. All I could see was how much he looked like his mother, Brenda. She and I lived a thousand miles away from each other, but Val was her easy surrogate.

He smiled, approached slowly, then gathered Pebbles into his arms and encouraged her to "Let it all out, sugar." No respectful distance there. I despaired and left them to it.

More wine was needed. I threaded my way towards Chartres, and stayed off Decatur where most folks were milling about, zombied by sadness. It was a sharp night made acrid from little saucers of untouched meat and milk left on stoops. Hopeful. Desperate. Maybe they'd come back. Cats always seemed very European to me, flourishing as they did in decrepit, ancient spaces as long as the food kept coming.

Little bowls of ground fish. Water pans with specks floating on top. I'd taken the route to avoid humanity, but this was worse. Miss Polly's sandwich hut sagged in the corner of a parking lot on Barracks Street, looking like an outhouse. Of course it was closed, but I had a bad feeling it might never open again. Miss Polly owned five cats, all of the matted hair, diseased eye variety. That's five we knew of. Having emigrated from the Ukraine sometime back in the sixties, she gave off a pungent and lonely paranoia that made her an ideal candidate for cat hoarding.

The echo and rattle of the night. Doors and trash bins slamming, high heeled clatter on the bricks, and then the two note cry of a woman as she called out: "Loooo-Laaahh."

I did not know Lola, but I worried for her all the same.

And suddenly I no longer wanted to be alone. I took a turn towards the water, the music, the lights. The all night sad party. I knew I was close when a Hummer came squalling around the corner with fog cutter headlights, music booming, and what looked like about fifteen laughing passengers crammed inside. Well, at least some folks were managing their grief. The vehicle screamed towards I-10. The driver was probably lost, but

I don't think he cared. When we get traffic, it's always madness on wheels. As that music faded, more routine down river noise returned. Music from competing locations spilled out into the humid night and combined into arrhythmic bird sounds, an appropriate affect given that few pre-Katrina bands were still intact. The players who returned and the ones who never left reassembled themselves into all-star collectives, and a lot of seventeen year-old ingénues found themselves filling in at legendary venues. Latin music was getting big, Latin players even bigger. Interesting times. Opportunity and broken dreams go hand in hand.

The world was vulnerable. Some argued that it was always so, that reality had always been subject to the whims of a select few. But that was s a political point, and useless. My worry was that imagination seemed so small and mean, sometimes.

A bit of background: Well before his impeachment, the President managed to usher in The Language Act. The Act was an efficiently administered piece of legislation, hastened by the bewilderment caused when cancer disappeared. Imagine being one of those poor souls who continued in poisonous treatment even after the disease was vanquished. Imagine being one of those joyous souls diagnosed but saved at the eleventh hour by a force of un-nature. Something had to be done to blunt these experiences.

The Language Act was a perfect law, all tongue and no teeth, because its violators were virtually undetectable and literally unpunishable. Hence, no measurable failure rate. Because to commit an offense against The Language Act was to speak imperfectly before certain death. The Language Act was direct. *Resolved: A dying wish must be expressed in simple, concrete terms. No wish may be issued with the intent to harm persons or institutions*. Helpfully, the government produced a pamphlet of exemplar wishes that were deemed both safe and constructive, such as: *I wish that the Atlantic cod stocks of the Grand Banks would double in yield*, or *I wish that this year's Trick or Treating is safe and fun for all children*.

Wishes against famine, disease, and war were omitted from the recommended list, and terms like *eco-sensitive* and *e.c.* or *eco-correct* began to pop up in speeches made by politicians and celebrities. "Eco" as a prefix no longer referred to *ecology* reliably, having now been hijacked by *economy*, and the two ecos were left struggling for the top bunk of popular concern. There was a campaign for Death Wishers to be responsible to corporate vulnerabilities as they crafted their final words. Broad stroke wishes might be well meant, but they were highly dangerous according to the administrative talking points. "Broad Strokes" became the new White House catchphrase, and at one especially delirious Veteran's Day speech, the President addressed a military academy to warn us all against "Broad Strokes with the Cat's Paw"—he should have said "monkey's paw," if he was referring to the old story about wishes gone wrong, but we knew what he meant.

No one took The Language Act to heart, especially since very few Death Wishes came true, and the successful wishes tended toward eccentric rather than calamitous change. We appreciated the return of the American Chestnut (when we finally noticed), but what the hell was a song bison for? Happily, the rumor of Bigfoot encampments turned out to be an internet prank. And at one point a very well meaning, but unclever lady died wishing "Everyone should have a thousand dollars."

And we did. But that's all we had. The thirteen thousand in my savings account vaporized, but I had ten one-hundred dollar bills in my wallet. Bums on Camp Street had the same, as did Donald Trump, every inmate in Angola, every baby in an incubator, and all the pygmies in the rainforest for all I knew.

I remembered the look on Val's face as he showed me his bulging wallet. "It's one of those wish things."

"Yes." By that time we'd learned, in the short span of the wishing thus far, not to get too excited by them. We strive for grace in our emotions.

"Is it fucked up then."

"Undoubtedly," I said. "According to the news, it's gone all cat's paw."

We then witnessed an extraordinary stretch of global silence during which the world learned what had happened and mulled the possible outcomes of a uniform economic event. Predictably or not, there erupted a burst of violence and trade and Libertarian pornography—like another Katrina, like another Tsunami, but worldwide this time. A lot of outright *taking* occurred, and I could imagine the leaders of the World Bank pulling on giant red levers to close the gates in the financial levees that safeguarded corporate empires. It was the same in certain tribal communities where every citizen was forced to hand over their cash to their head men, and it was a fifty-fifty chance as to whether the leaders would abscond with the dough or burn it in a ritual.

The bottom line being that while everyone had a plan for being suddenly poor, no one had a plan for dealing with a windfall. Luckily or unluckily, the credit industry and the free market prevailed, and within thirty-seven breathtaking days the financial status quo restored itself, for the most part. Like a bad run in the stock market, I was down 10k, but Warren Buffett was back to full power plus some. The rich are rich by nature.

Some areas were devastated, especially in so-called renaissance cities like Pittsburgh and Cleveland, both of which were driven back to their Reagan era second world statuses, but here in New Orleans we let the money, and the lack of it, wash right over us. We're on our own ship down here. We learned that the hard way. These days we've got enough rum and bread stored away to survive the longest of dark journeys.

2.

The cat-less night gave way to a still cat-less dawn, and I woke up a little cobwebbed from my indulgences. I stumbled into the kitchen and found Miss Pebbles seated at our sturdy old table, pulling the stone from a peach and flicking it into the trash while browsing through *Andrew's Hygienic Undergarments*, a men's corset catalog designed to mimic a pamphlet from the 1800s. Corset catalogs are abysmal, with spotty, all too realistic models photographed under high glare. Those thick ankles, raw skin, and *howdy-howdy* smiles are at odds with the dream.

A corset is a mechanical item of clothing that forces one to choose sides, if only because the sheer variety of corset styles and purposes makes one think about the dreaming wearer with tart empathy. Shall I assist young girls in their antebellum fantasies? Shall I enable tight-lacing fetishists? Shall I immobilize a damaged spine? Perhaps because of my own body image issues, I discovered that I felt something special for those men who sought to look more like women. I had no desire to look like or live as a woman, but I was aware that my attention to physical things (bodies, creation, barriers) squished its way through at least one feminine filter before it organized and labeled the world's objects.

But to be more direct about it, I was a man reshaping himself, trying to lose weight in a city where the streets run with clarified butter, red spices, and sweet, sweet oysters. I wanted to use my crafter's skills to assist other men as they reshaped themselves. To that end I had learned new things about old needs and desires.

A hand made garment can be the most perfect thing, as one thoughtful stitch follows another, accumulating into an aria. And opera is an apt metaphor here because that's how it felt as I ascended into grace, pulling hand dyed thread through layers of brocade coutil. So similar to yet more lovely than writing fucking code all day. But that was my old life, dead and buried. Back in Northern Virginia I was the info tech director for a major defense contractor, now defunct and disgraced. These days, I lived with and worked for my son. Not that I minded, but it was strange being the grown-up and not having that matter one tiny bit.

I did like seeing Pebbles in our kitchen, even as I fought off the implications. She looked very fresh in a lemon yellow tank top and plaid men's Bermuda shorts, leaning into our chrome and red Formica dining table that looked more like a 1950s Buick than a piece of kitchen furniture. Our kitchen was large with uneven floors, bright and sticky in the heart of our shabby Creole town home in the Marigny. We could never get that burnt grease and syrup smell to go away. Very different from the pretentious country kitchen of our old home in the suburbs.

I too was wearing shorts—sleeping shorts, and I looked a wreck. I yanked down my giant gray T-shirt and checked my fly. Nothing flopping, good. "Morning," I announced with confidence.

"Mmm, hey," she said brightly. I tried not to notice the glimmer of fruit pulp on her lower lip. The air was fragrant with chicory coffee, fresh brewed. A full pot, what a treat. One of the infrequent benefits of Val's Romeo lifestyle was that some of the ladies he brought home were ambitious. They made coffee, sometimes breakfast. One child was caught organizing our silverware drawer; we never saw her again.

But making coffee was perfectly acceptable. "Val not up yet?" I asked. I poured a cup and slid into the seat across from her. She flipped through the catalog, her modest pink nails making a mockery of every image she encountered.

"You think we slept together," she said. "We didn't."

"It's none of my business."

"He let me sleep on the couch last night. I was all weepy." She looked up at me. Eyes bright and blue. No carnal residue. I took her at her word.

"The coffee is excellent." I slurped to prove it.

She seemed to think this was an odd remark. "Can I come on your walk with you?"

"No." My morning constitutionals were sacred. Then I thought about it. Boom, boom, boom. "Yes," I said.

It was a romantic stroll in a very nineteenth century sense except that instead of picnicking amongst the tomb stones of poets (always an option around these parts) we took a tour of where certain cats once lived and prowled—the orange tom, the tuxedo twins, the half-pint-ever-pregnant tortie—and at one point the girl placed her hand atop my forearm.

It was sad and exciting at the same time. So terribly gothic. The gates surrounding St. Louis Cathedral were locked, protecting perfectly trimmed grass and red stone paths that wound around wild islands of flowers and trees. Normally the gardens would be crawling with cats. And later in the day after the gates were opened, this would be a place where people lay down for a bit of peace and shade—bums, tourists, students, artists, and cats, all shagged out like happy drunks. The sad tremor in Pebbles eyes suggested that she had read some part of my thoughts.

We wandered over to Woldenberg Park, half beckoned by the moan of a Russian barge and the morning-sweet scent of the river. Do other cities have so many oases? Each marvelous sculpture presided over its own wide territory so your heart could rest up before you happened upon the next. Robert Schoen's "Old Man River" being the most arresting of these—seventeen tons of Carrara marble shaped into an eighteen foot male nude rising up out of the shrubs somewhat unexpectedly. The figure is soulful and stylized, not realistic, but the rough square representing his genitalia produces a sense of virility unmatched by known anatomy. This morning his bits were covered though. An enormous drape of white fabric was hitched around the statue's waist, hanging down to where the figure's massive thighs disappeared into its marble pedestal. A middle aged woman in walking shorts, sun visor, and New Balance sneakers stood at the statue's base, tugging at the edge of the cloth, a bit shy about it, clearly wary that the authorities might swoop down at any moment. The drape slid down some, settling on the hips of the statue, making "Old Man River" look rather rakish and randy, as if he'd just popped out of the shower.

"Should we help her?" Pebbles asked.

"Whatever for?"

"Well she's obviously striking a blow against censorship."

"Do you really think so? My impression was that she was trying to sneak a peek."

"There's not that big a difference," said Pebbles.

I smiled inside. Her careless banter would be fighting words out of a less pretty mouth. "You know what I thought?" I said. "I thought the Old Man was done up as a waiter to promote a food festival or something."

Pebbles laughed. "So that's where your head is at. You need

some breakfast."

We made our way to the Café Du Monde where Pebbles ordered hot, greasy beignets and a pint of whole milk. I ordered more coffee. The powdered sugar fell down her chin and onto her bosom, as is customary, and my heart started to click-click-click; lust and hunger are dangerous companions. Pigeons strutted everywhere, apocalyptic in number. One walked right over my shoe top, a thing that had never happened before. "Away, little bugger," and I sort of soft-booted him into clumsy flight. Pebbles thought that was cute of me. I began to feel unreasonably handsome.

"So," said Pebbles, tugging about fifty little napkins out of the dispenser on our table, "Corsets, huh?" She began scrubbing her fingers free of all traces of sugar. She was done eating, but there was one beignet untouched on her plate. Unbelievable.

I braced for an emasculating interrogation.

She sucked her teeth. "Isn't that really complicated? I mean compared to making capes?"

"And what would be the transitional garment, in your view?"

She shrugged. Cream colored shoulders with freckles. Strawberries and cream. Damn. "Dunno. Belts? Hats? Oh wait—hoods," she said, convinced.

It was early for it, but a "character" waded through a sea of pigeons clogging passage from the Café patio to the steps that lead up to the Moon Walk. Moon Walk was what they called the boardwalk along the river, named for good old Moon Landrieu, the politician credited with revitalizing the city in the seventies. This morning, one of the beneficiaries of that revitalization was already inebriated, all bright and pink in a bass (the fish) covered shirt and wearing an odd round straw hat with a shallow crown. Someone must have told him before he came down south, *get yourself a wide brimmed hat,* and stopping short of buying a sombrero that's just what this fellow did. As I said, he waded through pigeons, making a general nuisance of himself. He shouted to no one in particular, "Satan hates Faggots!"

The disembodied reply was, of course, "So he must hate you!" Not clever, but there you have it.

"Fuck you wearing?" some other voice inquired.

The man insisted, "God loves me!"

"He must!" And this drew some chuckles.

I murmured to Pebbles, "The gentleman's attitude is unexpected."

She agreed. "From a distance, he looks more like the flexible type."

We would normally ignore the behavior of impaired louts, but that round hat distracted me. I could barely keep from staring. And then Pebbles put her finger right on it. "You get those at the craft store," she said. "You know, for centerpieces, dried flowers, that sort of thing? You hang 'em on your door. You're not supposed to wear the damn things."

"Yes, of course, of course. My lord, how does he keep it affixed?"

"Suction of ignorance is my guess."

We were having such a good time. A heavy Vietnamese woman in a smeared white apron and paper hat arrived tableside to collect our payment, and she too had an opinion on our early morning entertainment. "Mmmm-mm," she blew, as we watched that blessed fellow teeter off towards Jackson Square. "I ain' ready for that. Too early inna day." Her accent came straight out of Plaquemines Parish.

Food is too cheap at the Café Du Monde, and leaving a properly calculated tip is embarrassing. I urged Pebbles to leave with me before our server returned with my change. We should have gone back to Esplanade then, but as with all experiences pleasant and complete, it is human nature to extend the moment into something weird and iffy and potentially ruinous. We drifted towards the Cabildo, and as the sun rose to burn off any cool remnant of dawn, the number of joggers, breakfast seekers, and first-minute shoppers increased, all of them plowing their way through pigeons now congregated big time in front of St. Louis Cathedral as if the archbishop himself was fixing to toss out some communion wafers or holy popcorn or whatever.

During our stroll I learned a few things about my lady Pebbles. It seemed she haled from a dry county in Arkansas, a refugee from a two year Christian college through which she visited New Orleans as part of a program to help folks rebuild their homes. It was supposed to be a six week mission, but by the program's conclusion Pebbles hadn't done much of the Lord's work; instead she secured employment and a tiny walk-up on Esplanade. She was currently employed as a barista in an unfamous internet café, and it was her best job so far—she'd tried a little stripping, a little bartending, a little house cleaning, all the conventional service gigs, but pulling coffee meant she worked in a reliably air conditioned environment, and her nights were mostly free. Free for what? Free to sing the blues, of course. While she was waiting for divine inspiration to tell her what she was going to do with the rest of her life (and she did not want to return to college, thank you), she liked to sing at open mic nights. Checkpoint Charlie's mainly.

That settled it. I had to get out more. I told her I'd like to hear her sing some time.

"You sure about that? Because I'm damned awful. I just get up, wiggle around and yell a couple tunes for the folks who are too drunk to go home yet. They're real appreciative, but the musicians pretty much think I suck."

"And you love the blues that much?"

"Not really. But that's what people want to hear from white girls around here. I prefer honky-tonk, like Loretta Lynn when she was doing those 'Fist City' type songs. Those I can sing, but players around here don't like to rock so much."

Normally, if the day is fine, you'll come across a little pick up band installed on the benches in Jackson Square, maybe sharing the territory with a palm reader or a juggler or homeless druggie Bobby Rebar, dancing his fool head off. But we were too early for that, encountering instead a lone tuba player seated on an overturned white plastic bucket. He was an elderly Creole, somewhere between sixty and two hundred years old, and his instrument looked like it had gotten caught in the undercarriage of a runaway bus. He wasn't playing, not just yet, but his lips were poised over the mouthpiece as he eyed passersby, silently and unsuccessfully willing them to gather. You gotta give the people what they want though, so he commenced an unenthusiastic rendition of "When The Saints Go Marching In," one of the few options for solo tuba. Some folks slowed down to listen, but I had the sense he wasn't playing for them so much as he was calling to his tardy brother musicians: *Hey, help me out here!*

Unfortunately, he managed to attract our mad hatter, who sort of planted himself ten yards away, eyes ablaze as if receiving signals that no one else understood. He'd scored himself a refreshment, a large white go-cup full of pink frost, and he sucked on the straw like he needed a brain freeze to shut out the nagging voice of God. I began to worry for the pigeons at his feet.

There was tension between these men. Predator and prey. A bit of nervous fear in the tuba player's eyes.

The hat man sucked hard, as if that plastic straw was his portal to glory, and his face changed colors. He finally let go and gasped a squealing breath, the quality of which captured my attention and that of many others in the square.

Then he was down. I heard a flesh muted crack. An explosion of pigeons opted not to catch his fall in favor of forming an avian cloud to hide the shame of his collapse. But pigeons know how to rid themselves of strong emotion, and in a split second they dispersed, settling just a short hop away from the man's still form. He was face down. At first it appeared as if he were horribly, impossibly injured, but that was because he'd landed on top of his hurricane. The pink, icy ooze squirted an unfortunate trajectory across the bricks from about where his heart was located. It was not gore, obviously, but suggestion can be a powerful thing. Some good soul screamed for our prone lunatic whose head was now entirely obscured by his ludicrous craft store hat.

He moved his arms. Hands tentative as they sought the push up position, and that small sign of life sent a wave of relief among those who had paused to watch. There were six or eight of us, enough for a small concert. No doubt the tuba man was pissed.

When Pebbles touched my arm, I felt emboldened. "Sir," I said firmly.

Two palms to the ground, testing his weight. He groaned.

"Sir, do you need assistance? Should I call for help?"

"Let him sleep it off," someone suggested, and there was agreement from others. Hat Man had made himself popular, all right. I could only imagine that he'd made a full morning out of expressing his charming opinions.

He groaned again, made another move to raise himself. I did not want to touch him. I sort of leaned over, but away so he couldn't catch me with some drunken, round house move. A mule and carriage clopped onto the scene, and the driver paused to scare up custom. "Any y'all want to ride?" He seemed unimpressed by our unwell friend.

The hatter made a forceful move and heaved himself over onto his back.

"Shit," said about four people at once. His nose was smashed, and blood painted a thick, filthy stripe out over his mouth and down his chin and neck, pooling on his shirtfront where the bass no longer appeared indifferent to their situation. The pink libation clashed with the red blood, and it looked as if his torso had been used as a fish cleaning station.

I'm not trained in these matters, but I crouched next to him, and another man joined me. Several onlookers used their cell phones to dial 911, and all I could think was that there didn't seem to be a way to stop the bleeding without pushing *stuff* into his head.

Pebbles dropped some of her unused napkins from the Café down to us—I don't know why she kept them—and the man who knelt with me accepted them gratefully, but then he too became indecisive. He held the tissues in his hand and hovered over the wound, unsure of where he could do any good. Our man's nose was absolutely obliterated; it looked like he'd been shot in the face.

His eyes were open, zig zagging like an animal. Then they closed. "I think you need to stay awake," I said. A siren burst, not too far away. "Someone's coming sir. It won't be long."

Then the man honked like a goose, and flecks of blood and other particles sprayed upward. I caught most of the gory sneeze, and my helpful friend caught a bit as well.

"Oh my God, Victor!"

I clamped my lips and eyes shut, but it was too late. I could taste copper, could feel hot specks on my skin. I lurched back. The crowd gasped. We all shared the same horrible, unchristian thought, underscored by what the mad hatter managed to declare next, his voice a thick, nauseating thing:

"I'm dying. I know it."

I kept my mouth and eyes sealed. I didn't even want to God-damned breathe.

"Gimme your water!" Pebbles' voice sounded like a crow. Subsequently I detected a scuffle, which was probably her wrestling a plastic bottle out of some tourist's fanny belt. She was by me then, trickling water on my cheek. "Hold still," she said, her instruction hardly necessary. She daubed at my face with a wet napkin. I stayed still and tight. I had to trust that she could do this right.

"I die," croaked the man I'd felt compelled to assist. "And I wish, I wish . . ."

Pebbles tells me I was forgotten then. That the possibility of my infection from the bloody sputum of a homophobic raving drunk was released like a vapor and replaced with an entirely refocused sense of horror. I remember someone pushing me back, but still I refused to open my eyes. The uneven pavement below me was cool, but the sun targeted my clenched face and I saw red, literally. Like it was some kind of sick joke.

The small crowd descended upon the man who seemed prepared to utter his last words. Pebbles' napkins were put to immediate use, and there was no more uncertainty. The group wordlessly colluded on a *divers hands* approach to curtailing his freedom of speech by committing an act of involuntary man-slaughter. Paper napkins covered and filled all the holes in the poor man's face. He was unable to complete his wish, all right. He was also unable to breathe, right up until the paramedics came marching in.

And he was a drunken liar. Gerald Pollin was not dying, he wasn't even close to dying. And he carried no communicable diseases, though not for lack of trying. Apparently he'd come to New

Orleans intent on becoming someone new via sexual experiment, but so far no one was willing to lend a hand unless Gerald was willing to fill it with money first. And more than horny, Gerald was cheap. More than cheap, he was a drunkard. Two days into his adventure all the rejections he managed to collect took the spirit form of the ignorant woman who raised him, and he found himself raving in her voice. What a meager inheritance.

And what he gave to me was paranoia. For the first time since I moved down south, I felt real fear. I sat in an examining room with Pebbles who bided her time perusing a colorful pamphlet about stroke symptoms. She'd insisted on coming with me to the emergency room, but before that she'd tried to convince the paramedics to take me before poor Gerald. It didn't work, and her attitude was not very attractive, but there are rare moments when a screeching, shrill woman is the only person on your side, and you couldn't be prouder of the spectacle she was willing to make of herself.

There was nothing wrong with me, but we were waiting for the Alprazolam to take effect, and the doctor thought we'd be better off cooling our heels in private. Since Katrina it's a whole lot easier to get anti anxiety meds through legitimate channels, which is not to say I didn't fully deserve a little chemical help at the moment. And since cancer had been wished away, medical centers no longer processed patients like cans in a factory.

The edge fuzzed for me eventually, and the bitterness in my throat became stale. Somewhere else in this cigarette stain colored hospital Gerald Pollin was having his face restored as if it were the infrastructure of an ancient city, with pipes being laid and walls being reinforced. He, and the rest of us, would be better off with the Las Vegas approach: implode the fucker and start from scratch. I wondered if he'd had this sort of thing done before, and if the reason his nose seemed to shatter like marzipan wasn't due to a previous reconstruction. Whatever. He was in pain. If not now, then soon.

Gerald Pollin was an asshole, but he wasn't meaningful enough to make me feel this defeated. He was an accident. He was banal. He simply didn't possess the power to trouble me so deeply. And to be honest, I had a hard time fixating on him, especially after I sussed out his inborn limitations. There was no Demon Gerald, so what had me so rattled?

Pebbles recognized that I was ready to move. She asked, "We gonna call Val yet?"

"Uhm. What's today?

"Friday."

Good then. I hadn't missed Sunday. In a tourist driven economy you can lose track of days, because every day is an occasion for parties, both heartfelt and hollow. "Death Wishing," I said out loud.

Pebbles waited. She'd seen trauma before, apparently.

I told her, "A friend of mine is giving a speech Sunday. One of the Wish Local events. Would you care to accompany me?"

Pebbles settled in her bones, becoming all women at once, and what came out was very measured, closed off: "Will it cost anything?"

"No."

"Val coming?"

"He might just."

"Okay."

"What happened today—" I wanted to say something that would isolate the experience and rationalize the behavior of all involved. We weren't going to be questioned by any authorities, especially if we all remained silent, and even if Gerald retained memories of the trauma he was entirely unreliable. That left us with our own internal judges to appease. For the first time I was grateful for having been incapacitated by hysteria; I don't know how I would have behaved otherwise. All I know is that up until today I had been living a parallel world where Death Wishing was no more real to me than the latest scandalized celebrity. It was an earthquake, but in another country that only existed on the nightly news.

I wanted to say something about it all. But Pebbles was staring me down something fierce, and all of a sudden I felt as if I had no right to say anything at all.

I was nothing, right? Just a moony old man to her. She took my hand, and I hopped down from the exam table. She was going to lead me down the hall. She was going to guide this shuffling fool out the door.

I bit down: *and what did you do my lovely girl? What side did you take when Hat Man Gerald opened his poisoned mouth?* Oh yes indeed, paranoia had me now. Answers are never as important as questions.

Pebbles made a move to replace the stroke pamphlet in its holder (a minor relief that she didn't think we'd need to take it with us), but she ended up knocking the entire batch to the floor. She squatted to retrieve them and the whale tail of her thong breached from the waistband of her shorts. The Alprazolam granted me permission to stare at her backside, and I found myself reading a line of red words printed on the pink elastic waistband: *—llo Kitty Hello Kitty Hello Kitty Hello Kitty Hello Kitty Hello Kitty Hello Ki—*

I held my breath and made a wish. Girl was gonna kill me for sure. And Death Wishing? That mysterious bitch. I honestly thought she would pass me by.

3.

Esplanade was a shady avenue but not completely peaceful, lined with houses, small absurd businesses, a few wrecked places, and ancient trees that thrived on ashes and rain. A lot of garbage collected in its corners, but somehow our trash was a little less filthy and more homey than the rubbish on Canal Street, which was over exposed to traffic and impersonal commerce. Val's Vintage occupied the ground floor of our town home, and it was a dark, gloomy shop, luridly portentous with a lot of indirect and unhelpful lighting, some of it on the novelty side—neon sculptures, illuminated masks, and the like. I had a corner in the back, a workshop space filled with my fabrics, dummies, and an industrial serger.

Saturday morning that's where my dearest friend, Martine Bernier, teetered on a plastic milk crate, his ample midsection aglow from a gooseneck work lamp. My latest travesty was stitched around his abdomen. I'd started out running Val's website and a service: V3C. Victor's Cape and Corset Cleaning. It was a natural leap into corset construction. Seriously, you'd be surprised what a feller gets up to when his main vices, such as binge eating and drinking, are curtailed. Martine was a big man, taller than me but just as wide, and he'd stripped down to what looked like an old man's v-neck undershirt but was really some luxurious silk blend thing. Subtle, antique styling was all the rage amongst well-heeled clubbers. A tranny dabbler on the holidays, Martine was tickled to loan his body to my art. Even so, he could only handle posing for about a half hour at a time before he'd want to go out for a Pimm's or some other touristy libation. It also didn't help that Martine would tolerate no serious drawing in of laces. He couldn't take much pressure on his esteemed, well fed gut. Frustrating because I really wanted to test the engineering.

He'd found the whole business with Gerald Pollin distasteful, especially the gory details. I never even got to the to say the worst part out loud—Martine wouldn't let me. So there I was, stuck on the subject, going around and around the edges of chance. I asked Martine, "What's your take on this Wish Local business? My weight loss leader quit the program after twenty-four years to join up with them."

To which Martine said, "Change is a soul kiss from a strange boy on New Year's Eve; he doesn't know you from Adam and doesn't care, because the kiss is as far as it's going to go, Buster Brown."

"I am not going to even ask you what that's supposed to mean." Because I knew what he meant. He didn't want to talk about what everyone else wanted to talk about. I understood. Worry and action, those are a young man's games.

Martine was my age or thereabouts, French Canadian, with a pile of eerie blond curls and a square smiling face so sun-cooked that his eyes were always in squints. I couldn't even tell what color they were. He owned, but did not run as far as I could tell, a gay-themed greeting card and gift-wrap shop on Bourbon Street, and he had an inordinate amount of leisure time. A team of young, gorgeous athletes managed the business, and to be honest I had no idea how they made money. The card shop was ghostly empty most days, but Martine never worried.

He must have had some subsidy interest supporting them all.

"There's a presentation on Sunday." I pulled a thread through four layers of stressed, taut fabric.

"No," he said before I could invite him. I shushed him, vaguely threatening with the big curved needle. The reorganization of Martine was almost complete. We had managed to sculpt a meaningful inward curve with this latest prototype. Our previous attempts merely compacted his torso into a dense cube. But in this model Martine could almost breathe. He said, "You know who'd make a beautiful queen is your boy. An' he's got a girl's name already."

I nodded. I'd heard this point made before. "He already looks too much like his mother." I traveled around to Martine's backside—kind of a long trip—and took the laces in my fists, like a carriage driver picking up the reins. "Ready?"

"Never." He sucked in a preparatory breath. "You know, I look like my mother," Martine said, his voice a half step higher. "Oof. Easy Vic, easy there."

"Yes, well Val's already got his drag. All that gothic Anime cowboy crap."

Martine laughed easy, which was one of his most pleasant features. At this moment he guffawed, and I waited for stitches and grommets to burst. They didn't. "He's a dish Victor, a real dish. You're just jealous because he has like what, eighteen girlfriends? Are they all baristas? Anyway, he's a hell of a kid. Took your fat ass in."

Which was true. There aren't many twenty-eight year olds who want to keep their dads so close. "Did you know that Val was an overweight child?" I loosened the laces, and Martine grunted dramatically as his flesh returned to its authentic levels. It was almost beautiful to watch all that meat find itself and settle down.

"You're kidding me. Hard to imagine it."

"He was always a big kid. Funny what you're saying about his girlfriends. In high school he had all these girl study partners, but never one to date. I always felt guilty about that."

"His metabolism is your fault, is it?"

That wasn't what I was getting at, but I let it drop. I know I wasn't a proper parent when Val needed one; I was angry, remote, busy. Plus I was eating my way into an early grave because I sensed, but did not know, that Brenda was losing affection for me (and I was correct; she had commenced an affair with the academic dean who would later approve her for tenure).

"What you need to see is that Val is not damaged," said Martine. He was talking out his ass, something he did quite a lot. "He's a clever businessman living a romantic life in a magical city, and women love him. However you may have failed him, he has recovered."

"Right," I said, making it clear that he was full of it. "Immediately after Brenda and I called it quits, Val started to lose weight. About forty pounds in his freshman year of college. That's not supposed to happen. That's not healthy. You have kids, Martine?"

"Straight folk always make the same jokes, over and over." He pulled a brick colored polo on over his head, dragging it down with some effort, like a child. Tugging at the waistline, situating it here and there, he drawled, "None that I know of." He looked parched. An invite to the Napoleon House for an afternoon booze up and appalling service was imminent.

I started putting away my materials. Martine dragged his fingertips across the fabric bolts before becoming distracted by a circular rack of military jackets. He handled those too, with a professional concern, inspecting his own fingertips. "Cat hair," he pronounced.

"One more charming feature when you buy a dead man's clothes."

"Ugh." Martine shuddered and flicked an invisibility from his fingers.

Martine was right that Val created himself, and he'd done a damned fine job of it. As a teenager back in Viriginia, he had been one of those suburban white boys you hear about, given absolute freedom and an SUV in exchange for perfect grades. He claimed he was high his entire senior year, but I can't see how that could be true. He was accepted into two almost-Ivy League universities, but he chose to go to a state school near home.

Before I put it away I inspected the corset prototype, which was a bit damp from perspiration but otherwise intact and ready for more. Excellent. "Val lived with us while he went to college. He used to cook meals for us, Brenda and me. Three, four course meals, with paired wines. He was trying to hold us hostage via Sunday dinner."

"It didn't work."

I shook my head. "In fifteen months Val's mother moved out." I failed to add that I was embroiled in the federal investigation of the contractor that employed me. Or that Val was on his way to flunking out of that state college so close to home.

Val learned, and I learned later, that Louisiana would welcome our sorry selves. That we would flourish in its swampy, bacterial love. When the Wishing began, Louisianans were best equipped to deal with the drama of fortune, with Poles and Tibetans running second and third, respectively. Because to be successfully lucky, you must also be unlucky; you have to be yourself, no matter what the weather.

"Modeling's thirsty work Vic. Fancy a tipple?"

"It's all thirsty work, Martine. All of it."

I placed the corset on my worktable and snapped off the light. We moved, two large men, like rhinos on a narrow path, towards the front door of the shop. I locked up and dialed the little hands on the *Back By* paper clock to an unrealistic estimate. As we hit the sidewalk and accepted the bright glare of the afternoon sun, Martine and I moved as slowly as possible and almost in synch. Martine noticed this and started to hum a little goofy tune. "All we need now is some bassoon laden theme music," he said, and he was genuinely happy.

We passed by the A&P where we saw Bobby Rebar sitting on the ground, wedged in between the newspaper machine and the automatic doors. His scarred knees poked out of holes in his jeans, and his hair looked surfer blond except that it was all clumped with grease. Tears had cleaned paths through the dirt on his face. Bobby was a drug addict, homeless most of the time. His name wasn't really Bobby Rebar, but we called him that because he hung out in Jackson Square to dance to the jazz bands. His specialty was a dirty jig to "Hey! Ba-Ba-Re-Bop" that scared the living crap out of tourist children. We should have called him Bobby Rebop, but Rebar amused us more.

Bobby may have had an especially warm relationship with all creatures of the night, given that he was a stray cat himself. I nodded at him, said his name, but it was Martine who stopped and loaded Bobby's hand with quarters, probably about two dollars worth. The coins were out of sight in a flash.

"Wish local, indeed," Martine growled. "I can't get more local than I am right now."

4.

That night, as the sun set and the world went violet, I got drunk in my room, swigging from a bottle of refrigerated white that was still a little cold by the time the punt became an island. Gerald Pollin's horrible bloody face kept popping into my head, and I was on a self pity jag. I still wasn't sure what all had happened, but my suspicions ran dark. Was the world so off kilter? My quality of life had been so much better before Gerald, even a mere fifteen minutes before he appeared on my scene. Those golden moments with a beautiful girl on my arm—I worried I might never feel that good again.

Poor Pebbles. If I was this weak, how the hell was she coping?

And I kept thinking about Val, as well. I'd talked too much about the past with Martine. Now it was impossible to shake off the regrets that tumbled around my mind.

When he was a sandy haired, plump boy, I used to call Val the "bean counter." It was a dumb nickname, never meaning anything more than the fact that I found his food intensity adorable. No matter what was on his plate, it would go into his mouth with deliberate passion. He was such a sweet little guy, sweating at the table, fist wrapped around a fork with which he speared every pea and tater tot and spaghetti-o as if they were the last of their kind. But always one piece at a time. He didn't like to mix his food or collect too great a mouthful in one go.

The little things come back to haunt you, especially if you are a parent.

I punished myself with a small pizza, and once seques- tered in my room for a feast of shame, I discovered the order was wrong—a large by mistake, loaded with evil, fatty meats. There was definitely a force at work in my life. I ate and drank like a free man.

My room was a wreck, like a student's room. A low bed, piles of books, pale yellow walls, and a ceiling so far away that I hadn't changed the bulbs on the fan or dusted it either. Three of the six were burnt out, and it was beginning to look like I could grow wildflowers up there. I couldn't walk from one corner to the other because of the computer and all its paraphernalia. But my room did have one priceless feature. It was directly parallel to Pebbles' apartment across the avenue, and though a lush mag- nolia tree partially obscured my view, I could usually spot her as she passed by her window. Sometimes it looked like she lived in the top of the tree. I ate and drank and watched for my lady from Arkansas, but apparently she was out. I got myself pretty tight, pretty quick. Three more swallows would finish the bot- tle, so I vowed not to. I felt proud of myself as I set it aside.

And then it was dark. I woke still in my chair, head on the desk, my back aching. I'd passed out. An ATM receipt dangled from my lower lip. At last, Pebbles was home; the light from her apartment had roused me. I stood up, wobbly, and sent the nearly empty wine bottle to the floor where it kindly rolled under the bed and out of sight. "Damn it!"

She couldn't have heard me, and yet there she was, her palms lost in the magnolia leaves, arms locked for support as she leaned out her window. A street lamp lit her softly from below. Her torso was curled and cocked to one side. Her concern was muted by the glass and street that separated us: "You okay?"

Breasts. She leaned forward and I could see the bottom of her brassiere, that little triangle of fabric between the cups.

I struggled to pull my window up. It hadn't been opened since the Christmas parade. My fingers screamed around the painted metal handle, but I got that sucker unstuck, and a child-sized entity of humid air slipped under the sash, followed by an army of its kind.

I tried to be jolly. "Excuse me, *Darkling*?" Darkling? Where did that come from? My heart pounded. I burped surreptitiously to relieve the pressure. "I'm all right hon'. Just stubbed my toe is all."

"Oh."

"But thank you for asking." *Darkling*.

She stepped back and removed her breasts from that magic illumination. Her head tilted and her hair sorted itself into a geometric silhouette, and I got this tingly feeling like she was going to start dancing or something. She didn't. She withdrew until her face was in shadow. She said, "We still on for church?" She was referring to the Wish Local presentation I'd invited her to attend.

"Of course, dear." At the moment I couldn't imagine being in any shape to get up before noon the next morning. My head throbbed and my tongue was thick. But there was no way I would call off our second date.

"And Val? Is he coming along?"

I was about to tell her that Val had another appointment when he decided to answer her himself. "Where are we going then?" He stood right behind me in my unlit room, but I denied him the satisfaction of seeing me jump.

"And what are we doing in the dark, Daddy?"

He flicked on the small reading lamp by my bed, and suddenly I was exposed. All lit up for Pebbles, and all revealed to Val. He frowned at the sight of the yawning, empty pizza box on my bed. He sniffed out the wine on the air.

"Take a little nap, did you?" Val nudged me away from the window and leaned out. "Hey there Miss Pebbles."

"Hey there Val. Your Daddy and me are going to a meeting tomorrow. I thought he told you?"

I hadn't told him a thing, but calling me on that omission would be non-productive at the moment. "Oh wow," he said. "Yeah, I remember now. Slipped my mind is all."

Pebbles moved forward, leaned out and sort of exposed herself as she had before. Val cast me a quick, big eyed look that said, *I know what you've been up to old man.* I feigned innocence. I feigned disinterest. I'm a good feigner I think, but Val wasn't buying.

"Wouldn't miss it," he said. Then he looked over his shoulder at me and added: "Whatever *it* is."

My moment at last. "*It* is a Wish Local rally."

The smirk slid from his face, and a dot of panic lit his eyes. He was extremely suspicious of any organized efforts to cope with the Wishing. He mouthed so that Pebbles couldn't hear: *"You have got to be fucking kidding me."*

I shook my head no.

Somehow I had fully recovered from whatever parental guilt I'd been wallowing in earlier. Competition is a powerful healing force. Did he really think he was getting something going with Miss Arkansas?

He did indeed. He proceeded to make himself comfortable at the window where he wooed my lady out from under me, ripping off my balcony scene. Prince Val.

I accepted defeat and retreated to my computer, sinking into a black, fake leather office chair. A trash find: only three of the four rollers rolled, but the thing held my weight without complaint. Where was I going to roll to anyway? As Val chatted with Pebbles, I logged into the V3C site and answered a few inquiries.

Flirting is an illusion. It's a made up activity that works well in films, but in real life flirting almost always ends on a flat note. Because for flirting to work, both parties need to be social athletes, untouched by darkness, and in synch. And if they are already in synch, then there's no need to flirt in the first place.

All I know is that Pebbles said something innocuous, and Val reacted ungenerously. His voice went flat, and the conversation stopped. By the time I realized something was wrong, Pebbles was tilting her chin into her collarbone. She was embarrassed.

"Son?" I stood up, pretended I needed something near where he stood. "Excuse me there." I plucked a copy of *The Watchmen* off a tilting pile of old *Smithsonian* magazines and acted as if it were the very thing. But it was enough. Val shook off his spoiled mood as quickly as it had come. Pebbles was understandably confused.

I gave her my most apologetic look, but I doubted she could see it so far away and in the dim streetlight.

Nevertheless, the spell was broken. We said our goodnights. Pebbles went off to her bed presumably, and I shut the window. As the room cooled I watched Val collect my leavings. The pizza box was crushed under one arm, and the discovered wine bottle was now gripped by the neck like a club. He was pissed, punishing me by tidying up. That'd show me.

"What the hell was that about?"

"Nothing. Dumb stuff, it's not important. She said the Wishing felt like a dream."

"And you said?"

Val shrugged. "I said that was an offensive way to think."

"Jesus."

"I apologized."

"You really didn't."

"Oh? Well I'm sorry."

"Look, could you just steer clear of my fantasy? It's depressing to watch you hit on your future step mother and then abuse her in the next breath."

"She could go either way, Dad." He pointed to himself and then back at me. "You still have a shot."

"Maybe I do. You know your grandpa was a prick too, but he had an excuse. He was a veteran."

"She doesn't care if I'm nice or not. But I'll try to be sweeter, for your sake."

"You don't like her."

"Not particularly. She's just a kid. But she likes me, and she likes you. And you're nutty about her. So I'm probably wrong."

"She's been through a lot."

"You've been through worse," he said. Val left me then, almost making it down the hall. But he was back in my doorway after a few moments, gesticulating with the empty pizza box. Not done with me yet, apparently.

"Don't do this Dad."

I was back at the computer. The Net was all kittens all the time. It was astounding.

"Don't do this any more," he repeated, indicating the pizza box. His tone was unexpectedly gentle. "You are doing so well. And I'm very proud of you."

This caught me well off guard. I didn't know what to say. I am not a regular receiver of attaboys. I fumbled the etiquette. "I haven't really lost that much."

"Well, your man boobs are gone. That's a fact."

I touched my chest. Weight loss done right is a gradual

event, and one can't always gauge success on one's own. Sometimes only an outsider can re-do the inventory. "Really," I said, but I could feel the difference for myself.

"Yeah," said Val. "So no more pizza and pinot orgies. No matter how weird things get. You're better than that, okay?" Now he walked away for real, having put his stamp of authority on the evening. I felt proud and appreciative, and he felt victorious, no doubt.

What a controlling bastard he was. He'd make a great Dad some day.

5.

Yielding to pressure from an oppositional Congress and his own nagging curiosity, the President commissioned a blue ribbon committee charged with leading an open, national discussion of the opportunities and consequences of the Death Wish phenomenon. Populated by fifteen well-known thinkers, the committee members ranged from scientists to religious leaders to television actors, all of whom seemed to possess a certain photogenic moral certainty. The term "open discussion" meant that our celebrity representatives would hash things out on TV while we watched from the comfort of our homes. The discussion was heavily scripted, with the Dalai Llama yielding to Martin Sheen on the topic of the "resilient spirit of humanity," while Steven Pinker asked leading questions of Oprah Winfrey. It was a ludicrous pageant of platitudes and vague reassurances, but the forum was enormously popular, and in no time the United States government had a hit reality show on their hands: The Wish Tank.

In a shadowed, starkly furnished setting reminiscent of an old PBS chat show or a post-modern play, Neil deGrasse Tyson and co-host Francis Bean Cobain reviewed the latest documented death wishes and tried to make sense of it all while the panel cooked up predictions and recommendations for future wishes.

Four episodes aired over the span of six weeks before any of the panelists dared to bring up the subject of death, itself.

Cal Ripken: "So there is real pleasure in knowing. And knowing becomes its own experience."

Amy Carter: "Yes, obliterating fear. We are all futurists now."

Applause.

Sunday morning, bright and early. Wish Tank knocked the stuffing out of Meet the Press or any of those talking head shows. Val flicked it on and wandered away to another corner of the house, leaving it to blare in an empty room. We were getting ready to attend the Wish Local rally at St. Aloysius. Fresh from the tub and naked, I stepped on the scale in my bathroom. It seemed I was a pound lighter than last week, despite the binge of the night before. As if proud of me, Heidi Klum's distant chirrup confirmed, "Well that's completely awesome."

I scrambled, mostly naked and mostly wet, to my room and shut the door, reducing the Wish Tank repartee to unintelligible vibrations transmitted to the soles of my feet via the ancient hardwood floor. I dressed in pale khakis and a short sleeved bowling shirt—my Sunday best, to be honest. Most of the clothing in my closet was, at this point, either too big or too small. I had landed squarely in the buffoon range of my wardrobe, and everything that fit me was best accessorized with a can of beer. I almost put on a pair of deck shoes before I realized I might be taking things too far. I caught sight of myself in the bedroom mirror and noticed that I resembled a down on his luck homicide detective. As I retrieved my loafers from the hallway, I heard Ms. Klum say, "And apocalyptics? Where do they stand?" Steve Ballmer had a quick, sweaty answer to this, but I didn't quite catch it.

"Dad," said Val. "Let's go. This is bullshit." He said this

from the kitchen as he fussed over the coffee urn. Was I dreaming or did the boy sound almost enthusiastic? I detected familiar music and put my hand up in the *justaminute* signal, and dashed— as dashingly as a man of my size can dash—into the living room.

"Val, come here."

A commercial for my weight loss program was on, with the usual thumpy techno pop and a bevy of plump ladies dancing around as if nothing was more blissful than self denial.

"What?"

"Just wait for it."

Val slumped against the doorway and watched with me. Glistening plates of unlikely food, horse back riding, more dancing, huge pieces of chiffon catching the wind.

"There!"

Vibrant aqua script splashed across a white screen: The Freedom Plan. A beat before a husky female voiceover announced, "Now at last. The Freedom Plan." And a beautiful, large, blonde woman dressed in a flowing white muslin suit emerged from the background, strutting seductively towards the camera. It wasn't until she was quite close that one noticed the lit cigarette in her hand. Then a final image, as triumphant music swelled to a flourish: she took a long drag off the smoke and her eyes fuzzed in orgasmic satisfaction. "Real freedom," the voiceover groaned.

Now Val was paying attention. "Did she just—?"

"Smoking is back, my boy." Early that morning I'd groggily logged onto my online diet diary provided by the program, and there it was: in addition to my food fractions, water count, and exercise tally, I now had a field in which to enter cigarettes. "I'm allowed eight per day, as a matter of fact."

Val ran his fingers through his lank hair and chuckled. "Cancer goes away and Big Tobacco comes back. Shit. Wish I'd thought of that."

I decided to take the high road. "Well I'm not going to smoke. It's filthy." I straightened my shirt and changed the subject. "I suppose this is too casual to wear to the church?"

Val shook his head no. "No one gets dressed for church any more except hat ladies. You're okay."

We took a trolley and then hiked to St. Aloysius which is located in one of the least lovely, unreconstructed areas of West Side. The church steps were crowded with families exchanging goodbyes and making plans to meet up for late day dinners. But then I spotted Pebbles, seated on the steps, her arms wrapped around her rosy knees. She was wearing a dress, some light yellow cotton tube, but it was a dress. And she'd pinned a square of lace on top of her shiny red hair. A sweet gesture to propriety, but the frock was too short, and my eyes wandered over her brilliant white thighs. I think she noticed my attention, because she squirmed slightly and tucked in a little tighter.

She waved, looking lapsed and uncomfortable. Out of her element. She'd been waiting for quite some time.

St. Aloysius was a decrepit thing, had been even before Katrina, and was slated for demolition some ten years prior, but any structure that survived the Big K was suddenly a treasure. Even brutalist grammar schools from the seventies were subject to the preservationist urge.

I approached our girlfriend. Pebbles tried to smile but it came out crooked and strained. "They're already loading in," she said, nodding to a side entrance where a pair of ugly metal doors were propped open with a cinder block. I extended my hand and she took it, unfolding to her feet.

She flashed a quick smile at Val and looked away. Still stinging from last night.

Val stepped forward and patted her on the back. It was a

weird thing for him to do, but she stood still for it, all the time staring hard at the church doors so as not to frighten him off. Like he was an autistic child. Or a deer.

I asked her, "What sort of crowd?"

"Scary. I think."

As if to validate her impression, a trio of elderly women in tennis outfits strolled by. Two of them held hands, and they'd all bought their platinum wigs from the same cheap supplier. Sisters. Together forever. Next came a gentleman who appeared as if he'd stepped out of a cartoon OTB parlor. His checkered polyester suit was festooned with fabric pills, and he reeked of cigars. My enthusiasm plummeted. I was on the verge of suggesting we skip the event when an ivory town car took a reckless, squealing turn onto the street, rushed towards the front of St. Aloysius and lurched to a stop in front of its startled parishioners.

The vehicle was spotless with tinted windows and fresh new tires. When the driver emerged, he showed himself to be a caricature with blonde hair and golden skin under a black cap, sunglasses, jodhpurs, and boots. He flashed a grin for no one and everyone before taking a little nazi skip backwards to open the rear door for his passenger.

"Mirella?" said Val. "Now I'm impressed."

Mirella emerged in her Sunday best, a knee length, lime green leather dress tailored so precisely it looked as if she'd simply hollowed out another woman and buttoned the husk up over her own. It was a threatening garment with a narrow collar and hem that cut into Mirella's perfectly maintained skin. Mirella was one of those one-name-only individuals whose ethnicity was elusive; today she wore her thick black hair piled up on top of her head with a pretty Chinese stick run through it. Her eye shadow was the same shade of lime as her dress, but her heels were basic black, no less than six inches. Like weapons.

The most successful stripper-entertainer in New Orleans, Mirella was possibly sixty to eighty years old. Mirella might also have been a man. If not presently, then some time in the past. It didn't seem to matter. She held our attention regardless, occupying a realm beyond sex; she was a creature of the fourth dimension, with better practices and more interesting options than any of us fools could imagine. Her driver man cupped her elbow to guide her to the church. The crowd made way, and she smiled like the queen she was. She and the driver ducked through the propped open metal doors, and I no longer had any doubts.

"Let's get a decent seat," I said.

Pebbles asked, "They just gonna leave that car in the street?"

"No one's going to touch it."

Within, rows of folding chairs were filling fast. This was a banquet room and not the church proper, windowless and dim, save for the furthermost row of ceiling lights illuminating a podium on a slim talent-show style stage. I could not imagine Queen Mirella resting her perfection on cold, gray metal, and indeed she was nowhere to be seen amongst the unwashed. Rather, she was arranged atop a stool set off to the side from the rest of us, where she was quite fortunately backlit by an emergency exit sign. Somehow she managed to draw the light forward like a stole around her shoulders. Her man stood behind her, all but invisible.

Mirella posed her long dark legs at an alluring angle, one knee a little higher than the other and both legs pressed close to each other in a hungry kiss, almost entwining at the ankles but not quite. All she needed now was a microphone and a sax player.

Oh, and one more detail. She smiled down at the rest of us like the God-damned Mona Lisa. I remembered something that I'd heard back when Death Wishing still lent itself to giddy gossip: that Mirella intended to OD and wish the sky orange. And now to be this close to her? The hairs rose up on my neck.

Val led us to seats at the front, but close to the exits. Eventually there were fifty of us in that stifling, dark room, most being unrepentant "characters" from the mid-low end of the economy. Not a normal workaday soul in the group. Of course since Katrina, everyone looked a little rough, a little raped, and even new-bought clothes tended to hang from the shoulders like government issue from an island nation you never heard of.

Enter Rollie, my queen-like weight loss leader. That is, before she got caught up in the Wish Local movement. Rollie was in her sixties, had kept her weight off for twenty four years. She was no nonsense, almost militaristic, and I missed her like hell. I'm sure her social views were gruesome, but her courage and knowledge of exotic fruit were impressive. She strolled in from a moldy antechamber wearing a sculpted periwinkle linen skirt suit, white stockings, and periwinkle flats dyed the exact shade of her outfit. I think there was even a slight periwinkle tint to her short white hair. I wouldn't put it past her.

So Rollie in her breathtaking, ready-for-heaven ensemble, and Mirella in her assertive lime leather. The rest of us? Filthy monkeys.

And Rollie wore that same smile, Mirella's smile. The women nodded to one another, and we all held our breath in the presence of such supreme collusion. Val's appreciation was cool, but Pebbles gazed like a child in awe. She wanted to be one or both of these women when she grew up.

Rollie took the podium. No notes. No amplifying device,

no power point set up. Someone closed the door and we were sealed in.

"Welcome," she said. "Welcome, my family."

Val made a face.

"We've gathered today to acknowledge the truth."

"Amen," called a voice from the shadows.

To which Rollie cautioned, "I do appreciate we're in a church, but let's not allow mystery and faith to confuse our mission. We have work to do." Her remark provoked some uncomfortable shifting, and we looked to Mirella the way one might peer into a flight attendant's face during turbulence. Mirella was solid, unmoved, eyes forward.

Rollie said, "You all know about the houses on Tennessee Street, right?"

And how could we not? Tennessee Street ran through one of those tragic Ninth Ward neighborhoods virtually erased by Katrina. Think of that famous photo of the two hundred foot barge squashing a school bus—*that* neighborhood. Used to be a street full of kids, old women and gangsta rap. Then for a while it was just wreckage, feral cats, and crickets. Have you ever seen a city street that was utterly dark at night, and silent? Because there is no electricity and there are no people? Of course you haven't. No one ever had, until the storm.

"The Tennessee Street event marks the sixth documented wish to be implemented," said Rollie. She took a breath. "In Southern Louisiana. The government will issue a report this week that will detail the demographics of enacted wishes, and one of the things that report is gonna say is that a disproportionate amount of wishes come from our area."

That was newsworthy. We shifted, muttered amongst ourselves like worried hens. The Tennessee Street event occurred after one of the original residents brought in a pre-fab home to set it up on his old land and declared it time for the neighborhood to return. And it did, but not in the way that he expected. While it had taken him more than a year to reclaim and rebuild his home to a livable condition, his great aunt, who had lived on Tennessee since before the great white flight of the sixties, managed to rebuild the rest of the neighborhood overnight.

"Wish they was houses back on Tennessee Street," she said, and then she went to sleep for the very last time. In the morning she was gone, but where every row house and shotgun shack had been swept away by the surge following the failure of the 17th Street Canal, now stood a perfect, if boring looking, Dan Ryan style modular home. All the plumbing plumbed, all the electricity wired, everything waiting for the city to do its part and flip the big switch that would restore basic services to the community.

It was an emotional thing to watch on the evening news, as the shreds of disintegrated families were led back to their homes under the protection of their nation, for once. Women cried, men cried, we all cried to see it. And we all waited for the administrative shoes to drop on those people's heads, but that never really happened. There were tax issues to be ironed out, but in Louisiana government crawls at a snail's pace. So here was a new, shiny neighborhood. Two strips of little putty colored, mushroom houses in the Lower Ninth Ward to form a sliver that looked a lot more like a Northern Virginia suburb than the cradle of jazz.

Rollie intoned, "No, we have no problem with God, but His intermediaries? We can't count on them. Not priests, not government, not any appointee who was in place and failed us before. Do you remember waiting for help and charity? Do you remember how none of the structures of responsibility, from the levees to the ministries to the White House, were adequate after the storm? The only real help came from family, friends, and heroic neighbors. Don't get me wrong. I'm not here to talk anarchy, I'm here to talk about local interest."

I leaned forward in my seat. I wished I'd been able to convince Martine to come along.

"We have no science other than statistics to support the suggestion that Death Wishing favors our region. But the numbers are too important to ignore. We must take measures to ensure our own safety and, you bet I'm gonna go there—*prosperity*. This is no longer a question of believing or not believing in the phenomenon of Death Wishing. No one can live outside it any more."

At this point Pebbles slipped her hand into mine, making me want to utter my own "Amen."

What followed then was an impassioned but sometimes strained argument that the Wish Local movement was a deity free philosophy of opportunity, though the mystic subtext was undeniable. Rollie and Mirella came off as High Priestesses, even though they insisted they were merely community leaders. Back in the cheap seats of my mind, I knew they were just as prone to corruption and inefficiency as anyone else, but I didn't care. I was thrilled to be part of the drama. Rollie was an artist, and it was a delight to watch her work the crowd, slowly releasing and cranking the tension until all rationality gave way to stomping, hooting, and other forms of sweaty affirmation.

My favorite part was the end. We were on our feet, and Rollie stepped back to accept our wild applause, her eyes wet with triumph. Then we turned our attention to Mirella. She had come down from her display to balance on those wicked heels, and the light that cradled her seemed to pulse and swell. We quieted down. She raised her chin. Her eyes went liquid black. When she spoke her voice was burnt sugar: "Looking out on the morning rain . . ."

Pebbles squeezed my fingers.

" . . . I used to feel so uninspired," said Mirella.

And then she proceeded to sing the rest of "You Make Me Feel (Like A Natural Woman)" *a capella*. So terrible, but so amazing. I held my breath. I wept. It was the most powerful religious experience of my life.

6.

The rally had been very much like a good church service in that we were released into the wet heat of a Sunday afternoon, feeling utterly perfect for a moment. But all perfect emotions degrade. That's why church goers keep going back.

On our way to the trolley shelter, Pebbles walked between Val and me. She tested out a line from Mirella's song: "Now I'm no longer doubtful . . ." It's a tough song for anyone, and more than talent you need confidence. Pebbles didn't have a lot of either. She coughed at the end of the phrase, and I placed an encouraging hand on her back only to find myself touching Val's hairy fingers, already in place. He should have at least stayed on his side of the girl's spine.

And then she dropped the bomb. "We're supposed to think about what we want."

Correct, but difficult to embrace. Even convinced of the need to Wish Local, I didn't find it any easier to think of the world without me in it. And that was the real problem wasn't it? To think of a place and time beyond death that was a lot like this place, this time. I glanced at Val and found his face unreadable. I couldn't tell if he was worried, upset, confused. Pebbles, however, looked as if she'd risen a level above us. Her face was blissing, all cheeky sparkle, like she could see many kinds of wonderful futures, and it didn't matter that she wouldn't be there to enjoy them. I put it down to her upbringing in the church. All intellectual arguments aside, she had been raised right for the current situation.

Not so Val or even myself. We were doomed to wallow in rationality, at least for a time, until we could pull ourselves out and come to grips with duty.

I think I was supposed to say something wise at this juncture. Material responsibility is actually the least difficult duty of being a Grown-Up. Any boob can get a job, feed his family, and guard the perimeter. There's no craft in that part of life. Where it gets tricky is in that impossible area of making sense out of uncertainty and stabilizing chaos. It can't be done you see, but it's still part of the job.

I had no wisdom to impart. Worse than that, my panic was on the rise. "Here's what I wonder," I said. "Are we supposed to not tell?"

Val laughed. "You mean like throwing a penny in a well or blowing out the candles on a cake? You think that by telling your wish it won't come true?"

"Who knows? You say that like it's crazy talk or stupid. Truth is we don't know the rules, so nothing is crazy. Or maybe it all is."

"Telling doesn't make a difference," Pebbles said. "It can't." Clearly, she didn't like this line of discussion. She stopped us, pivoting around so she could put her hand on my chest. "I'm going to wish something to do with music. I don't know what yet. Victor? What are you gonna wish before you die?"

I felt woozy under the mad sun. Val stood apart from us, his arms folded, keeping an eye on the distance so we didn't miss our ride. "I really don't know," I confessed. "I don't think about death. At least I haven't before."

Pebbles nodded, more sympathetic than I deserved. She

turned to Val. "What about you then?" There was a little icy edge in her voice that said she still hadn't forgiven him for making her feel awkward the night before. Val didn't seem to know it, but the balance of power between them was shifting.

He unfolded his arms, ran fingers through his hair to stall. But then he came out with what was on his mind: "Why does everyone think they're a wisher? Rollie says there are more successful wishes here than anywhere else, but the odds are still insane."

"That doesn't sound right," Pebbles said. We started walking again, the three of us in a row. "I don't think the odds have anything to do with this."

"I don't either. Not really," said Val. "I just think that if you're a wisher, then maybe you'd know. You'd have some kind of feeling about it. And I just don't."

My heart sank. Val had me going with his talk of odds— a tidy little argument against having to decide. But knowing wasn't feeling, and feeling was king. He felt nothing about the Wishing, and he was off the hook. Me? I felt something. A little, tiny, scared something.

We reached the trolley stop and came upon a man spread out across the bench, not quite asleep but certainly not very conscious. He wore a red and white checked long sleeved shirt buttoned all the way up to his brown throat. He might have been a restaurant worker. He certainly smelled like food garbage. He shielded his eyes with his forearm, showing off pits stained with ancient perspiration. In black uniform slacks, he'd propped a bent leg up on the bench and let the other dangle. He seemed to be roasting himself. The mere sight of him made me dizzy.

I suppose the main problem for me was that I never spent a great deal of time wanting, at least not on a large scale, beyond my passion for whatever food or drink hovered before my eyes. My memory seemed full of holes. I remembered wanting only those things/people/goals that I attained, eventually. I did not remember the things/people/goals I must have given up on. Surely that meant I had some sort of brain damage.

What did I want to leave behind? Nothing? That was a hell of a thing.

I excused myself and hustled over to the nearest trash receptacle, where I regurgitated. Though not quite an accepted custom in New Orleans, public vomiting isn't rare either. Open disgust at such behavior is perhaps less appropriate than the act itself, although I have known spectators to respond with a round of golf applause.

Val and Pebbles politely turned their attention to the slow moving streetcar emerging like a villain or a hero out of the heat waves. I recovered before the trolley came, wiping my fingers around my mouth and pulling my skin clean. I was angry with my own face. The trolley gasped to a stop, vibrating at rest, impatient. I collected myself, climbed into the vehicle, and thumbed my coins into the box. I tasted tears and bile. Val wouldn't look at me. Pebbles couldn't keep her frightened eyes off of me. Neither suggested the hospital.

I sat by myself, feeling fat, useless, and rancid. "If" was just about gone. That was Rollie's real message. "If" was a luxury, attached to what would never happen. But now things did happen, and "if" was a loaded gun, a sacrilege, a reckless waste of heart and thought. If I die. And certainly I would. But I didn't have a wish yet.

I needed a wish now, and damned quick it seemed. No fooling around any more.

Back home, I called Brenda, my ex wife. She sounded bored by my question, as if its simplicity insulted her intelligence. "Of course I have a wish, Victor." Her tone made me feel like a slob.

"Well what is it?"

She answered with a prim little cough. One of her professor tricks that had devolved into a tic. "I wish that Val receive the entirety of my estate upon my death to dispose of as he pleases. And I documented this wish into a will. Isn't that ingenious?"

"Don't be a bitch, Bren."

"I thought about setting aside a portion for you as well, but Rick would find that irritating, and besides, the likelihood of your succeeding me in death—"

"Oh do stop." Rick was her new husband, the Dean who had secured her academic position. "Why can't you ever take me seriously?"

Brenda said, "I might if it didn't seem like you were descending into childish magical thinking. You know, Val can handle all that southern gothic crap, but you? You're getting soft in the head. Picking up some bizarre lisp and going around in capes?"

"I do not lisp."

She ignored me. "No wonder you're buying into all this mythology."

"I really appreciate you taking the time to inventory my decline."

She went quiet. After a moment she said, "Sorry."

"Brenda." And for some reason I catapulted back to a sex memory: Brenda on the butcher block table. Me thin. Val safely away somewhere—camp? My face went hot, a blush from embarrassment, not arousal. Irrationally, I imagined that she could see into my mind. I said into the phone, "Help me think about this."

Another sound from her throat, this time more human than pedagogic. "I don't know where to begin, Vic. This isn't like you."

"I'm aware of that. But I seem to be changing. Recent circumstances and all that. Why don't you have a wish?"

"You mean aside from the existential crisis, the consuming narcissism, and the outright dizzying lunacy that attends wish design? I'm an atheist for Christ's sake—"

"Yes, yes. Cut to it, love."

Brenda sighed. "Victor. I have new wishes every God-damned day. *Dozens* of them. I lay awake at night trying to imagine the repercussions of even the most fractional change."

I imagined her in that sleepless state, lying next to man who was dead to the world and oblivious to or perhaps even tired of Brenda's neuroses. She needed to be held more. "Oh dear," I said.

"Exactly. I'm a wreck."

"And Rick? Is he as conflicted as you?"

"Oh no," she said. "He's had his wish for fucking ever. Something about honeybees. Very responsible. Very targeted. Very linguistically simple, so he can say it even under the most challenging circumstances, like in a car crash."

I liked the idea of Rick in a car crash. I also imagined a number of other challenging, drawn out scenarios featuring Rick gasping, groaning, coughing out his bee wish. "Well now see, you are being helpful. I might not have thought about the com-promised speech aspect."

"So you're having trouble picking a wish?"

"I'm having trouble picking any wish. Email me your cast-offs, maybe I can use one of those."

"You're disgusting," she said.

"Perhaps I should wish for a stinkier cheese."

"You should wish for men to have babies."

"Or women to be less brittle." I regretted it as soon as the words left my mouth, but it was too late. She hung up. I don't know if she was furious, bored, hurt, worried, or driving out of cell service. That's new technology for you. No longer do we have the option of giving notice of our displeasure by slamming the phone into the cradle. A hang up doesn't even come with a click anymore. Your person is there and then suddenly she's not. I have found myself on multiple occasions continuing a line of heated argument long after Brenda had ended the call. It's a problem because she's missed my best, most elegant rebuttals that way. And that in itself is a curiosity—why are my finest insights always preceded by the idiot behavior that made her hang up on me in the first place?

A cruelty crossed my mind. A Grinchy thought. I could wish for her to fall in love with me again.

That night Val and I ate separately but together. That's how it goes, me working as slowly as possible through an orange chicken Lean Cuisine, and Val plowing through a carton of takeout pasta from Fiorelli's. It smelled insanely good, but Val had flipped up the lid making it difficult for me to get a real eyeful. He had a music magazine open beside his dinner. He pretended he was reading it. Dinner was awfully quiet.

Except for when I said, "You're growing fonder of the girl."

"Not really." He didn't look up.

"Why mess with this Wish Local stuff at all, then. Why take her seriously?"

"I don't." He closed the magazine and slurped a forkful of Bolognese. "I wanted to just lay low till all this blew over. Like you," and here he pointed his glistening fork at me. "But now it's all gone too far. It's beginning to feel like . . . Well, it's stupid of me not to pay attention anymore. Even if I'm not a wisher, and I'm pretty damned sure none of us are, I need to prepare."

He leaned forward, buffeting me with his garlic breath. No, garlic and parmesan. "I am not so arrogant that I think I can change the world. But I do know there's folks out there that are going to change the world for me."

His words alarmed me, but I misunderstood. "But Val, we can't live in fear. That's not what we came down here for."

Val leaned back in his chair and shook his head. "Not fear, Dad. I'm not afraid of this bullshit."

"Then what are you talking about?"

He closed the lid to the carton and tossed it into the trash. I could tell by the way it tilted in the air that there were still a few precious morsels inside. He hadn't eaten the bread that they usually packed in with the entrees. He was sparing me the sight.

Val then wiped the sides of his lips, pulling his face into a smirk that wouldn't take. "I'm talking about fortune, Daddy. Fuck fear. I'm talking about getting ahead of this damned thing."

7.

Several times over the next few weeks, Val left me to work in the shop on my lonesome for hours at a time, sometimes for whole damned days without telling me that he'd be gone or where he was going. And then he'd return home a sweating wreck, smelling like beer and grease, and unwilling to talk. I didn't find out until much later that he was hunting desire.

This thing with him and feeling—Val was pragmatic, rarely giving in to any passions other than sexual. So when he was visited by strong emotion, he always took it seriously. And under the current circumstances he was keenly aware that his lack of strong feeling posed a problem. He decided to drive, wandering loops around the wards, then out towards the suburbs. He didn't know what he was looking for, he was just going, hoping that some sort of instinct or fancy would take him.

That's one way to live.

He'd been disgusted by what he'd seen online, even from fellow entrepreneurs he considered friends and half-assed mentors. There were guys putting a new twist on the already twisted industry of viatical trading. Cooperatives were selling wish futures. Internet dead pools had been elevated to consultancy status. Val was ready to make his move to grab a bit of the future, but none of these ideas seemed right. Eventually he found himself touring the swampy parishes of St. Bernard,

Lafourche, and Terrebonne—not far from the city proper, but a whole other world.

Val cruised broken roads—dusty, glittering with glass shards, and half swallowed by hostile vegetation—that skimmed along the waterways and led to commercial marinas choked with rickety shrimp boats. Shrimpers are, next to Iron Curtain era barges, just about the ugliest watercraft you'll ever behold, overtaken by brutal rigging that leaves just enough working room for a crewman with the instincts of a dancer under sniper fire. Shrimp and oyster boats are not built with any pleasure in mind.

So when he saw boat after boat with For Sale soaped across the cabin windows, and knowing that the combined assaults of Katrina, Rita, and the oil leak had decimated the local industry, Val was overcome with sadness. Those marinas were watery ghost towns.

And that sadness rang a bell.

In Lafourche he stopped at a bar. It was a shack—fried gray wood, corrugated plastic roof. The front of the building straddled a dock sagging over black water, while the rear nestled in a green and thorny world knotted around barrels, engine parts, and another, smaller shack. The word BAR featured in black paint over siding where other words had been bleached away by the ages. If the establishment had a name, it didn't advertise it. It was eleven in the morning when Val stepped in. Nearly every seat was taken.

The sadness was even deeper than he thought. These men hardly even noted his entrance. Val had been expecting some guff, dressed as he was in chains, jeans, a hammer & sickle shirt, his black hair swinging down like a girl's. But nothing. One old timer who quickly morphed into a mere forty year old gave him a yellow-eyed glance, but that was it. Everyone was too depressed to start any shit, and that was very depressed indeed.

BAR had not always been a bar, that much was obvious. Electric beer signs were rigged up on pegboards to remind patrons that life was temporary. Behind the counter, a short woman with dyed black hair and bare, biscuit colored arms leaned back, smoking a cigarette and watching a television mounted *behind* her patrons. Unless they twisted around on their four legged stools (swivels are for pussies), their only view was of the woman and rows of hooks, weights, leaders, and bright orange floats in dusty packages—merchandise for tourists should they ever hire a boat. And that never happened. A long, narrow package hung on one side. Val could just make it out through the plastic wrap gone milky gray: a closed bail Snoopy rod, for little kids.

He didn't bother asking what was on tap. He took a seat and accepted a Budweiser. Along with the other men he stared at the barkeep. She stared at the TV set and smoked. She was watching a medical reality show that made no sense without the picture. Val thought, *I'm going to crack up. I'm going to giggle. And if I do that I'm going to die.*

The man seated to his left had silver hair, blue eyes, and cheeks like watermelon meat, complete with pits that looked like seeds. He was drinking beer after beer, but no hard liquor. And no money changed hands between him and the barkeep. Val decided the man was a captain.

He put his hand out. "Valmont Swaim."

The man moved at half speed but managed to grasp Val's hand. "Dan Cheramie." He made only brief eye contact before returning his attention back to its natural resting spot.

And that was when Val realized that there was something other than the bartender and unsold tackle to stare at. The bar's one un-shuttered window could be found at the end where no one could sit because that's where the door hit when opened. Through that dingy square of glass the sun streamed through, bouncing bronze light off the bayou in such a way that you couldn't detect a clear horizon. This was probably the only angle from which you could not see a boat or any rigging. A green heron angled over and settled into the branch of a live oak. A tacky scene if it had been a couch painting.

Val leaned closer to Dan Cheramie. He was about to ask the man if he owned one of those rusting boats out there, when the woman tending bar suddenly looked at Val. Hard.

"Watch it," she said around her cigarette.

And then Val fell sideways off the stool that everyone knew had a tricky foot rung that popped out if you didn't center yourself just right. On the filthy floor of the bar, Val felt pain like sunbursts in his hip and elbow. Around him there were shouts and boots, none of them coming at him it seemed, so he took a little break there on the floor, holding his head and curling his knees up to his chest. The air was cooler down there but heavy with the stench of old blood. Before he could get sick, he was lifted up on both sides by two sets of powerful arms, and as he was forcibly re-fitted to his stool, Dan Cheramie said "Jesus Christ," almost tenderly.

By the time Val realized that there was a fresh beer set up for him, his fellow patrons had retaken their seats, their faces animated, here and there a quick grin. Nothing meaner than that. One fellow advised, "You should sue Barbra's ass. Take her for all she's got."

Barbra nodded towards the beer she'd just served. "That *is* all I got."

Dan Cheramie patted Val on the back, and Val drank down half the beer, partly to cover his embarrassment. "Wood glue," he said to Barbra when he could find his voice. But she waved him off like that was crazy talk. She was back into her show.

The accident turned out to be the perfect icebreaker, and pretty soon Val was informally interviewing Dan Cheramie and his buddies, learning about how they spent their days, what they used to do, and what they wished for the future. Of the seven men present, four owned their own boats and were trying to sell them. Dan Cheramie was one of those four.

Val took on a third beer, and his heart grew reckless. He'd made some offhand comment about how beautiful it was out "there," indicating the view of the water and the sun, and Dan Cheramie took exception.

"No sir," he said. "That there is a barren field. A grave-yard."

At which point Val understood that these men weren't merely drinking their lazy days away. This was an endless wake, and they were grieving, twenty-four seven.

The idea that overtook Val was unstoppable. And it wasn't even an idea. It was a whiff of what was possible, vague and unformed, but it came with its own theme music. As soon as the thought occurred to him, Barbra had cranked up the AC and changed channels on the TV. The theme from *Bonanza* arrived on ribbons of cool, sweet air, and Val just couldn't help himself.

"Dan, let me buy into your business."

Dan turned, his neck a little stiffer with drink than it had been when Val first arrived. "Kid, there ain't no business. You want my boat, I'll sell you that."

"I don't want the boat. I can give you $350 a week to start. Make me your partner."

Dan rested his head on his hand and examined Val's face. Their conversation had not gone unnoticed by the other patrons. Val could see them controlling their faces, trying not to butt in.

When Barbra said, "You hurt your head, honey?" it was all they could do to keep from falling out laughing. Which, once upon a time they might have done, but these days? No one in that bar laughed about cash any more.

Dan took a sip or two. "Partner? And what I gotta do?"

Val shrugged. "If I knew I'd tell you."

RATS

1.

Weeks passed, with me stalled on the precipice. All I had managed to do was decide that I needed to make a decision. Progress enough for some, and once upon a time for me, but now I was feeling strange and dissipated.

No wishes had been measured for nearly a month, but the after effects of the elimination of cats were quite pronounced. If there were more birds by day, rats had come to rule the night. The vermin population exploded. I'm not sure how that happened, being no expert on the life cycle of rodents, but the basic mechanism seemed obvious. Alleys at night were all tick-tickety as an ice storm.

My neighbors who once owned cats were driven to dogs for pest management, with the most popular types being small and humorless, originally bred for ratting, rabbitting, badgering, what have you. Unfortunately your modern day Chihuahua becomes bored or wounded rather easily. Plus there was the problem of nocturnity. Unlike cats, dogs could not be released from their yards into the rat-filled night. There were good rules against that. And even if there weren't, a decently raised puppy declined the night shift. The only working part of the hypothesis was that a dog does enjoy killing a rat. The trick is getting the dog and the rat in the same room at the same time.

It was on one of Pebbles' performance nights that I spotted

my first tame silver fox. It was a Tuesday night, and Decatur was largely under-populated at that end of the Quarter. The only predator I had expected to encounter would be one demanding the contents of my wallet. Instead I saw the flash of mirror eyes ducking behind an orange construction barrel that was probably covering some dangerous, beery hole in the banquette.

(I should mention here that a brief coyote experiment had ended in miserable failure. Turns out, coyotes are lazier than house dogs, having quickly learned that the rats they pursued lead them to heaps of restaurant garbage that was always delicious, sometimes hot, and mostly clawless. After two weeks of *that* wild west adventure, the streets were strewn with stinking rubbish, and there were just as many rats as ever. Plus, the sight of a coyote skulking through an alley was almost as disturbing as encountering an alligator in your garden pond. It was an image that inspired cold fear, regardless of how majestically moonlit the beast might be.)

So I spied this alternative canid beaming at me from behind a rather obvious length of CUIDADO/DANGER/ACHTUNG tape, and I thought that it might be a lost runt coyote or some grossly proportioned Pomeranian mix. I crossed to the other side of Decatur and continued toward the bar, all the while watching my little watcher watch me. As I drew parallel to it, the creature sat down and allowed its lovely little front paws to protrude from the shadow of its concealment. This was followed by a soft yip.

I stopped and turned, and soon the little bugger trotted across the street to meet me.

I was astounded. This thing had all the features of a wild fox except that it was blue and smoky with dark tipped ears that tilted forward in a friendly position. Common sense tells one that a fox approaching a human with any intention at all is rabid, but this thing emitted a vibration of inner sweetness that I found dazzling. It came to my feet and said yip yip before taking position behind my ankle.

I walked towards the bar and he followed me. My little wing man. But at the entry to Checkpoint Charlie's we parted ways. He had no interest in coming inside, and after a few seconds of waiting at the doorway he cantered away.

I learned later that the little fellow was a sample of a tame silver fox, a Russian adaptation, imported as an experimental pet here in the states. These little guys were almost completely domesticated and could live like house cats in just about every respect, including using a litter box. They were jolly, loving, and happily nocturnal. They'd even lost their foxy funk. However, they'd retained a powerful caching instinct impossible to breed or train away. Efficient and enthusiastic ratters, they tended to stash their kills inside their masters' homes, preferring upholstered furnishings such as cushioned couches with nice tight crevices for storing bits.

The bit about the caching was either unknown or insufficiently understood, and many tamed silver foxes were released by their adopters to roam the alleys like little gentleman bandits. Homelessness is always an unfortunate lifestyle, but if you must live under the stars some streets are more amenable than others, and I like to think that the loners of New Orleans catch more breaks than most. Whether you are animal or man.

So it is especially fitting that the night I spied my first tame silver fox, I also encountered my old friend Bobby Rebar. He too was homeless, socially inappropriate, and quite sweet in his squalid way. Bobby perched on a stool just inside the entryway to Checkpoint Charlie's. "Robert," I murmured and gave him a dollar, as if he were collecting the cover charge. He jammed the bill in his jeans pocket.

The stage was uninhabited but crowded with instruments and amps. Checkpoint Charlie's is unremarkable except that it's one of the larger Quarter bars, and just about the only place you can go for rock and roll or guitar driven anything.

The players were on a break, and I didn't see Pebbles anywhere. The main floor tables were mostly empty, but there were a few folks on the upper level near the pool table. The bar was crowded though, with several skinny, hard white boys in shredded shirts pounding back beers. The band?

"Quiet night," I remarked, and I thought that Bobby agreed with me until I realized he was merely bobbing to the music in his head. He discovered that the stool could swivel, so he twisted around like the agitator on a washing machine. His heavy old work boots swung counter to his knees. That's when I noticed that his soles were caked in gore.

I walked briskly away from him, towards the bar, unwilling to process the meaning of what I'd seen until I'd managed to collect a beer from the barman, a stringy muscled, tattooed Cajun named Jean-Claude. I leaned in with all the young, hard men, thinking how much they looked like my Val, thinking that NASCAR might be an interesting sport to follow, thinking where the hell was Pebbles anyway?—thinking everything I could to crowd out the image of blood and meat packed into the treads of Bobby's boots.

"Hey, you made it!" Pebbles came up behind me, and put both palms on my back so she could use my hulk as a sort of pogo stick. She jumped up and down, lightly. She was excited. She was nervous. She was unbelievably attractive.

"So I didn't miss it?" I turned around to appreciate her. She'd tied her red hair into innumerable crazy short braids with little rag ribbons on the ends. Weird, but cute. She wore tight-tight jeans and a pale yellow T-shirt advertising Valvolene. I swear I don't understand irony any more.

"No way man," she said. She was breathless, flushed. Tipsy? "I'm up next. There's like three of us, though."

"Three singers?"

"Uh huh. And I'm soooo screwed." She grinned like she wasn't screwed that much. "One of the gals is married to the guitar player."

I concentrated on her face, but I could see Bobby Rebar's shadow in the distance, lurching about, doing all it could to distract me. I dived into Pebbles' eyes.

Down the bar stood a fellow who had managed to drink himself to his full Rock Star height. He slammed down his glass to signal to his companions that it was time for them to drain theirs as well. He strolled our way, made a wet click in the back of his jaw that may have been meant as some kind of sexy cowboy noise, and said to Pebbles—without looking at her, I think it is important to note—"Ready Babe?" He strode towards the stage without waiting for her response.

They all leapt, long leggedly, onto the dais as if they were clocking in at the quarry, weary to begin another shift. I think it is amazing that four individuals can occupy the same 150 square foot space without ever making eye contact with one another. Were they a band of gorgons? And my sweet Pebbles followed them, grinning like a pretty idiot, very much the little sister ingratiating herself to her brother's posse. She positioned herself at the microphone, shifting it by fractions until it obscured half her face.

As the band geared up, a party in the back made its appreciation known. Seated near the pool table, two middle aged African American women in lavender skirts and hats rattled tambourines. They were ready for action with very tall, pristine beers before them. Somehow Sunday had collided with Friday on this Tuesday night.

Pebbles smiled shyly, and after a few embarrassing outbursts of feedback, the band launched into an ear-splitting, indelicate Stevie Ray Vaughn song. Pebbles started to sing, but her voice was too weak, so she had to sort of launch it into the microphone in an act that appeared unsanitary. The result was very unmusical I thought, but the band disagreed. In fact they seemed to awaken from their self-interested gloom. Smiles broke out, and it occurred to me that Pebbles might well be giving the best performance of her life.

The lavender ladies shook and stomped, and to my enormous surprise Jean-Claude whipped out a harmonica so he could contribute as well. I was surrounded by sound, and my glass was just about empty.

And there was Bobby Rebar. He'd hopped off the stool, emboldened to take the dance floor with his customary child-frightening authority. Pebbles closed her eyes and leaned into her performance. It seemed that no one but I noticed that Bobby was dancing little smears of flesh and blood across the floor.

I felt woozy. What had he done?

Suddenly the bartender stopped playing. "Goddamn you fucking turd!" he shouted. Not at me, of course, but at Bobby. Pebbles' eyes flew open and she dropped the next line of her song, which pissed off the band. I felt sorry for her, but I was grateful that not everyone considered Bobby's grooming as par for the course, even by homeless drug addict standards.

"Get the fuck off my dance floor! What the fuck!" And Jean-Claude was over the bar, powering like a linebacker towards Bobby Rebar. Pebbles took a step back, recoiling at the sight of an enthusiastic fan being bowled over. The band continued unperturbed, stomping away like a quartet of oblivious Neil Youngs, and in the back the tambourine ladies had risen over their beers, shaking their instruments, caught up in transcendent passion.

The barman argued with Bobby, who was bewildered. There was some pointing at shoes, and Bobby lifted his booted feet one by one as if he'd never seen them before and had no idea how they came to be affixed to the ends of his legs. The exchange concluded with the Jean-Claude grabbing the back of Bobby's shirt and chump-walking him out the door.

A once-upon-a-time beautiful woman took over the barman's duties and I gestured to her with my empty glass. She provided me with an icy, crisp refill that was much more delicious than the original. I gestured to her and she stretched herself over the bar. "What the hell?" I asked.

"He's been stompin' rats."

"Oh my lord."

"Jean-Claude paid him cause he said he could get rid of the rats. But you can't give that guy money. He's crazy." She wiped down the bar with a rag that looked like it had been used to clean a mummy's ass. "Not like the guy has skills."

"No."

"All he's got is a sense of purpose."

And she didn't have to say more on this point. A sense of purpose is a dangerous thing in a broken mind. Yet I felt a pang of envy. Where was my sense of purpose? I was perfectly sane and quite capable of handling a mission.

Poor Bobby. Trying to find his place in the world. Bobby the rat catcher. And he couldn't even do that right. Still, it's not like they offered training at the community colleges for this sort of thing.

Now out in the street, Bobby was visible through the open doors of the bar, and he was doing a sort of Russian kick-dance in his bloody boots. Nearby, my little fox friend watched him with gentle appreciation. It's all about perspective. To a carrion lover, Bobby Rebar's rat gore festooned footwear was the height of couture. Jean-Claude re-entered the establishment, and the band slid into another howler. There was some confusion as the next girl singer attempted to take the stage. Pebbles stood her ground, arguing that she had one song left, given the scuffle that made the last performance imperfect. The band agreed with Pebbles, but the second singer remained onstage to gyrate cage dancer style. This was distracting to Pebbles, and she sang her final song ("Crazy Little Thing Called Love") like a nervous eleven year old.

Out in the street, cars swerved around Bobby, who insisted on dancing between the faded lines on Decatur's crumbling blacktop. His eyes were glossy and white, full of moonlight and neon. He was completely mad. Seemed like he had been born damaged, a piece of crap that floated in on the oily foam churned up on the banks of Lake Ponchartrain. Which is to say he came of age during the oil boom, fully expecting to follow in his family tradition of giddy-headed land rape. His daddy had a truck with some gizmo on it that resembled a satellite dish, and he and his family crisscrossed the Louisiana-Texas border convincing folks that the gizmo could find oil in their back yards. Then they planted well pumps that looked like giant versions of those little drinking bird toys. Up, down, up, down. These pumps pumped. But Bobby entered the industry right after it peaked, and it was a quick slide. He couldn't make it as an independent, so he signed on to the offshore rigs, which is where he picked up his hunger for substances. Then he worked commercial fishing boats and shrimpers in Placquemines and St. Bernard where his xenophobia flourished. But in all these locales and positions his weaknesses surfaced, and even though he was a cheap laborer, he just wasn't cheap enough. Not to offset his lack of professionalism and other unpleasant qualities.

So he ends up at the bottom of the world. New Orleans, with no job or home. But he's a survivor, no? We love our survivors. He stayed through Katrina and Rita. It couldn't have helped his state of mind.

Pebbles finished, stumbled off the stage to a smattering of applause, and joined me at the bar. She was flushed and happy. This was one of her good nights. She draped a sweaty plump arm over my shoulder and accepted the beer I had ordered for her.

"Whoo!" she exclaimed, her face almost as goofy as Bobby's. I was supposed to answer in kind, and when I didn't she was disappointed, sharply reminding me of the fact that I was a fat old prick. A man can be too sensible. Or, alternatively, a man could be like crazy Bobby, dancing in the street. I looked out the doors and watched Bobby whirl like a three year old in a new Easter dress.

Pebbles chattered with Jean-Claude and hardly noticed me leaving. She had a new drink bought by a stranger. Well good for her. I ordered two beers in go-cups and took one out to the poor fuck dancing in traffic.

Bobby and I stood in the street and discussed independence and luck, and every once in a while I nudged him back from his many appointments with Jeep-borne death. He held up his end of the conversation for a decent stretch, but it soon degraded, and ultimately his gibberish became too gibbery for me. Or maybe my mood had changed. At one point he sang, *Incredible Mr. Limpet* style: "I wish! I wish! I wish I was a fish!" and laughed his head off.

That was it for me. I went home. Didn't want to be there when it happened.

2.

By the next morning, the world had changed. The casual days of this thing were well over. We had gone a month without any death wishes actualized, but overnight the levee around the dry spell had been fully breeched. The death genie granted *three* wishes this time.

1. Every woman who had ever given birth to a living child now had a fully functioning third eye at the base of her skull. An amazingly practical wish, met with hysterical enthusiasm. The eye tended to be quite small and very light sensitive. It worked like picture in picture; when the little eye was open its perception appeared in miniature within a bubble lens, hovering like a sprite above the normal field of vision. When the eye closed, the image vanished. Within the day we learned that this wish was progressive. As new mothers had their babies, so too did they grow a little wrinkled eye. As mothers lost their children, that eye closed and became a horny callous.

2. Elvis was back. The 1968 Elvis. Ironically, he almost died within minutes of what would later be referred to as "The Second Comeback," when he materialized near a fjord in Qaanaaq, Greenland, the northernmost community in the world. His leathers protected him from immediate hypothermia, but the slick soles of his boots proved highly impractical on the ice, and he almost fell into a crevasse before the curator of the Hotel

Qaanaaq discovered him and took him indoors. Perhaps the most remarkable aspect of the King's return was that no one on earth doubted his identity. Not even for a moment. The second most remarkable aspect was the efficiency with which the US government, partnering with the Church of Scientology, retrieved the iconic singer to sequester him at an undisclosed location. It was almost as if they were specifically prepared for this event.

3. A new, disc shaped species of crustacean was discovered in abundance—not in open waterways, but well up into the bayous of Louisiana and Texas. The earliest guess was that it was a kind of shrimp—a decapod that was especially fat, meaty, and slow. Folks couldn't wait to taste it. Score one for the Wish Locals.

But to back up a bit. Death Wishing had been a one after the other phenomenon, leading most folks into a sense that there was something to that, a measured doling out of fortunes by a greater, wiser intelligence. I never fell into that fancy, and assumed that death wishes were random, rare occurrences, like when lightning strikes a child. After weeks of nothing happening, except adaptation to what had already been wished, I'd let go of the lightning model and was prepared for the possibility that I was off the hook, wish wise. If no more wishes were going to be granted, I could go back to my carefree non-existence.

But then the three wishes came at once. The ludicrous three. Even I was susceptible to a bit of weak, reactive thinking. I asked what everyone asked—why did they pile up like this?—before shaking off my supernatural assumptions to ask a much more reasonable question: why hadn't they before?

Brenda sent a phone picture of her little eye. It was dainty, brown as a puppy's. She, like many women, tied her hair in pigtails, hijacking the style of virgins. I showed Val. "Look, your Mummy is a cheerleader."

Val seemed happy enough to burst. He had a laptop ding-dinging on the kitchen table, and he kept looking from it to his mobile device. Giggling.

"Hey Pops," he said. "Your love life may pick up pretty soon."

"Oh yes?"

"Yeah. Blind women want to get pregnant. Talk about your perfect storm."

"Hilarious."

Though I acted the deadpan, in truth Val's giddiness unsettled me. After the emotional tidal wave that accompanied the elimination of cats, I wasn't ready for another big event. I hadn't taken my morning walk yet, but I feared that there'd be nothing but powerful feeling everywhere, in everyone, and that practically no one would see a percentage in maintaining a sense of dignity.

I could hear laughter from the street. Not all that unusual, our street is the place for dark fun, but this morning it tweaked me up. I had grown accustomed to a level anxiety, the words *when, when, when*, tolling a bell in the brain. Ever drowning out the flat music of *what*. Adaptive instincts being more powerful than anticipation, the initial concern of *what is death wishing, anyway?* yielded damned quickly to the necessity of living with the results. Wonder and its pause are pricey.

For most.

"Shit, I'm good," said Val. Staring at the computer.

"Shouldn't we get ready to open the shop?"

"You go ahead, Daddy. You open. You need to get used to running it on your own." He looked up at me and winked.

My gut fluttered. "What have you done, boy?"

"Don't worry, you'd approve. We'll talk later, okay?" He looked like he did when he was eleven and sold a comic book to a dealer for fifty bucks. Face so pale and bright. "Please, you work the shop today. I gotta—" Something on his screen sucked him in. "I gotta work this." He didn't look up. His blue eyes looked like alien eyes, no pupils, just kaleidoscopic ice, phosphorescent and energized.

I didn't argue. I collected my coffee, sipped some down to make room for ice and milk. I'd managed to gobble down a nectarine, and I knew the combination of caffeine and fruit would soon result in regret, but I had no appetite. At least not yet.

There was one last thing from Val though, just as I was on my way:

"Dad. If you see Bobby Rebar today, send him up."

"I doubt he'll make a daylight appearance," I said, picturing his bloody street dance from the night before. "Why do you want him?"

"I may have work to throw his way." An impossible suggestion, but Val refused to elaborate. I gave him a look, which he did not appreciate as he was re-absorbed into the virtual world of his ambitions. I left him to it, but I was troubled. Things always changed, but this time? This time felt bigger.

I climbed down the stairs into our cool, musty shop, flicking on a couple of lights here and there (I left my own corner of capes and corsets, the V3C sub-boutique, dark, as if I'd called in sick to myself), smacking the obvious dust away from those surfaces that caught the morning sun. I turned up the AC and scattered drops of incense oil on the filter, then entered our various security and credit card codes. I tried to cast myself psychically over the whole of the shop, but I wasn't comfortable being in charge.

I felt like I was wearing Val's boots. He had grown less and less interested in the shop lately, and I'd always suspected that as soon as his next ship came in, he'd abandon or scuttle this one. (Little did I know how apt the metaphor.) Whatever he was working on upstairs excited him into a quartz-like attention, which meant that I was likely to find myself under or over employed soon.

So I puttered and muttered and completely forgot to open the front doors. Proof positive that I was ill-suited to run a business. Eventually the doors rattled, and so did I.

The morning sun blinded me as I horsed open the doors and wrestled the security bars aside, and before I knew it I had admitted a small gang onto the premises, and I mean that, literally. It was a gang, and they were small. Three boys and one girl, local kids, tweeners in pristine banger wear, all baggy and bright. Huge damned basketball shoes that looked more like alien pods than footwear. One more year on any of them and I would have been terrified. As it was, I was only nervous about their number. They spread out in the shop, making it impossible for me to watch them all.

They were a diverse group of hoodlums, I'd give them that. Two of the boys were African American, but the other boy was smoky skinned, almost iridescent, with dramatic sharp features and slightly ginger hair. Everything had gone into that pot. I recognized the girl. She would grow up to be a great, doe-eyed beauty once she shed her tomboy ways. "Esme? Esme Fateh?"

"Hey Mister Victor," she said, smiling quick. Esme was the middle daughter of a Palestinian scholar at UNO. She was desperately trying to pass herself off as Latina. The boys snickered when I called her name, as if she'd lost a bet. All four of the children began to rifle through the racks of jackets and shirts.

"Esme, what do you all need?"

A shaft of morning sun had divided the shop into two dark territories, and now that shaft was suddenly eclipsed. Martine stood in the doorway, filling it right up. He was a little out of breath, but smiling.

"These creatures have been making the rounds," he said. One of the boys frowned at the characterization. He pulled a wool sergeant's jacket from a hanger and poked his little stick-like arms into the sleeves. He whirled, wobbling under the weight of the coat. His tiny comrades scowled their disapproval.

Not that then.

Since Esme had chosen not to answer me, I asked Martine, "What are they looking for?"

The big man shrugged. "They won't say. Big secret apparently. They've been in every open shop in the Quarter, now they're hitting the Marigny. And they haven't swiped anything yet. At least not that anyone's noticed. I reckon they've already been paid for this mission." This last part he sort of shouted, as if he'd been trying to get a rise out of this crowd for some time.

Apparently they'd come a cropper here as well, and the colorless boy gave the signal: "We gone." Search suspended, the children gathered near the entry. The sergeant's jacket had slipped off the hanger to the floor, which jolted the boy who'd been modeling it. He looked sorry.

"Leave it," I said.

Martine removed himself from the threshold. It was not his intention to block the children's egress. He merely wanted to monitor their activity. They seemed scared to pass him.

But then Esme said, "Hey wait."

She was peering into the dark corner of V3C, and for a second I was embarrassed. I felt sure she was entranced by the outrageous silhouette of Louis/Louise, the dressmaker's dummy now wrapped in my latest industrial strength corset. But I was wrong. Esme had no interest in something so familiar. Instead she moved towards a rack of light-weight matador style capes. She probably couldn't really see what they were at all, but found herself attracted to the sparkle of the beads and the metallic thread trim.

I turned on a desk lamp for her. There were three capes, one red and black, the other two neon pink and lemon.

"What are they?" she asked me directly.

"Matador capes. Bullfighter capes."

"How much?"

"Oh, the red one was made in China, that's only fifty dollars."

"I like the pretty ones," she said.

"Yes, I made those. They're a bit more expensive. It depends on the detail work, the fabric." In fact I hadn't priced these capes, so I was at a loss.

Martine to the rescue, with an outrageous number: "A hundred fifty," he asserted, farm auction style.

Esme didn't blink. "These all you got?"

"I can make more."

The child instructed one of her partners to model a pink and yellow cape. I took control of that process, bringing down the garment and re-hanging it after she snapped a cell phone picture.

Esme kept up the efficient little scout routine right up until she hit send on her phone. Then her face broke into an excited grin of triumph that restored my faith in immaturity. The four scoundrels rushed out of the shop, whooping wild as soon as they hit the street.

When Esme returned that afternoon she was alone, and she brought with her a hand written order for an astounding fifteen matador-style capes. "But they don't want the pink," she said, obviously disappointed. "They want this."

She handed me a wrinkled page from a magazine. I asked,

"Who are they, Esme? What sort of low-end, wannabe rack-eteers send out an agent from the sixth grade?"

She ignored my question in classic twelve year old style, as if I were incapable of forming intelligible sound unless I was speaking directly to her concerns. All the rest was just dog barking. I unfolded the page and almost laughed out loud at the image I was supposed to copy.

"That's what they want," she said. "Maybe different 'broi-ders, but all white and sorta short."

I ended up laughing anyway. Couldn't help it. "This is the wrong Elvis, sweetheart." She had given me a picture of Las Vegas Elvis, with the white sequined cape, torn from a glossy magazine. I owned a poster from the same era, tacked carelessly to the cork board behind the serger. Layered over my Elvis were other images of caped role models—super heroes, vampires, highwaymen, and carnival kings. It was an evolving, artless col-lage. Elvis was nothing special, and I wasn't a fan in particular. He was just a guy with a cape. For that I felt a dim, yellow guilt.

I returned the page to Esme. She found my amusement insulting.

"Tell your friends it's the wrong Elvis," I said.

She reached into the deep pocket of her stiff, overlarge jeans and extracted a wad of twenties, neatly folded and bound with a rubber band. Somehow I had expected this. Drug money, no doubt. I was terrified of what she carried in the other pocket. "They said half now. This is a grand." Her tiny, slim fingers made the wedge of cash look like a lot more money than it really was.

So she was being backed by scum level drug dealers who couldn't do basic math. Punks who dealt meth and grandma's prescriptions and who didn't know which Elvis had returned. I wanted no part of this. "No thanks," I said.

Esme didn't want to hear that. She was on her phone. "He says it's the wrong Elvis." She listened for a while before hanging up without a word. She walked over to my worktable and tossed the cash onto it. The child would prevail.

She turned and smiled at me, really sweetly. I melted, powerless against manners. Already I was working out my personal rationalization: I had never done a background check on my customers before, so why should I care now? And if I thought I could forestall Esme's corruption, I was certainly a fool. She was already much harder than me.

"Well?" I asked.

"He says there ain't no wrong Elvis."

Ah, then. A true believer.

3.

When I finally closed the shop at six or thereabouts, I was a little deflated, a condition that surprised me given that I was in possession of a small mystery and a wad of cash. But in my new capacity as unofficial manager and sole employee of Val's Vintage, I'd been shut in all day. Couldn't even step out with Martine for a quick lunchtime cosmopolitan or sangria. And now that it was after hours, I needed to plan a trip to gather supplies for Esme's order. My day and night were essentially shot to hell. No wonder Val could be so humorless sometimes.

I marched upstairs—well, climbed anyway—prepared to tell Val in no uncertain terms that I was uninterested in taking over the business; working all day, even not working very hard, just didn't suit me any more. I found him in the kitchen still, but this time on the phone. He was sort of half smiling, half scowling into the receiver, reciting percentages and tonnage. Then something about freight and ice.

He mouthed a word to me: "In-sur-ance."

I shuddered and backed away. I waited for him in the television room where I watched the news coverage of the day's developments. It was a good day to be a telegenic psychologist. Talking head experts giddily careened back and forth between the day's two hottest stories, speculating on the inner terror and delight of a man out of time while predicting the social revolution that would stem from new female empowerment.

This stuff. So soon. I wasn't surprised at how rapid, fantastic, and detailed the projective analyses were so much as I was upset to be practically a whole day behind in gossip, having spent it all in the shop. Every station ran the same footage of Lisa Marie Presley being escorted through Heathrow airport, grinning uncharacteristically, stopping only to toss her hair and wink at the paparazzi—coming and going with her new little eye. She was a mother after all. No hint as to where she was headed.

Thinking as a father, I hoped she'd be gentle with her old man. She was already thirty odd years older than when he'd last seen her. The extra eye might be too much.

Very little time was spent on the new shrimp thing. Oh there were a few panicked environmental experts trudging through muddy backwaters in hip waders, sputtering about the dangers of such a massive non-native species invasion, but these folks were neither interesting nor sexy. Invariably, whenever one of these scientists had worked up a lather of hysterical reason, the camera would stray away from the expert's face, sort of wandering over the shoulder to pan over a shimmering horizon of water and clouded sun, made more beautiful by the silhouette of an egret or pelican. It didn't matter what the poor scientist had to say; just look at the water, look at the sky. Everything was going to be okay.

I turned the set off. Val was still on the phone. Pebbles hadn't been over the entire day, as far as I knew. I grew restless for company. There was a weight program meeting scheduled for the dinner hour, and I decided I would attend as a drop in. Evening meetings were always dramatic, with weigh-ins sabotaged by cafeteria lunches and desperate snacks, followed by stories of workplace master-slave humiliations. I had gathered my wallet and house keys when I encountered Val, bright eyed and flushed, blocking the threshold. He was finally off the phone. Looking successful. I said, "I'm on my way out the door, son."

"Dad, wait."

My neck prickled. Irritation. For some reason I stared at Val's bare feet, his toes sort of curled over the strip of molding that married the wood floor of the living room to the linoleum of the kitchen. "I'm guessing you had no occasion to put shoes on today, is that right? Why'd you even bother changing out of your pajamas?"

"Heh." Val walked past me and plopped onto our green vinyl couch. The sun had dropped to burn around the edges of the blinds, and the living room was gold and dusty. Val's face was shadowed, but his eyes shined through. He was going to tell me he was rich or something. I tried to prepare an efficient reaction.

"We're gonna be rich, Daddy."

"Oh yes?"

"I mean it this time," he said. "What are they saying on TV about the shrimp?"

"The shrimp? The new shrimp? I don't know, the usual doom and gloom. It's the new snakehead, it's the new crack baby. We'll all be slain in our sleep."

Val grinned. "Yay Elvis."

"I think you mean viva Elvis."

"I tell you what the coon-asses are calling it, Daddy. They're calling it the buttershrimp. *Buttershrimp*. Now how does that sound?"

"I'm afraid you've caught me at a delicate moment, food wise. I was just going to a meeting for a little pick me up."

Val leaned forward. "You don't understand. The Cajuns are already catching and eating this thing. Cooks up like a crab except when it's done the shell practically falls away, and inside is this thick medallion of sweet white meat."

I shrugged. "And of course, it tastes of butter."

"Well yeah."

"Excellent news. I'm off."

"Not so fast. Seriously, you need to take a seat and listen to me."

I was too tired to fight. I sat on the edge of a footstool to make my inclinations clear, but nothing I could do or say made much of an impression. Now that I had given in he proceeded to tell me the story of his water bar epiphany, and how he dropped thousands on getting two boats back in shape for a market that didn't exist—until today.

I had to admit I was shocked when he described the costs so far. He didn't tell me where he'd gotten the bankroll, but I could only assume that the house and shop were at risk. And I didn't understand it, I couldn't see him just taking a plunge like that. "Whatever possessed you?"

"These were family businesses," he said. "I was sitting there thinking, 'man there's a whole lot of pain in this place,' when it occurred to me that the entire community had to be in pain, with every mind fixated on the end of the waterman's era."

I was drawn in by Val's poetry. "A powerful place, then."

"A locus of desire. Of *particular* desire, Daddy. But I'm not talking magic. I'm trying to respect the numbers. Density creates probability."

You can't argue with gamblers. They are so sure they have reason and method. I asked, "Where are your boats?"

"The first one is in Lafourche. Next day I went out and scored another in Terrebonne. Both captains are Cheramies."

"And how are they related?"

"They're not sure. Cousins likely. They never met."

I doubted the role of coincidence in my boy's selection of partners. He'd likely brokered his deal with the first Cheramie only because the man was nearest when the scheme was born. He probably picked the second Captain Cheramie for luck.

But he wasn't asking my counsel. The shrimpers were a done deal.

Before I left, Val asked again after Bobby Rebar. He still needed to see him. Apparently the Captains Cheramie were short on crew, so short that even mad men could apply. I assured Val that I would pass along the tip and then congratulated him on his impending emperorship.

By the time I got to the meeting, it was half over, so I slipped in quietly and sat in the rear of the overly air conditioned room. The weight loss group met in the most generic of commercial meeting spaces, and once you stepped upon that gunmetal Berber or placed your ample self in a stackable metal chair and breathed in the processed, ghostly stench of the weekend's real estate seminars, it was easy to pretend that you weren't in Southern Louisiana at all. The room was soulless, a safe place, a sterile pocket; no one was going to waft in with a bag of hot beignets or cooling pralines, or whip a ladle of etouffe your way.

(That happened to me once, actually. Before Katrina. An antique shop on Royal hosted a wine tasting in a maze of mildewed rooms jammed with anxiety of provenance. How does one acquire a sixty piece golden tea set from a sunken ship or slave shackles from the very same? Several slurps of wine later I found myself in a room packed floor to ceiling with hideous Capo Di Monte vases, dead ending at a closet full of stinking books and one plump, famous chef. Monsieur Prudhomme got to work behind plumes of humid spice and a portable cook top, and his assistant readied a plastic bowl. Suddenly I had a bowl of crawfish etouffe in my hand. Some on my shirt, too. From behind, a strange hand checked the quality of meat on my bones while urging me to move along. That was a good day for me. I loved my little dish of crawfish. I loved my little sips of wine. I loved the sweat pouring down my back. I staggered out of the antique shop onto the banquette sucking a plastic fork, and I decided right then and there that I would come back to New Orleans to live this life, every day, all day. But oh, the consequences.)

Four women occupied the row in front of me, each one with a rear end like a suitcase. I made a point to be subtle with my gaze, as being in the back of the room no longer guaranteed anonymity. The woman directly in front of me checked me out with her sleepy third eye. I smiled and waved. If she smiled back I couldn't tell. Once my threat level had been assessed, the little eye closed and was almost fully camouflaged in curls.

This was going to be a challenge, wasn't it?

In the front of the room the new leader, Ruby the simp, pitched the latest range of candies from the company, droning on without enthusiasm. She was a small African American woman who inflected every statement as a question, which was one of the reasons I never found her appealing. Also, weight program participants can be a bit self-centered, and if the leader is not properly charismatic, gossip and crinkling breaks out throughout the room, making it even harder to pay attention.

That's what was happening now, only at a much ruder volume than usual. The room was packed, mostly with women in their business wear, shoes popped off and cell phones resting on their laps. As Ruby attempted to describe how to cure depression with a PB Lite bar, several sets of women gabbled well above the whisper stage. Well, who could blame them really? It was silly for Ruby to think that her members would be interested in anything other than The Elvis and their new eyes.

To her credit, Ruby soon gave up on her prepared remarks. She did not wield authority well, and she may have also been disadvantaged by the fact that she was so lean and compact that you could never imagine her as an overweight person. "All right, all right," she said, putting away an insultingly simple chart that described hunger danger zones. It was a pie chart of course, which made me smile inside. It was time to solicit stories of food peril and triumph. Ruby said, "Anyone want to talk about how their week went?"

Several hands shot up, but one woman stood in her stocking feet and began to speak without waiting to be called upon. While her accent was syrupy her tone was all business: "Those three shootings in Midtown today? They was gang done."

Ruby was speechless. No one else was. Everyone started talking. The lady in front of me said, "I heard that as well."

I leaned forward and inquired of her, "What shootings?"

Her wee eye opened, and she turned her head to tell me, "Three folks shot dead in the space of an hour. And not all together either. Different places, they were snatched off the street and killed in alleyways. It's terrible."

I gasped. We had a high murder rate in New Orleans, but three such fatalities in one day?

Ruby had officially lost control of the meeting. Her face was peaceful, resigned. She'd expected no less. She began to collect her notes into a satchel. Half heartedly she asked, "I meant do any y'all have any new recipes you tried?"

The woman who spoke before was still standing. She said, "Ruby, are you for real? No one can concentrate on losing weight anymore. Not when things are like they are."

A chorus of agreement noises rose from the group, except for one person I could not see who said, "Take it easy on the lady." This comment drew just as much support.

"I'm not trying to be a bitch, I'm just saying this whole thing, this whole system of denial and minute calculations— doesn't it strike you as a little foolish?" She placed her hand on the back of her head. "My body changed over night. *Over night.* I don't think I'm in the mood to stop and take my calcium pills before I run out of a burning building."

"A man came back from the dead," said the woman in front of me.

Ruby cleared her throat. She put forth one last effort: "You mean to tell me that you are willing to give up what you know for what you don't know? Miss Tracy, the building is not on fire, but even if it was, that's no reason to eat a hot fudge sundae."

Good shot, I thought. The group was on the edge of abandoning reason, but only on the edge. The woman sat down, unsatisfied, but she heard what Ruby was saying. Sensing she was on to something, Ruby continued, "This is a challenging time, no doubt. And that's when we slip up worst, when our world becomes irregular, good or bad. Celebration and grief— we use food to even out our feelings."

Another good point, but I don't like being confused. I spoke up, addressing myself to Miss Tracy. "Excuse me." I stood and was startled to see so many tiny eyes flutter open. A handful of members turned, some of them out of habit rather than necessity. "I came late, so maybe I'm missing something? The killings in Midtown. Are they related to the Wishing?"

Ruby's features collapsed. I had disappointed her greatly by going off topic again. Miss Tracy was eager to explain, "Three people shot, just blocks apart, over a very short time. They thought it was a crazy person, and then witnesses came forward. It was boys, a couple of them, wearing all that shit they do. Pardon my French. They grabbed people off the street, forced them to say a wish, like for a pile of cash, then shot 'em in the head."

More than a few of the members crossed themselves and murmured parts of prayers.

"I'm sorry, and I hate to be argumentative," I said, and that was two lies in a row, "but how could anyone know all that? What kind of witnesses came forward? There are no witnesses in New Orleans."

"It's what I heard," she said.

So it was just a rumor. So far. And one that the people in the room were all too eager to embrace. I needed a beer. I saw that Ruby was quietly making her way out the back without dismissing the group. The chatter was high and grim, so I started making my way out too, though watched by many little eyes. The woman who had been sitting in front of me twisted up and touched my forearm as I struggled past the folding chairs.

"It's not so far fetched Mr. Victor," she said. She knew me but I did not know her. That happened all the time. A man in a weight loss program is a minor celebrity. "It's an unhappy world. I work at the Sunny Grace Village, you know that place?"

I did. "The assisted living facility adjacent to the city hospital."

"That's the one. Well, volunteerism is through the roof sir. We got a two to one helper-resident ratio on the weekends. And I heard there's a waiting list at the hospices. Think about that," she said. Her eyes, the regular ones, were shining. I did not know what she felt—glee, grief, thrill—but it was intense. "It was only a matter of time."

I had this feeling she was entirely right, but only in her world, not mine. In my world folks were too lazy and hot to foment fear and work an angle. And then I thought of Val. He was in my world. He was making ready, wasn't he? What she was telling me was that folks were seeking out the dying and otherwise short on time, not because they cared but because they wanted something.

And then she said, "It's not all so bad, you know. I'm sorry I frightened you."

She stood and took my hands in both of hers. Was I frightened? Why yes, I believe I was. Others made their own way out of the room, not happy but certainly energized by the new facts of life. The woman would not let go of my hands. People regarded me warmly as they filed past. Southern Louisiana, where fools are not only suffered, they are beloved. It appeared that I had made a scene.

"It's not so bad," she repeated. "There's no extortion involved. The ones who have been forgotten, or remembered too hard."

"Just what are you talking about?"

"You must know what I mean. When you reach a certain age, your animation fades and all the things that we used to be able to do—smile, frown, smirk, show wonder—escape us. And it turns out that these small muscular things with your face, those are the signals your loved ones need to be reassured that life is still life. You make it to ninety-seven or 'sumpin like that, your face goes still and it scares your family. If they visit at all they act different, 'cause it's like talking to a tombstone. Those people have company now, Mr. Victor. And lots of it. Young, old, all kinds of folks, coming around hoping to make a positive impression. It's like anyone has an inheritance to pass on, so everyone else better kiss your ancient, wrinkled butt."

I pulled my hands away. "And you think that's a good thing?" I asked.

The woman's face creased with sympathy. She was watching a child learn new tough truths. She said, "I been helping old folks check out ever since my own mama passed. And one thing is for sure. Having your hand held is number one. Holding a hand transcends the motivation for doing so. I'd bring God into it, but I'm thinking you would be unpersuaded. So let me put it this way—the body loves and the mind looks for reasons not to. Well it's a silly fight because the body always wins, 'specially when it's shutting itself down."

I felt like she was telling me to give up, give in. I'd spent the last several months controlling my body, rising above its urgency. "Stop talking to me," I said. "Please. What you are telling me is a horror story."

She shrugged to underscore the fact that her capacity for mercy was unlimited. But I was already storming out, grace abandoned.

4.

I lurched into the Spotted Cat and ordered a bourbon that I tossed back like they do in the movies, but it was the vision of Pebbles that went to my head. The Cat is a narrow venue with couches in the front window, positioned just a hair's breadth from the tiny stage, while the bar takes up the back half of the space. Quite intimate. The first band was packing up and another was stumbling in, hauling battered cases repaired with duct tape and decorated with novelty stickers. The patrons had spilled out into the sparkling street creating an informal gauntlet around the entry. I did not know my lady was present at all until she emerged from a sagging, red lit antechamber in the rear of the building where the restrooms were located. She looked like a dirty dream: tiny denim skirt and a white T-shirt that so loved the illumination of the Jagermeister sign, I was tempted to order a round.

She saw me. She smiled. Of course she smiled. God, I loved her. Well, I loved that she existed.

She bounced up to me, and I took her hand. "Twirl," I commanded. She did.

"Good, no tail lights."

She laughed. "I can't begin to tell you how wrong that is, Vic."

And that was a sharp thing, prettily dispensed. She climbed onto the stool next to mine and I ordered her a sweet drink, a crantini or something like that. There were quite a few women my age in that bar, most with men already, but they were still capable of blasting me to kingdom come with a look. It occurred to me that one of the reasons I adored Pebbles was that she fluttered over my surface and rarely interrogated me. Whereas a woman of a certain age, even a stranger, might say something as meager as hello and suddenly I was fixed to a slide and placed under a microscope.

And then I did something stupid. I touched Pebbles' knee and confessed, "I'm frightened."

She placed my hand on my own knee but squeezed it affectionately. I felt like an ass. "What happened, Vic?"

What happened? You just pulled my heart out and put in on the bar for strangers to use as an ashtray. "The world is becoming brittle, love. Strange," I said. "A lady told me that people are starting to hang out at old age homes in hopes of squeezing the last drop of good will from a death wisher."

"Not cool, Vic."

I was so bumfuzzled that I couldn't tell whether she referred to my information or my response. Regardless. "What do you think?"

Pebbles was not asked that question very often. Her mouth was red with whatever goop they put in her drink to give it that neon look. "I think we're all discovering new paths," she said.

Surprised by her cautious reply, I gave her an out: "No gig tonight?"

"It's early hours yet. Might roll over later, see what's up."

I ordered another round, pushed a big tip towards the bartender. "You sound . . . I don't want to say blasé, but something's different isn't it? You're distracted."

Pebbles used her fresh drink to avoid eye contact. She took a sip. "Whoa, this one's pretty dang hoochie."

"Pebbles, dear. What's going on?"

A man the color of shadows sat on a kitchen chair on the stage and began to tune his banjo. The man, his clothes, the banjo, the chair—all so shabby, so *uniformly* shabby, as to provoke suspicion. Pebbles swiveled on the barstool, drink in hand, at the first sound of strings being plunked. But she spun towards me, not away. That was a good sign.

While she watched the musician, men seated at tables and couches watched her. Probably had an easy up-skirt view, even with her knees pressed together. Her sandals dangled from the straps between her toes, exposing her dark heels and curved arches. When she spoke, her voice was low and pure, cutting through the bar noise.

"I feel like, I feel like tonight is the last night, Victor. Like something is gonna end tonight, and I need to be out here."

Her face had changed subtly, as if the last trace of baby fat had been absorbed, the jawline lengthened, and the planes of her face refined. As if she had aged, but only by a year or so, just enough to temper certain immature excitements.

She was serious. "You need to be out here," I repeated.

"I don't know why, Victor. I guess I want to remember. I want to remember really good."

A thin, elderly man with long white hair and matching beard juggled scuffed bowling pins outside, his prowess framed by the large window. He wore a black top hat and a black vest but no shirt underneath. His white chest hairs curled against his oaken skin, and he dispassionately executed a series of complex and dangerous moves, all too near the street lamps, his drink-bold audience, and the plate glass.

He did this every night at about this time. Never varied his routine. We watched anyway. Tourists, spying him for the first time, were disturbed. His eyes were dark and cruel, his exposed chest all too human. No jolly circus stray was he.

"Today was too much," I said, feebly.

"Well I'm not afraid. Does that help?" She took my hand again, held it high on her lap, a tight expanse of denim between my fingertips and her hot thigh. Every eye in the room was drawn to the gesture, but she meant nothing more by it than to comfort me.

The juggler stopped abruptly and for a wild moment I thought he too objected to the tenderness bestowed upon me, but I soon realized that he was responding to a heckler. Bobby Rebar had distracted the juggler's audience, having positioned himself just a few yards away. He was mimicking the artist's moves, enhancing them with grotesque flourishes and ape noises. The juggler ceased his own act to tell Bobby to fuck off, but that kind of thing never worked on our hero. Instead, Bobby started pulling empties from a trash bin, flipping them into the air, which sent the crowd scrambling as the glass bottles shattered in the gutter. The bartender picked up the phone and spoke a few efficient, emotion-free words into it. Even Bobby appreciated the danger of his antics, so he switched to a mangled plastic grenade shaped go-cup and a soggy something-filled take out bag. He tossed them both into the air at the same time, watching blike a child at the beach who has thrown his very first fistful of sand into the clouds.

The grenade bounced off his forehead. The bag exploded olives, meat, and bread at his feet.

"That was lucky," said Pebbles.

"Believe it or not, I have business with that gentleman."

I slid off my stool and away from her touch. She looked at me like I was crazy.

I collected her hand and kissed her fingers, now curled into a weak fist. "Later love," I said. "If there is a later." Which I thought was bloody cool of me.

The next morning brought no drama, despite Pebbles' eerie premonitions. And Val was pleased with me as I had managed to recruit Bobby to the shrimp biz, spiriting him away from the bar just before the police arrived. I also brokered a deal with Skeletor (my private nickname for the ancient juggler), who was initially quite miffed to see an offer of employment coming to his idiotic rival. Skeletor's mother was a Cheramie, and his family had worked on the bayous for generations. He had no problem going back to that life, especially in the current sluggish economy. He did not know if or how he might be related to either Captain Cheramie, but he was willing to fake affection and/or obedience if that's what the job entailed.

We allowed Bobby to sleep in the shop that night. The offer of work and money had an immediate sobering affect on him, and he was so grateful for a sandwich, a shower, and a reasonably clean cot in an air conditioned environment that at first I thought he was making fun of us. Then I thought he was planning to rob us blind. Eventually I grew too tired to be suspicious, and I went to bed, fully expecting to be awakened in the night by some roaring, destructive expression of his mania. This did not happen.

In the morning Bobby was refreshed, serious, and shy. It was a pleasure to serve him eggs and coffee before Val carted him out to his new position in Terrebonne Parish. He would also collect Skeletor on the way and return him to his ancestral home.

So it was as easy as all that, was it? The overnight cure for poverty, madness, and substance abuse? I would have worried more, but Val's new business was none of my business. I had his old business to deal with.

Tidy enough. Now Val had two boats, two captains, two crewmen, and a father who cared. I was unable to open the shop until noon though, since I had to make several trips to get supplies for Esme's order.

I made Martine drive me around because, as I've mentioned before, he had nothing better to do. It was a dull expedition out to Kenner, then Metairie, poking around retailers and wholesalers looking for the best price, but Martine was an avid bargainer, and we succeeded in loading his vehicle with excellent product for a good price. So good in fact that Martine deserved a cut of the profits, especially given that he set the sale price for the capes in the first place.

I told him as much. We were detouring through "Fat City," a club and bar district in Metairie that some claim rivals the distractions to be found in the Quarter, but wordlessly Martine and I agreed that this place was too open, too scoured, too raw and angry for our comfort. Perhaps unfairly tainted by a generalized strip mall ambiance and the tacky ghost of David Duke, Metairie always made me nervous.

"Let's get back to our moldy old caves," said Martine as he merged into the four lane insanity of the causeway.

"You deserve compensation," I insisted.

Martine was thoughtful, never coy. I let him ruminate. Finally he said, "You really think Val's gonna dump the business all on you?"

I sighed. "I really don't know. But he seems to misunderstand the depth of my personal investment. Why, you thinking of mounting a hostile takeover? Does that even happen in the boutique industry?"

Martine laughed, swerving away from one lunatic cabdriver and almost grazing another. The near accident went unacknowledged. Everyone on the causeway was driving eighty miles an hour. "I am interested in the corsets, I have to tell you."

"It seemed you were possibly over-fond of the modeling gig. Do you think there's a market?"

"I've no idea. I don't study these things. Just go with my gut, ha!" He turned in his seat to grin. Very dangerous move. "Seriously though, I like the way that thing feels. Gives me a little boost, you know?"

"Good," I said as we whizzed past four cop cars that had pulled over a construction van filled with Latino day laborers. "You can have it when I'm done. That'll be your compensation, eh?"

"Oh Victor, that's too much."

"Not at all. It'll be fantastic advertising, especially if you become even pervier as you age. Which is guaranteed."

"God bless ya. Speaking of me getting pervier Vic, you are looking damned fine these days."

"Excuse me?"

"It's a joke, of course. I want something old as you, I'll look down my own pants for it, thank you. But really, you've lost a boat load of belly. We gotta get you some new clothes."

I was pleased. "I'm making new holes in my belts."

"I'll take you out later, we'll go to the mall or something. Like real Americans. But you gotta take me somewhere first."

"Oh yeah?" Our exit was fast approaching and Martine drifted across lanes like he was driving a speed boat on an empty lake. I grabbed the door handle, as if that would help control the vehicle should we go tumbling beyond the berm. I couldn't imagine what place he had in mind. Unless he was making another dirty joke. Two in a row; did that add up to a pass? It would for me.

He dropped his hand to his lap and made an up and down gesture that I looked away from. Then back. He grasped a great big handful of lower tummy fat in his hand and shook it. "Take me to your leader, love."

I finally got past my misunderstanding, but I bookmarked it for later consideration: was I homophobic or narcissistic? "You want to go to a meeting!"

"Yeah man. You've inspired me."

"That's wonderful Martine. I'd be delighted to take you." I really was thrilled that he'd asked, but I tried to keep a lid on my enthusiasm. It must have taken a lot of courage to ask. I was touched. When I thought about it, I realized that of all of my current relationships, the one I had with Martine was the most physical. And intimate. And it only made sense that as I manipulated his body into unnatural, new shapes, he watched the reshaping of my body with a similar attention. We used to be the two fat bastards at the bar, amusingly twinned to cruel and uncaring observers. Now we were just bastards I suppose. One big, one not so big. Martine had reckoned it was time to make things even again.

"Stop grinning," said Martine.

"I can't," I said. "We just left Fat City."

5.

It took me four days to construct eight capes, during which time a rash of stranger killings erupted in a number of areas, both urban and rural. I guess there was something to the gang issue after all. Apparently, it takes a group to convince its lowest members to engage in random violence, because even if the profit motive seems obvious, killing in cold blood needs the encouragement of others.

I was terrified, staying in the shop to work on capes, and trying not to watch TV. When Esme came to collect the first batch, I promised her that the rest would be completed by the weekend. Her cool, bold facade steadied my nerves. She was all business, and unaffected by fear of sudden violence.

And then, five days after the wish killings began, they suddenly stopped. Violence for profit needs a quick payoff to develop into a proper industry, and none of the wish murders had produced desirable results. And worse, the victims tended to be chosen for opportunity, which meant that they were often marginal operators themselves and therefore part of the gangsters' customer base. Let's say some young, blank-eyed hood grabs a tranny hooker off Canal, puts a gun to her throat and terrorizes her until she speaks just the right combination of simple, raw words: *Give Timmy White a trunk of gold Krugerands*. At which point he kills her, then waits around just long enough to learn nothing has changed. Except that there's a dead lady-man at his feet. Now Timmy has to go to his boss to let him know that not only did his effort fail, but one less addict walks the streets. The economics became very clear, very quickly.

Thus, by the time the rest of Esme's capes were ready, the phenomenon had burned itself out like a hot virus. Gang leaders engaged in public relations clean up the best they knew how, appearing masked on news programs to reassure the public that it was once again safe to buy drugs on the street. But I was still nervous to see Esme arrive for the final pick-up with a tall, shadowed stranger in tow. It was late Sunday afternoon and brutally bright outside, but within the shop it was cool and dark. The environment was perfect for being silent, interior. I sat on a stool back near my workspace, and when Esme brought her buyer with her it was a violating experience.

He moved with her from shadows into revelation, tall, but he was just a boy. Curly tousled hair, white and lean, with muscles and bones that were only just coming under control. What was he, seventeen? Ratty T-shirt, rattier shorts. His knees shined with layers of scars.

Mick Breglia. He wasn't allowed in the shop.

"You aren't allowed in the shop, Mick."

He held out a wad of cash. So crude. Esme grinned.

"Oh. Thanks." I accepted the money and gave them the rest of the capes, which I'd packed into twine-handled shopping bags.

Mick was a thief. As was his whole skateboarding crew. But they stole dumb stuff, like pens and candies and trinkets you could get for free during Mardi Gras parades. The value had less to do with the item stolen than it did with the addition of difficulty that transformed a conventional skateboard stunt into a caper. Mick and the boys liked to whiz up and down the banquette, weaving around pedestrians and delivery trucks, and whooping as they executed leaps and slides before surfing into shops to snatch what ever was loose and handy. In our shop it wasn't so much the stealing—although they did clean us out of *think-pink* rubber bracelets—as the knocking down of racks loaded with clothing. Mick and his boys were banned throughout the Quarter and Marigny.

And now they had capes. Marvelous. I counted the cash and tried to ignore the fact that Esme and Mick were still standing there, barely suppressing hormonal glee.

I said, "It's the wrong Elvis."

"It's the best Elvis," Mick argued. He peeked into the bag. "Brother you are fucking awesome."

"I appreciate that. And I appreciate your business. Let me know if there is anything else I can do for you," I immediately regretted the waste of my dry wit. "May I assume that you and your rolling comrades are planning some bit of theater? A memorable rampage through the city?"

Mick raised his bag in triumph. He declared, "We are the Phantoms!"

Esme raised her little fist in support. "Wish Phantoms," she chirped.

Sounded good. "Wish Phantoms? You'll have masks then?"

"You know it."

"Tremendous. Invest in quality, flexibility."

"Already thought of that," said Mick. "Nothing but the best."

"And may I request, ah, professional courtesy?"

This confounded the boy. Too many syllables.

I gestured to my surroundings, the shop in general. "What I mean to say is, we here at Val's Vintage, and its subsidiary interest V3C, would appreciate an exemption from the coming mayhem."

The boy did not get my drift. Esme looked annoyed, the way a moll does when she's run out of fingernails to file and buff.

"Give us a pass, Mick-o," I said. "Let's be friends, and all that. Count the capes, you got a lagniappe."

That he understood. "No shit?" The boy grinned and grabbed my hand, pumping it with experimental force, as if he had never shaken a grownup's hand before. Done deal. He didn't know it yet, but we were networking.

The two bandits left the shop together, giggling and whispering like they were going steady, which was not a terrible thought. He was much younger than his years and she much older than hers. Sure there was nearly a three foot difference in height between them, but perhaps the physical stuff didn't matter so much when it was all so volatile and in flux.

Maybe there was hope for Pebbles and me after all. A self deprecating joke of a thought, but it made me wince inside. I'd managed to hurt my own feelings.

My fear, stemming from the instability of recent events, made me emotionally prone. I was weakened and distracted, laid bare. I no longer merely fancied my neighbor Pebbles. I had grown attached to her, in love as insane as that sounds, and I retreated into an obsessive state, inhabiting a continuous fantasy of lust and sweetness. The real world softened for me, became less detailed, and that felt good. I slept-walked through conversations, especially with Val, coming to consciousness only when the real Pebbles pierced the veil.

The next time she visited, she brought me two thirds of a seedless watermelon, the cut edge protected in plastic wrap. It was an enormous thing and a delightful treat. Bachelors tend to live without watermelon, it being a family sized food that doesn't keep. But the girl carrying a gigantic piece of fruit was the only thing normal about her visit. She showed up dressed in a natural linen skirt, tailored blouse, and damn it, sensible shoes. Her hair was combed like she was going to church, and there wasn't a single note of whimsy in her accessories. She was beautiful, though. I spied the baby cross resting on the inner rise of her left breast and then the gold chain to which it was connected, so delicate I almost missed it.

"Are you going to a job interview?" I asked, taking the melon from her. It was the size and slipperiness of a six month old baby. I had to shove a lot of stuff to the back of the fridge to find a place for it.

"No," she said. Subdued. It was overcast that Monday morning, and everything seemed more serious because of it. "I'm going to a meeting."

The front of my shirt was damp with the dew of the rind, my hands sticky with juice. Pebbles handed me a dishtowel.

"I don't think I should talk about it," she said. Couldn't look me in the eye.

I couldn't take my eyes off of her though. She looked something. More mature. The thought excited me. "That's all right," I assured her. "But if you want to tell me, maybe you should?"

Now she seemed hurt. Shot me a dark, odd look.

I took it back. "Or not. Just tell me you're okay."

She couldn't verbalize it. I had to use all my strength to keep from launching into worried dad mode, the urge to patronize nearly as powerful as desire. But I knew when to back down, not interfere. Lovers are equals, I kept chanting in my brain. Brenda would be proud. Or sad. No, amused, because I was doomed to fail.

"Tell me." Too much edge.

Pebbles left.

In his first televised appearance, The Elvis did not speak. I think the strategy was to get the world accustomed to seeing the dead walk by giving us only glimpses at first, exposing us little by little to the impossible. Our first look was eighteen seconds, which was how long it took for the man to descend the stairs from a private jet, jog across a small stretch of tarmac, smile, give a thumbs up, and duck into the black tinted safety of a waiting Suburban. He wore black jeans, a Hollister hoodie, and a Marine Corps baseball cap. The clothes looked good on him, perfectly natural. But he was also wearing sunglasses that were too modern, too chic and narrow. We'd have to get used to change.

I watched that smile over and over again, on every channel. Here was a man who knew about love. Was born with enough that he could give it away like this, in smiles. Then I watched those milliseconds before and after the smile, his appraisal of the immediate present. Plane, tarmac, limousine. Everything had changed, become smaller and more efficient except for this. Getting to where he needed to be was still the same old story. Was that a comfort, I wondered? Or an extreme disappointment?

I spent the day grinding on my misstep with Pebbles, but in the early evening my self-hatred abated enough to enjoy the long walk to the weight plan meeting with Martine. We got him weighed in, pre-paid for a three month trial, all his little pamphlets and records in order before we toddled into the lecture room like happy sailors. And there my general good humor soured.

Here I meant to show him a pageant of hopers, an array of hefty enthusiasts all bound together in a single goal, but the turnout was so slight I thought they'd changed the schedule on us. Normally, there would be thirty of us struggling and wheezing to find comfortable positions on the metal chairs, but this evening there were only about eight attendees. And no Ruby in sight.

Martine shuffled through his packet, organized his coupons and such, but that only held his interest for so long. After a few minutes he announced, "Well I'm not that impressed, Vic."

"Of course you aren't. This isn't the way it is supposed to be. Excuse me," I leaned forward and spoke to the back of a woman's head. Her little eye fluttered open, as if I'd awakened it. "Where's Ruby?"

She shrugged without turning around. The old habits had begun to erode, and many women had given up on the custom of turning to face their interrogators. They'd adapted to the new equipment very quickly, but it still felt rude to those of us without the modification.

"I been waiting a while," she said to the space in front of her. "Mebbe we'll have a sub?"

I was embarrassed. Martine would surely abandon the project before it could properly begin. One of the ladies from the front desk waddled in, all apologies and smiles. "I'm sorry y'all, but Ms. Ruby hasn't arrived just yet, and we're not sure what the problem is. Let's give her another five minutes, and if she doesn't make it I guess I'll take care of things." She sounded a bit brittle about this possibility. I had the distinct impression she wished we would all just go away.

"Where is everyone?" I asked her, but she only shrugged and returned to her post at the weigh in desk, despite the fact that there was no one left in line.

That Tracy woman from the last meeting showed up, though. She smiled at me in greeting and took a moment to notice Martine. She made her eyes glitter at him. More man meat. He recognized her intent and grunted pleasantly.

He whispered, "How many of these gals did you bang again?"

"Shh."

Tracy grinned at us. "Nobody comes to these things anymore, Mr. Victor. I told you, for some it's a waste of time. I been to three different meetings this week. They're all the same. Like goin' to church in the seventies. And," she continued, looking around the room, "it looks like old Ruby has finally given it up. Course, that seemed kinda inevitable."

The half dozen other women in the room seemed content to wait, all occupied with magazines, knitting, cell phones and the like. I was not willing to waste Martine's time like this. The desk lady came to the threshold a couple of times to stare at us and bite the lipstick from her mouth. "Well, this is stupid!" I declared, and Martine patted my knee. He felt my disappointment.

Tracy smiled at me. She was a snake, so happy to be proven right. But she wasn't right. Just because everyone agreed to give up didn't make it right.

Tracy said, "You do it, Mr. Victor."

The little eye in front of us spasmed. Its voice: "Yes, that's a marvelous idea."

It was not a marvelous idea at all, and I was on my feet almost immediately. Surprised myself. Surprised the hell out of Martine. Because I did not leave the gathering in a fit of pique. Instead I rolled myself up to the front of the room and took position behind the podium. Neither Ruby nor Rollie used the podium, as they liked to put their bodies out there on display. I didn't have that kind of confidence.

I had no idea how to begin. I was looking at faces, not just rear ends and hair and little eyes. "Could you all sort of gather together here in the middle instead of being so spread out?" No one moved until Tracy did, and then they all heaved themselves up and over, complaining gently as they did so. I could tell they were interested in witnessing this train wreck.

The desk lady came to the threshold, and great relief spread over her face. She leaned against the frame, her thin arms folded across her chest. She wanted to watch this happen as well.

I tried to remember the parts. *Introduction, news, how was your week, inspiring story, goodbye.* "My name is Victor, I've been coming to meetings for six months and I've lost . . . I've lost, how much?" Desk lady scrambled out of sight, returned in a wink.

"Thirty six point four pounds, dear."

That got a round of applause. Even I hadn't dared to say the number out loud before. "Really?" I asked her. It was a genuine question but they all, even Martine, laughed at me. It didn't matter.

"Well okay, thirty six pounds then."

"You need new clothes," said Tracy, reminding me that while she had nominated me for the job of meeting leader, she wasn't going to be lead very easily.

And even Martine chimed in, "That's what I told him. Man runs a clothing shop fer Gawd's sake."

I let them banter. It used up time, and they were happy to abuse me. Eventually, my tension melted. When I finally reclaimed the spotlight, I was calm and authoritative, harkening back to the days when I had to explain content management systems to boardrooms full of drooling executives. My audience settled right down. First, I went into a brief discussion of what I understood about the nutritional benefits of the buttershrimp. Everyone had a recipe already, so we ate up time sharing those; my hand cramped as I attempted to take dictation on the whiteboard. Then I opened up the meeting for diet week confessions, and I was delighted that no one derailed the discussion the way they liked to do with Ruby. Tellingly, there was no mention of the wish killings, Elvis, or anything that had nothing to do with food and weight loss. We were in a safe zone, willing and eager to play by the rules for once.

When I ended the meeting, on time mind you, I was chuffed. I hadn't felt so accomplished in a long time. Even Tracy congratulated me on her way out. Martine waited on them all to clear out, his ass firmly planted in his metal chair. I was pretty sure he planned to give this weight plan thing a real shot. He beamed at me. Totally smitten.

That felt really good.

6.

That night I dreamed of making love to Pebbles. I was lean and young, and we were back in my marriage bed in Northern Virginia. She locked her legs around me, breathed hard and called me Elvis, which was perfect. I even got to finish without any upsetting Freudian intrusions. I never had a better dream. I awoke in the dark to the sounds of glass breaking and a security alarm. Not our shop, but someone else's, nearby.

I fought the sheets, and by the time I made it to the window I recognized the wrong, strange light three blocks away. The vegetarian café, it looked like. Probably broken into. Over at Pebbles' all was dark except a certain pale, rose illumination far back into her apartment. Possibly the kitchen. I thought I saw a shadow stir, but then no. My clock read 3:27am. I put on a robe, just in case she had been awakened by the ruckus.

Then I saw the culprit, a vampiric figure slithering down the middle of Esplanade, confident as a ballroom dancer. His half mask was basic, but it glowed in the dark, and around his neck and wrists he wore those bendy neon light stick bracelets, green and pink, which cast dull rainbows across his short white cape. I could hear the brutal rumble of his skateboard wheels, but in the night he appeared mystically propelled, surfing shadows as if they had substance. As he skated below my window, he offered a salute. Mick was disguised, but he was unmistakably himself.

"You bastard," said Pebbles.

She leaned out of her apartment window just across the street. My heart dropped. It was hard to see her face. Mick raised his middle finger to her as he disappeared into darkness: "Wish Phantoms, bitch!"

"Why'd he wave at you? You know him?" she asked. Her voice was direct, but not loud.

What was the prudent answer? I didn't reply quick enough.

"You made that cape, Victor."

A siren, at last. Thank God. "Cops," I said, stupidly.

"That shit just broke into Tammy Benoit's business. You don't care about that?"

"Of course I do."

"Val!" the girl yelled. I wheeled around, half expecting to discover my son behind me in my room. But no.

I said, "I can't help what happens in the clothing I make. Please be reasonable, love."

She wasn't listening. She had grown so much stronger, stranger over the past few days. And now she was angry with me. Where had that come from? I asked, "What was your meeting about, Pebbles. Please tell me."

She repeated, "Val, get out here."

He appeared by *her* side, assuming a position in the frame of her window. A shadow like she, but sulky. A discernable posture of guilt.

I wanted to collapse. It wasn't fair.

"Dad." So not a question.

I hoped to God they didn't see the streetlight shine in my eyes.

Pebbles zeroed in on Val. "You said he had a cape order for some gangster. That wasn't no gangster. That was some white kid punk. And he just smashed Le Potate. Goes by on his skateboard and gives your pops a howdy—"

Feeling exposed, I retreated from the window and dropped back onto my narrow bed where I listened to Val cut her off. "What are you getting all wound up for? Dad didn't break any windows." Not the sharpest argument, but I filed it away for deferred appreciation.

As far as I could tell, the argument ended there. Sirens grew louder, and I could hear dogs barking and old women emptying into the street. Red light swept the far corner, rhythmically, followed by gargled, crunchy radio voices as the police coordinated their efforts at the scene. I waited until I felt sure that Pebbles and Val had retreated before I got up to close my shade against the noise and the light.

Miscalculation. They were still hanging out the window to monitor the confusion at the end of the street. Val did not notice me shutting myself away, but Pebbles did. There was a bit more light now, what with neighbors waking and cop cars leaving their lights rolling. Pebbles stared across at me, her eyes wide and sorry. Well, wasn't that something, then. A dime's worth of sorry feeling after a dollar's worth of anger.

Hard thing to do, pulling down that shade.

Well that explained it. Pebbles had finally captured Val, and now she was coping with her achievement. I knew how that happened, how happiness could become guilt that transforms into anger.

When she gave me the watermelon, it was happening then. Her leap. But first she had to give me fruit. It was a clearing of the decks gesture. The melon was her way of signaling the break with me, the end of our flirtation. A reasonable and humane effort. But more, she'd settled her outstanding debts, made way for the new era. That was one hell of a watermelon.

But I still believed there was a deeper irritant, some other undiscovered issue. I tracked back along her moods. I don't think she had been seeing Val yet, that last night at the Spotted Cat when she spoke of vague portent. She had been on the verge of change, about to take incontrovertible action that night. And I had to believe that action was bigger than sex, that her regret stemmed from something more substantial than trivial betrayal. And then there was her mysterious meeting. The deeper feeling she showed that morning, the concern that was not about her, me, and Val; that was a different specter altogether.

I met Martine for breakfast at the Primrose Cafe, a cramped, busy diner that had remained dormant after Katrina, and had only recently reopened. I wasn't sure if the owners were the same, but they still offered platter-sized pancakes, a Primrose specialty. We were not indulging, and Martine ordered what I ordered: dry wheat toast, egg substitute, and bacon. It didn't matter, as the ascetic fare would still be delicious, and the cook would fry it all up in the same butter and andouille grease as the rest of the menu. In addition to two person booths and wobbly tables, there was a narrow counter with stools behind which the coffee machine gurgled and the dirty dishes accumulated. Back there a small TV ran without sound, tuned to the local Fox station. Apparently more footage of The Elvis had been released. I saw desert landscapes, a horse, the man walking alone. Hands in pockets, a cowboy hat.

I told Martine about the kerfuffle at Le Potate, and that Pebbles and Val were now "together." Not entirely reformed, my friend sipped at a large Bloody Mary that he claimed made the egg substitute tolerable. We had timed things perfectly, getting into the diner early for a decent table. Tourists now loitered at the entry, waiting for seats to open up. Martine and I had a cozy booth near the kitchen, in the heart of the action, with plenty of delicious breeze from the swinging door. He examined me over the narrow rim of his glass. "The girl is your life's mystery."

"Oh thank you," I said, and proceeded to confess everything

to him. My feelings for Pebbles, my humiliation, even my dream. "I am so terribly blue, Martine. And more in love than ever. My shame is of course compounded by the likelihood that my dream had been synchronized with their *consummation*."

Martine's face crinkled with sympathy. He drank a long draught, then ate a weak mouthful of eggs, taking no joy in it. But he continued to eat. I chewed on my toast, sniffling as I washed it down with coffee. The heartache came in nasty little waves. "Oh God, please don't let me embarrass myself."

Martine scanned the diner. "In front of this buncha piggies? Look at them getting their feed on. You go right on ahead and bawl your eyes out if you want."

"Nice attitude." I meant it. One of the first signs of commitment to weight loss is a them vs. us competitive spirit. Outside the diner faces from the crowd breathed on the glass, eyes widening with each heaped and steaming tray that the staff brought out. A blur passed by our table to drop off the check we hadn't asked for.

We were in no hurry to leave. On the TV, a replay of The Elvis footage, but this time I caught the crawl: Somewhere in Montana. The camera swung wide to show a nearly empty, featureless landscape, and a horizon that promised no more moons. But then the reality was revealed. A fleet of black SUVs and a cadre of suited, sun-glassed men, all waiting on their captive from the past. The Elvis did not seem too put off, though. He had a beatific expression not seen in his original incarnation. Perhaps a bit of this impression was due to the absence of pomade in his hair. Instead, he had a good cut that left the pompadour with sculpted rather than slick sides. And the color was warmer, going to its natural brown. No doubt about it, he was a lovely looking fellow. No images of him with his family yet. That tugged at me. Montana, eh? Poor bastard.

To our server's dismay, Martine ordered a coffee chaser for

his now empty Bloody Mary. He sort of shifted sideways in the booth as if he might just hang out till lunchtime, watching the world munch by.

"You know those little fuckers hit half a dozen shops last night."

He meant Mick and his Phantoms. I chewed on the information. The bastards. In my capes. "Do you think there's anything I can do?"

A couple of seats at the counter had opened up, stool tops still spinning when two young men in slicked back black hair and sideburns claimed them. One of the men wore sunglasses. Though dressed alike, it was unclear if the men were acquainted. The Elvis was catching on. Martine noticed too.

He said, "I don't think they'll listen to sense, Vic. But with the capes it won't take long to connect you to them."

Pebbles had been so angry, and I wondered how my fellow shopkeepers would take my apparent support of the Wish Phantoms. "It was a legal transaction. A job. I had no way of knowing."

"Won't stop folks from hating you."

"I know that."

Martine was thoughtful. He always knew how to fix a problem. "Whatever deal you made, unmake it. Ask Mick to hit the shop. And soon. Let them have their way with you now, before they get a taste for it. Before the sadism kicks in."

That night, Val ate dinner with me, which was surprising. I made green salad and scattered black beans, corn, and curried chicken on top. He ate it and didn't complain. Another surprise. But in between bites and phone calls, he managed to say, "We need to talk about last night."

Last night was my least favorite subject, and by invoking it my son reminded me of the many inversions in our relationship. I was his father, but that job had become a mere sinecure. He was the boss. He was the landlord. And now he was my beloved's lover.

Val was on the phone throughout most of the meal, and it was beginning to look like we'd never have our heart to heart. His laptop was open on the table top like a third place setting. I saw the reflection of numbers in his eyes, and his phone twinkled constantly, the blue chasing light all around the edge like a tiny police car.

Why all the urgent wheeling and dealing? It seemed Val's buttershrimp empire was in peril. He needed to hire a new crew and lease new boats. "We're gonna lose days," he moaned.

Because Bobby and Skeletor had played pirates with the old boats, ramming into each other out in South Pass, while the Captains Cheramie slept off lunch in the cabins below. The Captains survived without injury but were relieved of duty, and Skellie landed in jail. Bobby, however, went Batshit In The Bayou and escaped capture. Now he was on the run, although it was unlikely that anyone was chasing him very hard.

High tides, low tides, temperatures, all that. It sounded to me like it was going to take three times as many folks to replace the Cheramies, Bobby, and Skeletor.

When Val hung up, he looked at the dregs of the salad as if it caused him pain. He rose, went to the fridge and retrieved a stale tortilla from an open package. He tipped the remains of his meal into the wrap and consumed it in two bites, then rinsed the food down with an Abita Amber. "We gotta talk about Pebs," he said when he was done.

I sipped at my vodka and lime soda. About ninety fewer calories than beer, isn't that a kick in the ass? I shook my head like it was no big deal.

"Fuck you," said Val.

He had my attention.

"She's gone all religious, Dad. But really bad, and I don't have time for it." He gestured to the computer, indicating his priorities. He needed to focus on shoring up his new venture. "You probably know this, but it turns out I'm in love with her."

Strange, but that helped. I thought of her breasts, how lovely they were that morning she gave me the watermelon.

"Watermelon?" I offered. There were a few mushy slices left.

Val declined. "I'm sorry. I know this must seem like a kick in the head."

A kick in the head, a gut punch, a knife in my heart, whatever. I went to the fridge and grabbed both pieces for myself. I could live on watermelon, I had decided. Watermelon and vodka. "I saw that she was wearing a little cross," I said, sitting back down at the Formica table. Val leaned back, letting the beer do its digestive work.

We were going to talk about it, but not IT.

Val shook his head. "Nah, this isn't just some fundamentalist thing. It's Mirella and some 'cult' thing sprung up around her."

I hadn't heard about this, but I recalled Mirella's majesty at Rollie's speech with great fondness. That seemed like a long time ago. "'Wish Local' is it? I know Pebbles was persuaded."

Suddenly, our storefront gates were being vigorously rattled. That happened all the time, as people liked to shake the metal as they stumbled from bar to bar. Val ignored the sound, didn't jump inside the way I did. Per Martine's counsel, I'd gotten the message out to Breglia via one of his pimply associates. All we had to do was wait like virgin brides. Every thump, every creak in the centuries old building was alive with threat.

"I guess Mirella's sick. Really sick. Cirrhosis or pneumonia, but something that's getting worse every day. She's what, four hundred years old?"

"Val."

"Anyway, this punk ex-priest has got it into his head that Mirella's the next Death Wisher, and he's been recruiting followers to hang out at Mirella's home and her club. Hell, even her doctor's office. It's completely sick."

Probably, but I doubted Mirella minded the attention. "And Pebbles has joined them?"

"Yeah. She's totally into this bastard—Pere Qua? He goes by that, seriously. She's even missed work to attend emergency prayer sessions. And you know she doesn't sing any more."

Under other circumstances, a blessing. I could see it though, her latching on to some substitute for the religion she'd been raised in. Though she'd voluntarily left her mission with the Christian college soon after coming to New Orleans, she'd probably felt un-moored. It was only natural, especially after the dramatic changes the world had seen, that she would fall prey to charismatic forces.

"How long have you been sleeping with her?"

"Not long." He wasn't going to fight me on this. Got up to get another beer. There were shouts outside. Normal street shouts.

Val drank standing by the fridge. "Do something Daddy. She loves you. I love her." He was serious.

"She loves you."

Val shrugged. "She's a kid. She says so. But what does she know?"

I was unmoved by his humility. "You think this 'Pere Qua' is dangerous?"

"Everybody's dangerous these days."

"I'll talk to her," I said. "But you have to do something for me."

"Hmm?"

"Stay out tonight. Stay over with her if you like, it doesn't matter."

The beer stopped flowing past his lips as he tried to read me. "What's going on?"

"Appointment vandalism. Wish Phantoms. Val, I'm very sorry, but it has to happen."

He thought about this. "Because of the capes." I braced for his anger, but it didn't come. In fact, he looked almost peaceful. Took another swallow. "We're insured," he finally said.

Val really did want my help with Pebbles, but I doubted he completely understood his own motivations. Nothing dampens passion quite like another passion, and it was a sure thing that Pebbles would sacrifice their physical relationship to nurture her spiritual growth if it came down to it. Plus, by assigning me the delicate mission of dismantling her faith, Val kept me busy and intimately involved. No time to sit in my room, no time to stew in my loneliness.

I called Pebbles to get the ball rolling. She had to tell me in her own way what she was up to.

"I'm tearing up the town tonight, darling," I said, pretending that nothing had changed. "And I miss your sexy voice. Do promise you will be at the open mic tonight? I'm your stage door Johnny, I'll bring you posies."

That made her laugh but in a brief, sad way. Someday she'd remember that Val had never seen her sing, but that I'd always been there for her.

"I'm not into that any more, Vic," she said. A little strain in her voice, like she had to protect herself. "My nights are"–she oomphed—"I'm sort of studying a lot, and I'm with this group. A kind of fellowship thing. Val didn't tell you?" Saying his name to me was hard for her.

"No more singing? I'm devastated. What'll I do with m'self?"

"Just putting that part of me aside for a while," she said. "While I get my head on straight. I have to start taking life a whole lot more seriously."

"You may be in the wrong part of the world for that."

No laugh. "So really. Val didn't tell you I've gotten back into, um, religious stuff?"

This was breaking my heart all over again. "Not that I can recall, dearie. What do you mean, you're going to church?"

"Not as such. I'm just with a study group now. We have discussions, support each other. We're activist, I guess you'd say."

"Well that sounds grand, Pebbles. Like my meetings, they've been essential to my mental health. I've got Martine going now and last week I ended up leading the meeting. It was very exciting."

She didn't respond. Either she had drifted away or she knew what I was up to. Bold measures were called for.

"Sing to me Pebbles."

"Don't be a goof."

I poured all my frustrated lust into a single word. "Please."

"I'm thinking, I'm thinking," she said. Then, after a couple of dark seconds she launched into the second verse of "Dream a Little Dream of Me." The song just happened to be entirely within her range, much to my surprise. Singing softly into the phone and without the pressure of a band behind her, she managed the tricky bits with ease. The experience was lovely.

But she didn't finish the song. She got to "say nighty-night and kiss me" and choked on a sob. "Sorry, Victor." She hung up.

I let her go, un-pursued. This was enough for now.

I was half happy, half sad. I owned some tiny chunk of her heart, still.

CLOUDS

1.

I started the night at Snug Harbor's ten o'clock show, which featured a lanky white-boy vibraphonist, said to be a protégé of the great Terence Blanchard. Seemed like it would be a serious, sober experience, a proper foundation for the long night ahead. I swear I had no intention of hooking up.

I selected a bench table along the balcony where I could look down at the players and watch their finger work. The audience was mostly couples holding hands at candle-lit tables and sipping near-lethal Monsoons. At the moment the stage was empty except for the piano and two sets of vibraphones. A large mirror affixed to the wall allowed anyone in the club to see the piano keyboard. The vibraphones had just been uncovered and tested by a disheveled tech who would later re-appear as the performer himself, hair combed and in a suit jacket.

Feeling tender and dreading the long hours ahead, I ordered a diet cola and settled in. That was when I spotted her. How long had she been playing the eye game with me? The woman was tiny and fit in summery dress, and her hair was jewel colored under the club lights as it hugged her toned shoulders like ivy on a schoolhouse. She'd been around the block, but in a good way. With her sat a light skinned African American woman, definitely younger, wearing a blue silk blouse that gaped over her bosom, but her tight denim skirt was an inspiration. I wondered if I could make a corset out of Levis. The friend was a big girl, but not the sort who was so silly as to think she had to do anything about it. Both of them played with the straps of their handbags and sipped at beers in short glasses as they shared a portion of fried oysters and wiped their fingertips on napkins after every mouthful. A girls' night out.

Perhaps it goes overboard to characterize my sexual reticence as terror, but even I would admit that as the years passed since the divorce my prudence had evolved into pathology. Martine often criticized me for using him and Val, and more recently the inaccessible Pebbles, as the front line in my sexual defense zone, so I lied and told him tales of chubby, sweaty trysts with the ladies in my weight loss program. I don't know if he believed me, but he loved the stories and left it at that. Brenda was never that cool. In those tense months after we broke up, she thought I was punishing her by not dating. She accused me of hiding inside my fat. Which was true enough back then.

Even if I wanted to, there was nowhere to hide now. The way this lady gazed at me required a response. I raised my drink in salutation, and that was it. Done deal. She spoke two syllables to her friend who promptly collected her purse and drink, got up from the table, and went downstairs, not even making eye contact with me as she passed by.

So now it was just me and the woman fate had chosen to break my dry spell. She mouthed "Come here," and waved me over. I decided not to struggle and slid into the seat pre-warmed by her friend. I said, "I'm Victor," and inadvertently dropped my gaze to the three or four uneaten fried oysters left in the basket. The sharp scent of Tabasco entwined with the heavy aroma of grease. My stomach clenched and my balls tingled. This was going to be weird.

"Go ahead," she offered, giving the food a wee push in my

direction. "I'm Donna."

I immediately imagined her naked. I immediately felt bad about that. She smelled like lavender shampoo, beer, and fried seafood. She was a friendly woman, so much so that for a while I was worried that the night was going to cost me money. Half way through the vibraphonist's performance she shifted over to my side of the table so that we were hip to hip on the bench. Then she rested her hand, palm up, on my thigh, exactly midway between my hip and knee. It burned there throughout the rest of the set. I could not come up with a reciprocal gesture that seemed imaginative and worthy, and when we finally made it back to her place after the show, I went shy on her. She too seemed humbled by the fact that we were alone at last. It's easy to flirt in the magic darkness of a jazz club, but now that we were consenting adults in the cool domestic silence of her apartment the electricity between us found its ground. I was moments away from succumbing to doubt and fear when she invited me, quite kindly, to bed.

I didn't tell her that I hadn't been with a woman in seven years. I'd had a rich fantasy life, but I hadn't been physical with anyone since Brenda. Well, since a bookstore clerk right after Brenda, but that was so miserable it didn't count.

Donna went in ahead of me, leaving the bedroom dark. She understood that I required permission at every turn, so once she'd slid under the covers she called out, "Okay, now." The bathroom light was left on for navigation purposes, casting just enough indirect light for me to make my way through the unfamiliar room.

As easy as she was making this I still panicked. I came up with the crazy notion that I should just lay with her and hold her through the night in a gesture of tender appreciation. I banged my knee, not very hard, against the edge of a coffee table, and the accident produced an immediate, full blooded erection. I grabbed a small chenille pillow from the sofa and proceeded into her bedroom where I tried to remove my socks, shoes, and belt with some measure of grace. I stripped down to my shorts and hoped to hell that my lady did not have good night vision.

The shape of her on the bed. "I'm just happy to hold you," I said, and all the times I'd made similar promises to girls in college came rushing back to me. As I recalled I was not very good at keeping those promises.

"That'd be nice," she replied. "Anything, really."

A response that should have given me some relief but didn't. I worked my way under bedding that seemed more complicated than necessary, with sheets tucked in tight and silky bits folded over fleecy parts. But I finally got in there and inhaled the powerful mixture of her perfume, the alcohol we'd consumed, and the fresh laundered scent of her linens. We kissed, which was its own roller coaster ride, and I collected her in my arms, easing her over onto her side so we could spoon. I kissed her shoulders and placed the chenille pillow between us.

"What's that?"

"A pillow. From your sofa."

"Why?"

"Seemed less rude than the alternative."

She was quiet for a moment. Then, "You call it The Alternative?"

After which the pillow was tossed aside and we went ahead and did what we were supposed to do under the circumstances. I concluded our non-traumatic lovemaking by rubbing her feet until she fell asleep. Donna told me she was a waitress, which was a relief. I know a little about women but a lot about waitresses. Hash slingers crave foot rubs as much as frat boys love blowies. She dozed off with a smile on her face.

I woke before she did. I think. Regardless, she let me sneak out the door unimpeded. Leaving like that was not my style, but after so many years on the inactive list I didn't really have a style anymore. I crept home through streets that were mostly empty except for delivery vans and delivery men, and my dread of whatever might have happened to the shop during the night dissipated in light of the fact that I had gotten laid. I was annoyed at the prospect of tidying up, but mainly my thoughts settled on pleasure, and every trash can, every brick, every angry bird seemed charming and suffused with an erotic glow. The sunrise stalled on the horizon, and the pretty sherbet light painted every surface in every direction.

Which was wrong of course. The morning light was wrong. I saw a beer man roll a keg to the middle of the street. He stopped there, stood the keg on end, and looked up. I looked up too.

Orange clouds. Beautiful, but not at all right. Gorgeous sunrises and sunsets are common in New Orleans, given the coastal atmospherics, but this phenomenon had nothing to do with meteorology. Orange God-damned clouds. Against a blue-eyed sky. It hurt to look at it.

"The fuck," said the beer man.

The sun climbed, yellow and brutal, but the color of the clouds did not change. Although there were slight variations in depth and intensity, most of the clouds were pastel, like giant circus peanuts floating overhead. Others were sharply hued, conjuring citrus and melon flavors to bloom in the back of my mouth.

Ridiculous. Who would wish such a thing?

"Fuckin' artists," was the beer man's assessment. Probably so. As in all movements, it was only a matter of time before fashion overtook practical concerns. A candy fist of a cloud took a swipe at the sun, and its shade traveled over me, steady with the breeze. The beer man had seen enough and continued with his work, horsing the heavy cylinder into a brick and fern-filled courtyard where a man in a white apron waited. He held open an ancient, slatted door, which the beer man disappeared through. The aproned man then shut the slat door as if light itself were the enemy. If he'd noticed anything new about the sky he didn't show it.

I pulled out my phone, checked the time: 7:05 am. I called Val, who answered after the first ring.

"Are you home?" I asked.

A pause, some sleepy noises. "Um, no."

"Might as well stay put," I said, knowing he was in Pebbles' bed. "I'll be home in a tick. I'll let you know what I find." I hung up without giving him the weather report.

Orange clouds. Hard not to stare. I wondered what orange fog would look like.

I reached Decatur and leaned towards Esplanade, and one by one, folks ventured out from the protection of their homes, shops, and hotel rooms to stand on the curb and consider the sky. Not much in the way of chatter; the community had run dry of theories and assumptions. I think mine was the only body on the move as I veered my way around sidewalk gawkers. Some folks came out onto their filigreed iron balconies to get a closer look.

A man with a sun burnt scalp leaned on a street broom in front of an espresso bar that reeked of hot cinnamon pastries, and I wouldn't have given him a second glance except for two things I noticed as he tilted his flushed face to the sky. One, he looked familiar. And two, he wept openly. Tears streamed down his cheek and dangled from his squat, ruined nose. As if orange clouds were too beautiful and too terrible to behold.

I passed behind him, and recognized him a split second

before I saw that his name tag read: *Gerry*. Poor Gerald Pollin, he of "Satan hates faggots" fame. Sad fuck never made out of New Orleans after all. He was dressed in a uniform shirt and black work pants rolled in clumps over no slip shoes. His face was a mess, his skin blotchy as if he had just gotten over chicken pox. And his nose? My God that nose. It looked like a Chinese dumpling. Or a circus peanut.

I hurried away from him, away from his reality. I could not imagine any circumstances other than tragic ones that would have kept him in New Orleans. Perhaps I was foolish to think he'd recognize me, given his many impairments on the day that we met, but I felt rotten in his presence. Guilty and angry. I resented that he felt this event so keenly. To be honest, after our encounter in Jackson Square I had wanted him to evaporate, to stop existing altogether.

I stopped, looked back at him. He wept into the blinding sun. How dare he.

The lock was broken, and both sides of the gate were pulled apart. Other than that, there were no external signs of damage. The shop door was closed, and inside it was dark. I tried the door, but it wouldn't budge. I pressed my face to a window and cupped my eyes to see. It was a mess inside—racks toppled, the counter glass shattered, cash register missing. A heap of something in the middle of the floor, covered by my favorite cape, a big black velvet affair with a Saturn shaped broach and pumpkin colored satin lining. And, sticking out of one end of the heap, a pair of boots.

Shit.

I stomped past two obese rats, sluggish as they slipped into the shadows of the alley. The door to the house was locked tight, and I clumsily sorted through my keys.

"Everything cool, Dad?" Val was shirtless, standing in the frame of Pebbles' open window.

"There's someone in there. Maybe hurt."

"What do you mean?" And then he was distracted. "Whoa! Look at the clouds! Hey Pebs, get the hell out here!"

My heart raced as I jammed my key into the lock and twisted. My hands shook, but I got the door open. Turned to Val. "Forget the clouds," I shouted. "Call the police."

Pebbles joined Val at the window. She appeared to be fully dressed, in another skirt suit. She fussed with her cuffs as she squinted up at the morning sky.

Val looked down at me. I ran into our house.

Pebbles screamed.

I climbed a flight to get to the kitchen and then crossed to the door in the rear that lead to the back stairs. Down again, into the shop where shards of glass crunched under foot. A wicked stench permeated the air.

There were pins, beads, and hangers everywhere. To get to the suspicious heap, I climbed over toppled chrome racks, still heavy with clothing but now bent out of shape. One of the bigger racks was jammed against the front doors, which was why I couldn't get in that way. A barricade? I yanked my cape off the heap, releasing a massive, rolling cloud of foul stink, and even before I could bear to look at what lay beneath, my heart filled with relief. The smell was gruesome, but it was definitely produced by a living thing. Bobby Rebar, to be exact. He sat up, spring loaded, covered his eyes and blinked as if it was too bright, even though the shop was still dark.

The cot that Bobby had used when he stayed with us before was on the other side of the room, sort of mangled across the wall. It was a folding cot, but not in that particular configuration. As an alternative, Bobby had fashioned a sleeping pallet out of military coats, and had used my cape as a cover.

He smelled of shit, blood, urine, and shrimp.

"Robert."

"I took care of it," he said. "I fought 'em off. The whole fuckin' army of 'em."

"I can see that."

Bobby was not exactly wild-eyed. Coming down fast, most likely. He wore a USL T-shirt, crusted with some dark, platter sized stain across the chest. USL stood for University of Southwestern Louisiana. A fine institution that had changed its name to The University of Louisiana at Lafayette, or ULL, many years ago. The last time I'd seen Bobby he was wearing this shirt, but it was clean then. That had been weeks ago.

I heard Val thumping down the stairs. I warned him, "There's broken glass everywhere." He stopped, one step up in the doorway. Black jeans, shirtless. Still barefoot.

"Jesus Christ!" he said. He scanned the wreckage, palms braced on both sides of the doorway. "Bobby?"

Bobby was scared of Val, and for good reason. The glass and the pins were the only thing keeping my boy from leaping upon and throttling his deranged former employee.

"But I fought 'em!" argued Bobby. He stayed on the floor and hugged his knees to make himself smaller. "Kicked their evil asses."

"Robert," I said again, trying to settle him down.

Val said, "What is that God-damned smell?"

"We're insured," I reminded him. "You call the police yet?"

Val nodded once as his eyes traveled slowly over every inch of the shop, cataloguing the damage in the ledger of his mind. He was already in a calm, practical state of mind.

"You didn't hurt anyone, did you Robert?"

"I fucked 'em up. Evil shits. Stomped 'em like rats."

That was worrisome news, but the only blood was on Bobby's shirt and possibly under his thick gray fingernails. A siren in the distance. Bobby heard it, grabbed up a military jacket in fear.

I was about to tell him not to run, that he was already a fugitive for his pirate games and that he might as well accept some hospitality from the city, but Val spoke first: "Get the fuck out of here, Bobby. Run like hell." He dug into his jeans pocket and extracted a twenty dollar bill. "Here."

Bobby was on his feet like a gymnast, vaulting over the wreckage and snatching the money from Val's outstretched hand.

Val jabbed his finger towards the shop door, still barricaded. "Out," he emphasized. "I'll be in touch."

Bobby looked very confused. I suppose I did as well.

"Do it already," said Val. "Don't come back for a couple days." He bent a lazy elbow over his head to scratch between his own shoulder blades. "But *do* come back, 'cause you are so gonna clean this shit up. You know that right?"

The sirens. Val pointed in the air.

With some help from me, Bobby dislodged the rack that had been wedged against the front entrance, and then I saw the locks were broken as well. The doors swung wide and lazy, and soon the mad, filthy vagabond disappeared into the bright morning.

From the open doorway we saw orange clouds drifting over Pebbles' apartment building and the lady herself—at her window in her lovely coffee colored skirt suit, staring up at the sky. She didn't notice the gates rattling or Bobby's escape. She was crying, looking at the clouds. Just like Gerald Pollin.

I had to turn away. Val sat heavily on the second step of the stairway leading back up into the house. He was examining his toes. I said, "I have no idea what you are up to, but when the cops catch up to Bobby, he won't keep anything back. If he can speak at all. They're going to want to know why you let him go, under the circumstances."

Val chuckled with no pleasure in it. His toes were hypnotic, apparently. A police cruiser lurched to a stop in front of our broken door, and the siren died. I waved to the officer who remained in the driver seat as she reported in by radio. She waved back, smiled a sad smile for my trouble.

"And Pebbles?" I asked. "Why the high emotion?"

Val nodded. "Mirella's dead." We listened to the sound of the cruiser doors being opened and slammed. "That's why the clouds are orange," he said.

2.

Val's lie was simple, creating a wide, comfortable margin for our conspiracy. Everything had happened as it had except that Bobby Rebar was never part of the story. We came home to a mess. Wish Phantom mischief. Now it was up to our local patrollers to spread the gossip: no one was safe, not even the costumer to the Wish Phantom King. Of course the news would not have the impact we hoped for, competing for attention with the new clownish sky, Mirella's departing gift.

But a gift only to New Orleans. Mirella was true to her Wish Local affiliation. The sky outside the city limits was unaffected. What was initially written off as the lady's capricious vanity evolved into a legend of beneficence. New Orleans, that unique destination of appetite fulfillment, now had another feature to tout: a one of a kind sky. Even from her deathbed, Mirella was a tourism genius.

After the police concluded their investigation of our break-in, I began to clean up what I could, sweeping the pins and glass into piles, and squaring the bent metal racks. I got a few standing upright but others were beyond repair.

"Oh what a bore," Martine drawled. He stood on the threshold of our broken entry, a silhouette of dramatic proportions. I'd been expecting him to pop by, eventually. Val scampered early on with more interesting business to attend to, leaving me to welcome numerous visitors, mainly other Marigny shop owners, throughout the day.

"It's hot in here. Beastly."

I suppose it was, but I didn't feel it as intensely as I used to. Still I had to concede that the shop had lost its usual cave-like conditions, what with the doors wide open. I apologized. "Can't afford to run the AC with the door broken."

"Well no, but why labor under these conditions? Come out and have drink with me."

Was it noon already? "I haven't yet figured out how to secure my inventory, such as it is. I have to get the doors fixed."

Martine was impatient. "Hire one of these brat shits to watch the place. For Gawd's sake Victor." He waved his arm towards something I couldn't see. I carried my broom to the front and stepped out on the banquette.

I was astonished. During daylight hours there were normally two or three vagabond teenagers huddled in the recessed doorways of unopened clubs and shops on the block, sometimes playing guitar, sometimes doing a little on-the-street body modification, sometimes reading palms, and always with a box or a paper cup out for you to drop your pennies. Often they propped up homemade placards that said something provocative and unfunny like "will work for pot." But today there were three or four times as many of the creatures, all squatting or curled up against the brick walls under margins of shade that grew thinner and thinner as the sun rose.

Raccoon eyes, all looking at me. Slack mouths. Pretty, ragged clothes. Scarred arms, tattooed arms, hennaed hands hugging knees up. Vampire children, waiting for something. Scraps? The scene conveyed a pre-apocalyptic portent, especially as a single, massive orange cloud scudded towards the river.

Martine smiled like something hurt him in his guts. He whispered, "What did you do?"

"Me?"

The children weren't talking. Not out loud anyway. I saw a couple of girls lean in to whisper into each other's razored, limp haircuts. I approached the nearest creature, a bony, black haired wraith with olive skin and lateral straight scars on one forearm; she was just getting started on a life in the margins. I had never attempted to initiate communication with one of these wicked kids before, so I was a little nervous.

"Excuse me, sweetheart. What's your name then?" I said. The child's companion was gender-free, a crab scuttling back from me.

At least the girl did not spit at me. "Miriam," she said. I believed her. Miriam wasn't gothic enough to be an invented identity.

"Miriam, I'm Victor. Why are you here?"

Her eyes widened, and I could see she was worried about giving the wrong answer. "Gotta be somewhere."

Martine grumped. "Vic, do you remember that *Star Trek* episode where all the adults are dead and the children run society?"

"Hush Martine. Miriam, I mean why are there so many of you—your crowd—here today?"

Miriam smirked, squinted against the sun. "I don't know these kids."

"That's not what I asked you."

Miriam didn't respond for a while. Then quietly, "Call the cops if you want."

I gestured back to my ruined shop. "The police have come and gone, on other business, but I expect they'll make the rounds again soon. I don't think I need to call them out special. Do you?"

Miriam looked at me as if I were speaking a foreign language.

I sighed. "I should like to take a break, my dear. With my friend."

Miriam took a look at Martine, then at me. Did some dirty math and narrowed her kohl smeared eyes at me. I pictured strolling away with Martine, turning the corner out of sight, before all the cruddy street kids descended upon the shop like ants on a rotting peach.

But Miriam understood more than she let on. "I can watch your place. Maybe swap for merch?"

I was unconvinced.

"Ask Mick. You know Mick? Ask him, I'm a good girl."

"Mick Breglia is your reference? Very amusing."

And that's when I recognized the boy, directly across the street, under cover of the awning that led to the foyer of Pebbles' apartment building. He was wearing long pants today, and a frayed tuxedo jacket buttoned across his bare, bony chest. He looked ridiculous, but older. No skateboard with him. Smoking, but then they all were. Couldn't afford food but they all had a few smokes on them. He straightened and stepped forward so I could see him. Raised his hand.

He'd been there all morning. I just never really looked. King of the ragamuffins. After he was sure that I recognized him he came across the street, half burnt cigarette clamped between his teeth, hands in his pockets. His hair was greasy, unwashed. Still wild with curls though.

His chin was scraped and his cheek, on the same side, was darkened with a bruise along the top of the bone. As he grew near, he nodded as if we'd come to some sort of final agreement. But then, as he grew closer to me, his expression grew darker. He looked a little confused. Blinked at me.

Miriam said, "Mick, tell him I'm okay."

"Hush up," he barked. He stared at me as if I were the one all beat up and scuffed.

I said, "I'm sorry for your trouble, son."

He looked at me sideways, like a dog. "The way it happens sometimes."

Mick's tone made Martine nervous. "Is there a problem, boy?"

Mick ignored him, continued to scrutinize me. He leaned forward and whispered, "Fuck. You Superman or something? 'Cause I know I clipped you good at least a coupla times, dude. I mean I'm sorry about that, but you were over the top, you know?"

He thought it had been me last night. I couldn't imagine anyone confusing me with wiry little Bobby, under any circumstances, but for a split second I was flushed by the by the unintended compliment. Mick encountered Bobby (was Bobby wrapped in the cape?), and he thought it was me. Then we scuffled? Oh this was too marvelous. Mick thought it was some kind of set up. Theater.

"I do get excitable," I said.

"Mick," said Miriam. Mick was making a career out of ignoring her. I wondered where little Esme was, this time of day. School, I hoped.

"Miriam has offered to watch the premises while I take lunch," I said.

Mick snorted. "Miriam ain't got the basic skills to watch a TV show." She slumped with a smiley frown, as if Mick had just said she was too cute to work. "I'll be here, boss," he said. "Go enjoy. No worries."

No worries. Boss. I gestured to the population of goth urchins, all of whom watched our negotiation closely. "What's happening here, Mick? Why the gathering?"

Mick flicked his butt into the street. Miriam tracked it like a terrier. "We're family, man."

I wondered how inclusive the "we" was.

He continued, "And these are strange damn days." He tugged at the jacket, reseating it across his shoulders. A new garment to him, but not to me. I recognized it as part of our stock. Val would have gone ape-shit over the boy's audacity, but I understood where Mick was coming from. Cost of doing business.

For some reason I trusted the freak. Not because he was trustworthy, but because I was beginning to understand his evolving code. Mick Breglia didn't know it, but he was on the precipice of actual manhood. That goofy light in his eyes—the one that had Esme and Miriam so entranced—was about to dim.

Martine saw what I saw as well. He asked, "Is there something brewing boy? We gotta be on the lookout, you think?"

"Relax, man." Mick spread his hands across his ridiculous lapels—a move picked up from watching stuffed shirt types on TV no doubt, with poor Mick unable to distinguish gestures of power from satire. "This street here, it's our home. We'll look out for you."

Martine had his routines, such as his mid-day lubrications, but he was also full of surprises. We did not go to a bar for our liquid lunch. Instead he led me to a wine shop on Royal where he purchased a fairly expensive (for lunch anyway) bottle of Spanish red. Unbidden, the clerk uncorked it and handed him two clear plastic wine glasses. Martine filled each more generously than etiquette dictates, handed me one and took the other for himself.

"We'll be on our way then," Martine said to me, gesturing

towards the door with the re-corked bottle in hand.

I sipped the wine down to a slightly more respectable level. "On our way where?"

"Pay our respects to the Lady Mirella."

"Ah," I said. Too soon for a conventional viewing and such events were rarely BYOB. No doubt we were on our way to Mirella's club on Bourbon Street. If only just to see what was shakin'. I almost asked Martine the thing I was always on the verge of asking him: *Lady* Mirella? Did he mean that in a non-ironic, non-fabulous way? Did he have any inside information? I'm sorry to say that my curiosity was adolescent, but given Martine's lifestyle, career, and gossip network, he was as close to a sexual expert as I was going to get. Nevertheless I kept my mouth shut and generally full of wine.

Martine topped off my glass from time to time as we made our way in the midday heat. In Jackson Square horn players played Dixieland to compete with the rock and hip-hop that poured out of the strip clubs. On Bourbon itself the back and forth between t-shirt shops blasting jazz and air conditioning out onto the street, along with stumbling crowds of tourists, made it seem like we had stepped into the theme park version of our daily lives. Martine's shop was on Bourbon, and his feelings were uncomplicated with regard to the street's less genuine aspects. The fake party, complete with its fake sex, fake jazz, and fake voodoo, lived comfortably alongside the real stuff. And vice versa. The only real problem with Bourbon, Martine was fond of arguing, was the illusion of its relative safety, both physically and spiritually.

But today Bourbon Street had made itself special. We were several blocks from Mirella's club, where we could see that a crowd had gathered already. And up in the sky—

"My Jesus!" Even Martine was impressed. We stopped.

Orange clouds, one over each block of Bourbon, identically shaped, and in a direct, straight line. No drifting, no dissipation. They looked like Halloween cookies gone wrong, with sort of bulb shaped top ends and pointy little tails.

"Is that an animal shape?" I wondered out loud.

"I honestly don't know."

"Looks like a cat a little bit. Or a stomach." I sipped more wine. "A cat would really be too much, though."

"Agreed." Martine recovered his cool. "S'pretty, though."

We moved towards Mirella's again. I counted five distinct clouds before they started piling up in my field of vision. Maybe the shape was that of some female organ. Which thought, I'm embarrassed to say, reminded me I had news for Martine.

"Went home with a waitress last night."

He reacted by slowing down our already sluggish pace. Looked at me with an expression I couldn't measure as positive or negative and tapped my arm with the wine bottle. "Really? Good for you, sexy." He carried the bottle by the neck, letting the wine slosh. Looked like the more we drained it, the heavier the bottle became. I was disappointed that he wasn't more inquisitive—didn't he want details? The wine and the heat had made me touchy.

Mirella's club occupied an ancient building with a carefully faked French façade of gilded columns, dark wood panels, and lit glass featuring bright pictures of busty, friendly women, and of course, life sized images of Mirella in various sequined gowns. The club was not open so early in the day, but there were dozens of people out front, forming not one, but two distinct crowds.

"I smell barbecue," said Martine, and indeed it seemed that one group had assembled around a smoking oil drum style rig on wheels. A man I did not recognize was working the meat while several others camped out in nylon folding chairs or rummaged through coolers for beverages. The thrum of gossip was a cheerful sound. Nothing mournful about it.

"Hey there's Rollie," I said. Martine had only heard tales of my personal prophet, so he was interested to see the lady in the flesh. Rollie was in the center of things, holding court and looking very noble in a blood red halter blouse and blue denim skirt. Little white ankle boots, like for a baby cowboy except for the spiky heels.

"Impressive," Martine said. "Sleeveless at her age."

"She's my hero."

"I can see why. But what's with the sob sisters?" Martine gestured to the other group, separated from the picnickers not only by space and distance, but by a moat of nearly palpable gloom. These mourners had arranged themselves away from the marquee entrance in a formation that looked more defensive than communal. No food, no drinks, no place to rest. Just a gathering of dour faced individuals, all looking a bit churchy and disappointed. And silent as the grave, gathered around one man who had backed himself into a tiny bit of shade cast by the club balcony.

I recognized Pebbles' round rump in her chocolate skirt. She looked miserable as she concentrated on whatever it was the man had to say.

"You ever heard of a bloke named 'Pere Qua'?" I asked Martine.

"I have indeed. Is that the fucker?"

"I believe so."

"I heard he was a priest before he became a hustler. Looks like he's found a way to combine his vocations."

Pere Qua, or whatever his name was, looked like a swamp deity. His hair was long and ragged, brown rapidly fading to white. His beard had already turned, a stiff white brush sticking down, bright and clean against his dirty features. He was one of those medium small men who looked a lot bigger, with square work-built shoulders and thick forearms.

Martine said, "Looks like Mel Gibson."

"Excuse me?"

"*Apocalypto* era. 'Sugar tits' Mel."

When Pere Qua spoke to his people his eyes glowed, and his teeth shined in way I would never mistake for a smile. Pebbles, along with everyone in the group, hung on his every word. He was probably one hell of a dancer.

"Mr. Victor!" That voice. Rollie leapt from her folding throne. She was luminous, loud, and at me damn quick. Just before she embraced me in her naked, firm arms, I saw a flash of Pebbles responding to the sound of my name. She saw me, didn't like that I was there.

Rollie smelled like vanilla cookies. Wench. But then again, I reeked of red wine. She clamped onto my shoulders and pushed me back to look me over. Big grin. "Why you're skin and bones!"

I flushed, buzzed and embarrassed.

"Been keeping up with the program," I said, suddenly shy.

She pulled the kind of theatrically knowing grin you reserve for children and other dim audiences. "Why, I hear you're running the show these days."

"An overstatement, I'm afraid."

A busker with an accordion misread the opportunity and placed himself between the two groups in front of Mirella's. Closed off to vehicle traffic for a fair chunk, Bourbon Street permits room to experiment. He shouted as if we had gathered there for his pleasure: "Oh yeah, the Zy-de-co!" before he launched into a frenetic version of "Bernadette."

Inconveniently, a bit of dancing broke out amongst Rollie's group. Pebbles' friends were annoyed and clustered even more

tightly around their leader, like scavengers around a wilde-
beest carcass. And Rollie's reaction was practically genetic. She
snatched me for a compulsory two step, and we were off, skipping over the bricked street as if bewitched by matching pairs of
red shoes. Martine howled. Luckily, Louisiana dance tunes run
to the short side.

That tune ended, another began. I made gestures that I
might be dying and managed to convince Rollie that I should
stand down. Nothing makes a few glasses of red wine go to your
head like the noonday sun and a bit of twirling about. Rollie was
heated up, aching for another dance. She pulled a beer from a
random cooler and pressed the icy bottle to her cheek. Her eyes
were blazing pearls, and she looked pretty doable.

I glanced to the orange clouds. "Mirella," I said. I had no
breath for more.

She pulled the cap off the bottle and took a swig. Remarkable. She said, "Oh yes. Right on target."

Somewhere in the melee I'd lost my wine cup. I was fiercely
thirsty, and it must have shown on me. Rollie practically shoved
her bottle into my mouth. Sweet, cold Dixie.

I thought I should work up the juice to dance with her again,
but as soon as I caught my breath my senses returned as well.
"That bunch"—and here it hurt to betray my dear Pebbles, but I
had work to do on Val's behalf—"Who are they?"

Rollie took her beer back. Tipped it, drained it dry. "That's
rot over there. Rot and fear."

Native Louisianans never give you information as requested. There's always a parable guarding the door to the facts.
They might tell you a thing directly as a matter of gossip, but
conventional Q & A is always a struggle. I scratched my neck
and smiled as if she'd told me something wise. "I'm sorry to hear
that. See, I have a personal interest."

Rollie raised an eyebrow. Permission to continue the interrogation.

I said, "That lovely young thing in the brown skirt?"

Rollie found Pebbles, appraised her. "Healthy," she said.

"Indeed." I let the suggested lechery wander out on a long lead before I walked it back. "She's my son's fiancé."

Rollie loved that. "Oh dear."

"Yes."

"And she's in with those fools?" Rollie shook her head. "That's unfortunate. That shifty fella, Pere Qua? Looks like the Devil as a day laborer. Born Jamie Boudreau, became Father James, and now I guess he thinks he's being cute. You know he's fallen clergy, right? It doesn't take too much imagination to figure out what for, either."

"Little boys?" First thing to pop in my mind.

"Oh goodness no. The kiddie fiddlers they keep. Throw their butts into rehab before shuttling them off to a mission in Timbuktu. No, Pere Qua likes girls. Lots of them, soon as they develop right up until they get too smart for him. Can't keep his grubby fingers off 'em."

Martine chuckled, and Rollie shushed him with a frown.

"He was a little too friendly a little too often. And not nearly careful enough. He lost his calling when it became clear that the Church wanted to interfere with his lifestyle. Apparently he'd put together his own little severance package, and then he went God knows where for a while."

"I heard Angola," said Martine.

Rollie didn't know Martine and was offended by his interruptions. I had forgotten to introduce them. She gave him the eye. "It's possible he was in prison. But it doesn't look like he learned anything useful there. He comes back, shows up at one of our Wish Local events, and the next thing I hear is that he's started his own street movement. 'More spiritual' is his hook. More dangerous, you ask me. Certainly less fun.'"

I said, "But why dangerous?"

"He told his people that Mirella was the next Death Wisher, which was a good call. He told them to pray for her peaceful passage. He promised them she was going to wish the 'unification and enlightenment of the chosen.'" This last bit Rollie derided by wiggling her fingers in the air.

"And she gave us orange clouds instead."

"Yes sir. But here's the rough part. Mirella loved herself a party, even in the hospital. Visitors streaming in and out, almost no security, and even if one of her boys tried to stop some stage door Johnny from disturbing her rest, she'd let him in. Anyway, Jamie Boudreau was at her bedside the few times I'd dropped by, so that must mean he'd talked to Mirella quite a lot during those last days."

Martine said, "You mean he ministered to her?"

"You get in that condition, you take comfort and company from anyone offering. Her boyfriend got a little antsy near the end, and she sure didn't have a regular confessor."

I said, "So he pressured her to make a particular wish. What did you say it was? 'The unification and enlightenment of the chosen'?" I did not wiggle my fingers. "What the hell does that mean?"

Rollie shook her head. "It's bullshit is what it is. And that's not what he asked her to wish. That's just what he promised them." She jabbed a thumb to the Pere Qua cluster. "I spoke to Mirella in the last hour of her life, and she was laughing about it. Because in the end, he wasn't ministering so much as entertaining her. He didn't know that of course."

Rollie drew a breath and lowered her register but not her volume. "She told me he asked her to kick start the end of days.

Well, he didn't ask so much as command her to wish for it. Because he thought he had her hooked."

"He didn't though," said Martine.

Rollie smiled, "He pressed and pressed. But I think she'd had her heart set on orange clouds for quite some time."

I thought about Pebbles' open grief as she saw the orange clouds above the city that morning. All dressed up in her waiting-for-Mirella-to-pass clothing. The apocalypse? Really? Not what I would have thought 'unification and enlightenment' to entail.

Martine read my mind. "If you tell Pebbles, she'll never believe you."

Rollie agreed, and she was warming to Martine. "You can't go up to a believer and tell 'em their hero is corrupt. They either shut you out or find a way to embrace the core of that corruption. And the rot has set in with that crowd. Set in."

Poppycock, I thought. Pebbles was just a tender girl looking for someone to make sense of an unstable world, and religion was a familiar filter. That didn't mean she was possessed. The fact that she had hooked up with Val was proof that she still had one foot in the corporeal world.

But Rollie thought I should just leave it. So did Martine. I couldn't of course. "I have business with Qua."

Martine said, "Are you crazy?"

Not the sort of question you answer with words. I walked away from Rollie and Martine, left them gawping as I snuck up on Pebbles.

No one from Pere Qua's group noticed that I'd joined their number. Jamie Boudreau's accent was thick, nasal, drifting in and out of French-ness as the subject required. His beard looked like a separate, thoughtful creature, nodding on his chin as he spoke. "We must study on the mystery and know that this is just one component in the design." Almost singing certain phrases, Boudreau's cadence was rapid, his words mushy and sensual.

When I touched Pebbles' sleeve she twitched like I was a bug flying into her breathing space. "Hi there." I smiled like a dummy. She pursed her lips to shush me, but at least she let me stay.

Jamie Boudreau/Pere Qua went on with his sidewalk sermon. I could not tell if his words were off the cuff or just hastily prepared: "I don' know what kinda dance we're dancing, but I do know how to let the Man lead."

I tapped Pebbles' arm, pesky-like. She whispered, "Go. Away."

"Nope."

Pere Qua noticed me, and a few of the faithful flinched. They were a twitchy, flinchy lot. "What're you all doing anyway?" I acted totally oblivious to the intensity I had penetrated.

Pebbles pleaded with me. "Victor, please go away."

"Sir." Pere Qua's hard blue eyes mowed a row through the huddled mass. He said to me, "We are an open prayer group and you are more than welcome to join in, but at the moment you are disrupting our congress." He grinned in a predatory I'm inclined to kill you even if I'm not hungry kind of way.

I had no idea what I hoped to gain from being a jerk, but I was still a bit high and disrupting congress was fun. "Jamie boy," I said. "You look like a wolf to me. Are you a wolf?"

A tall bony kid in a new Kmart suit whipped around, blood in his eye. Pebbles stepped in between us. I grinned at the kid, put up my mitts like a fighter in a cartoon. Pebbles smacked my hands down. "Victor, these are my friends. Please, you have to go away." Then she leaned forward, sniffed. Sighted Martine in the distance. "You're drunk, aren't you?"

"It's Bourbon Street, honey. What do you expect?"

Boney Moroney pulled Pebbles aside. Pere Qua watched us with a gambler's attention. He placed his arms around the shoulders of two women—mother and adult daughter?—as if to protect them from my toxic presence.

"Perhaps you should move along then sir," said the tall kid. He breathed through his mouth, over excited by conflict. "You shouldn't interfere with decent people."

I was about to argue with his characterization of Pere Qua, but that wasn't going to win me any points. So I tried pathetic. "Pebbles, darling, I don't feel well. I need you to take me home."

Pathetic didn't work. She said, "Get away from me you old fool."

Ouch. "Monsieur Qua," I hailed.

"Victor, shush!"

But I had the man's attention. I'd had it from the get go I think. Guy like that doesn't miss much. "Monsieur," I said, attempting to talk over the heads of those who stood between us. "I admire your work. Takes some brassy balls to hang out while an old woman fades away. Takes a special kind of some-one to pour venom into her ears as she lays dying."

Then the tall kid again. "Step off, sir." Boney stood straight, cast a shadow like a building.

"Girard, please," Boudreau said, calling the boy to heel.

Girard backed off. Pere Qua had let the women loose so he could approach, and he stepped right up to collect my hands in a car salesman's grip. He was shorter than me and smelled like oiled wood. "My friend. Victor is it? Victor. You seem a little confused."

I saw why he kept his hair so long. Jail tat across the back of his creased neck, gothic lettering. Couldn't read it, didn't want to. He continued to hold my hands in his, as if he was trying to send a transmission through my body. I was not receiving, but I let him hold on as long as he wanted.

"Pebbles?" I called.

"I don't want to talk to you." Pebbles clung to Girard's long, cheap sleeve.

"She don' wanna talk to you," said Qua. "Now that's gotta *hoyt.*"

"Oh make up your mind, sir. A second ago you were all Evangeline Parish, now you're from the wards? What's next, you gotta Transylvanian accent you want to trot out? Pebbles, this man is an obvious fake."

Pere Qua squeezed. He wanted to break my bones without anyone else seeing. He said, "Now what's that fine lady been telling you?" He meant Rollie. "She's a lovey, but she does tell tales. Part of her charm." He shifted to block my view of Pebbles.

He shouldn't have done that, is my only defense. I leaned into the man as if to share a secret, and then I stomped on his left foot with my right.

He broke his grip and let out a pain bark. Boney launched forward, but the thing about guys with long limbs is that it takes too long for them to wind up and land a punch. You could write a haiku while you were waiting. I didn't, but I did experience the suspended moment in all its richness, the arm pulled back, the knuckles aligning, the sure release.

Pebbles shouted. I ducked away, and Girard fell forward. Impressive follow through, but he landed in the street, skidding on his elbows and knees because no one came forward to catch or restrain him. Martine swooped in and grabbed me by the upper arm, but I weasled away and used the cover of confusion to make my way back to Pebbles, who was now alone.

"Come home with me," I said to her.

Pere Qua steamed towards me.

She was shaky. "They're gonna cream you," Pebbles said.

Indeed, he looked ready to do me in. He got his fingers near my throat and grabbed my collar, wrenching it so I had to rise up on the balls of my feet. A couple of dudes backed him up, built so like him they could have been cousins. Girard sat up in the street, rubbing his shredded points.

They were not going to cream me. They were going talk me into the dirt. Something about the practiced delivery of Pere Qua's rage calmed me; he had to put on a show of injury and offense for his people. This was what martyrs and near martyrs like to call a "teachable moment." I relaxed my feet flat and let him do all the work of suspension. It was uncomfortable as hell, being slightly hanged.

Martine said, "Victor, what the hell are you doing?"

I honestly didn't know. I was going on instinct, and instinct told me not to give Jamie Boudreau a single moment of satisfaction.

"He's testing us," answered Boudreau.

"You nailed it." He twisted my collar tighter, forcing me to cough for air. Which was more than Pebbles could handle.

"Please," she said. "Let him loose. He's just an idiot."

I gasped like a strung fish.

"I'll take him home, he's just a silly old man."

Pebbles seemed on the verge of breaking, but this being the day of Mirella's passing, emotions didn't count for much. When we were away from this lot I intended to point out to Pebbles that she should probably cut out that ageist shit, especially since Monsieur Qua and I had probably seen all the same presidents come and go.

Qua's face relaxed. He liked my pain, but my humiliation was sweeter. "Sister, you have a good heart," he said to Pebbles. He released my collar, and I stumbled back against Martine's ample support.

"We'll pray for you," said Pere Qua. And Pebbles appeared by my side, looping her arm around mine. Her muscles were tensed, her bones sharp. Qua did a slow, balletic, almost stoned turn to his followers, who had bowed their heads to murmur in concert. They sounded like bees trapped in an attic.

Pebbles hauled me away, and I waved to Rollie. She batted her eyes in reply and returned to her group, striking up a conversation about sheep that didn't require the enthusiasm she'd mustered. Martine brought up the rear as we wheeled back down Bourbon towards the river. He was amused by Pebbles' take charge attitude.

"Prayer is good," Martine remarked. And then he asked a fair question: "Who they prayin' for again?" When no answer came, he said, "Guess it doesn't make a difference."

And that got up the girl's nose. "Of course it makes a difference. Of course it does." And that was all there was to say about the subject. Which was sad, because Pebbles didn't even know what she meant or why she felt it so strongly.

So, a big fat nothing on the existential question of the day, but at least I accomplished one small thing: I got the girl out of there.

3.

Orange clouds over New Orleans. That was a magical thing. No such feature in desert Montana, however, where cold blue sky hit ruddy hot dirt, and a layer of shimmer seemed to describe the tension between the world we once knew—a world of killing storms and other cataclysms that could be explained if not always predicted—and the one we knew now, which was capricious and truly unstable. Come the next morning, we could all wake up as turtles. And I might've been in favor of that since I'm pretty sure turtles can't make wishes.

So Montana. The big sky state without orange clouds. A black helicopter rose up from a valley hiding place, skimmed low over the horizon and scattered dirt and bent brush, to angle toward five strong men on horseback who paused to watch the commotion. The helicopter swooped overhead and upset the horses, who lurched and stomped.

One of the men was simply handsomer than the others, under any circumstance, even in silhouette. He radiated a god-like warmth that was at once loving and sad. Loving, because that was his vocation. Sad, because that was his job. Even if you didn't know he was The Elvis, you would understand that the other men did not work for him so much as they worked around him, that their livelihood was based on maintaining proximity. But with this helicopter overhead, there was confusion and anxiety. It made a slow arc in the eastern sky for a return run.

Now the guns. Hard to control the horses, and perhaps that was the point. The helicopter dipped, and from within several shots were fired from what appeared to be a military weapon designed to delete small gatherings efficiently. The Elvis's protectors drew handguns but were mentally unprepared for assault from above. Before they were able to position themselves, every one of their horses collapsed into bloody, suffering heaps. Screaming. Then not.

Two men had been shot and pinned under their beasts. They were as good as dead. Another was merely pinned, his hips crushed against a long angle of ragged stone that had breached the desert crust a thousand years ago. The Elvis, somehow unwounded, scrambled for his life, running back down the trail they had taken to get to this place. The last man did his job, stood free and took aim at the helicopter.

The pinned men would die out there. So would the shooting man, but he would vex the helicopter before its violent passenger took him out, giving The Elvis just enough time to lose himself in the brush.

Despite the urgency of his predicament, The Elvis had a moment of doubt before calling for help, awkwardly thumbing a cell phone he had barely learned to use. Who to call? His protectors were from the government. But his would-be assassins looked like they were from the government, too. He canceled the call. Who wanted him dead?

Who wanted him alive?

He didn't know anyone anymore, except his family. Every time The Elvis recalled a time when he was older than his daughter, he became overcome by equal measures of joy and grief, which made him holy and suicidal. Which helped, in this case. He decided to call someone he knew wanted him dead, someone who had created an empire from his death, because at least that was a fixed point from which to start the discussion. He called the Man from the Record Company.

By the time we made it back to the shop, it was late afternoon. The vampire teen squad had dispersed, and two Latino day laborers, hired by Val in a fit of intelligence, busily repaired the broken gates. I invited Martine and Pebbles in for iced tea, and surprisingly they both accepted. Up the back stairs and into the kitchen, we found my lad brooding over his computer as he sat at the Formica table. Pebbles leaned in to kiss him hello. Tongues, but she did all the work. Val barely twisted to meet her lips. My gut clenched, and Martine shot me a warning look. I was going to have to get used to this.

"What's that fantastic smell?" asked Martine. Indeed, the kitchen was flooded with a warm, spicy aroma that made all the hairs on my body lay flat. A familiar pot on the stove. I lifted the lid, released the steam, and peered in at a mess that looked like garbage covered with red oil. Beans and rice.

So Val wasn't so self-absorbed that he'd given up on life. Still cooking to keep his family together. A big loaf of French bread lay violated on the counter, as if Val had torn it in half with his teeth. Pebbles wedged herself between Val and his computer, and tried to sit on his lap. He only barely accommodated her. I couldn't tell if he was being insensitive to her or if he was embarrassed for me. Regardless, as a divorced man I could've told him the mistake he was making might beccome a habit if he weren't careful.

Martine was not shy. He started mounding the beans into a bowl. Grabbed some bread, asked after the butter.

I said, "Thought we were weighing in tonight."

"I'm grieving," he said. "Red wine?" It was two in the afternoon, and we had already polished off one bottle. I guess Martine considered the day shot. Val pointed him to a cupboard and Martine moved through our kitchen with uncanny familiarity. He retrieved the jug of chianti, poured himself a water glass full, then sat himself down with his feast.

My own portions were more moderate. Except for the wine. I poured a water glass full, as well. The day *was* shot, I realized. I sat next to Martine, the both of us directly across from Pebbles perched on Val's narrow thighs.

Val stared into his computer. Pebbles' bowl waited on the counter, but she wasn't about to give up her territory, and I wasn't about to serve her. We wanted to hurt each other.

Pebbles said, "Victor made a real ass of himself in front of my friends."

"Oh yeah?" Unsettled, Val's gaze flickered from me to her to the screen. He couldn't afford to take sides, seeing as how he'd set me onto Qua in the first place.

"He got drunk and violent and he attacked the Father."

Martine smirked, literally fulla beans.

Val sat up. "Daddy?"

The chianti was shitty, not worth savoring. I shrugged as I swigged. Pebbles went on like a tattle-tale. "He stomped on that good man's foot and called him a liar. If I hadn't taken him outta there, Victor would be moaning in the gutters of Bourbon Street."

Martine agreed with the girl. "Ice pack on his balls time. It was that close."

Then Pebbles said to me, "Whatever possessed you?"

Val wasn't about to let me answer. He closed his computer, eased the girl from his lap and nodded to the beans. "Get yourself some. Bring two forks." A domestic order, the beginning of the end, and Pebbles was only too happy to comply. While she prepared their dish, Val pretended to scold me: "You need to be more careful, Dad. You've been acting out. What with last night, and then this confrontation today?"

I blinked. Last night I was rolling in the arms of a very kind woman.

"The phantoms," he reminded me.

Ah yes, had to keep my lies organized. Almost forgot that I'd done battle with Mick Breglia. And then there was a different lie for the police.

Pebbles brought her bowl to the table, sucking her finger. "That's right," she said. "That's all over town, how you beat down twenty teenaged skate punks. My God. I suppose you are still full of yourself about that." She forgot the second fork so they shared one. "What really happened, Victor?"

Seemed like the right time to drain my glass and pour another. It was nearly siesta time anyway. "It's hard to say."

Martine jammed more food in his mouth. Of course I'd told him everything, which was about the worst thing I could have done. He loved secrets, but they hurt so much to keep.

"Twenty?" Val was amused. "Jesus. Well it wasn't twenty, that's for sure. It was just a couple of guys, right? And they didn't expect you to be there, so you had the upper hand."

"That's a bit closer to the truth," I said. There were a couple of us, sure. I had to fight off the urge to tell them all that I'd just come off a one night stand, and that I was feeling damned good about that. But the bees were humming in my head, and I remembered Pebbles' prayer cult, the way they started their incantations as we walked away. Too much wine. Too fast. Again today. As I reached for more bread, I managed to knock over my glass. Pebbles mopped up the spilled wine with a rag, sucking her teeth in disapproval. Martine gave me teddy bear pity eyes. Was I blotto? My, that had happened very fast.

But Val was cool about it. He nodded. "You don't have the fat to drink like you used to. Don't try to keep pace with Martine." Then to my friend, "Sorry, dude." Martine shrugged it off, drank to us both and heaved up to claim a second helping of red beans.

Val came to my side, offered his arm. As we made our way out of the kitchen, and up to my room, he whispered into my ear, "Thanks for bringing her home, Dad."

Val put me to bed. He also woke me up, shaking me by my shoulders around nine-thirty p.m., which time I learned that I was the last person on earth to hear that The Elvis had been attacked, possibly by terrorists, possibly by our own government. The attack was not the work of some lone crazy, but an organized, well-funded assassination attempt. And of course, The Elvis was no run of the mill pop star; he was the reconstituted American dream. So it was a pretty big damned deal, sending shock waves of bizarre emotion throughout our community and probably the world. We'd been hit again, by improbability.

Whereas before all specific news of The Elvis had been carefully rationed out to us by the federate misers who kept him secure, which is not the same as safe I guess, suddenly a flood of information was released by both his family and the representatives of SonyVerse, the media behemoth that now employed him. That's right, the renewed King signed a new deal, immediately after which the corporate flaks gave the people what they wanted in lieu of actual musical product: information.

What seemed clear was that the level of sophistication of the attack, plus the intel required to locate The Elvis in the first place, suggested that his enemies had serious resources. The PR team at SonyVerse were giddily qualm-free about blurring the lines between traditional extremist boogeymen and the CIA.

The message being that in these uncertain times, corporations were best equipped to do what the government could not: protect and serve. And yes, a new album was in the works. Possibly in Target stores by Rocktober, with T-Bone Burnett producing.

"Dad, Daddy. You got to get up. The streets are full of people." I fought cobwebs, and rubbed my shoulder where Val had squeezed it. He left the light off in my room but pulled aside the curtain. Then we were side by side at my window looking out on the crowded street. A sight we have seen several times before during festival season, but the crowd assembled on Esplanade was hardly celebrating.

"It's like this everywhere," said Val. "Everyone went outside."

I swallowed. My mouth was rancid, and my eyes hurt, but I was sober. "There's no music," I said.

Val nodded. His eyes were red. His clothes reeked of pot. "No music."

We watched for a while. It was a zombie movie out there, without the brain eating. Women in nightgowns walking their tiny dogs, and even the dogs seemed glum. Men wearing little more than their tattoos and perspiration. All of them wandering around as if there used to be a wonderful café around here, somewhere, and they had to find it. Pretty soon, the urge came upon us as well. We tumbled outside into a tuneless, worried night.

I followed Val as he wandered ankle deep in the desiccated grass that covered the median like a comb over. The beat flat patches winked with glass fragments reflecting streetlight and stars. I thought of his bare feet; whatever bacteria lived on the slivers was sure to be the thriving kind, and of some rare, multi resistant variety. His hands were sunk in his pockets, and he stared into shadows. He did not have a plan for this eventuality. He looked up to Pebbles' apartment window. It was dark.

I said, "Look, you can't tell the clouds are orange at night."
It was true. The stars were smeared with cloud cover, but the
night sky betrayed nothing of the recent Mirella modifications.

He tried calling Pebbles. No answer. Then he sent a text.

A group of quiet shadows walked between us, as if we were
in the way. I could smell soap and perfume, but the faces were
just moonlit puzzle pieces. By the time they passed, I saw that
Val was in pain. Pebbles had sent her reply.

"She's gone off to be with her group. To be with Pere Qua."

"I'm so sorry, Val." I felt like I might have to sit myself
down very soon.

"She should be with me right now." Val jammed the phone
back into his pocket. "Or I should be with her. We only just got
together and already I'm not there for her."

A woman sobbed in the darkened distance, and everyone
paused to listen. I half hoped she would break into song. It didn't
have to be an Elvis song. Could be any song. But that never happened. After a while I assured Val that there probably wasn't
much he could have done. "After all, I was there for her, every
day. And it didn't make a bit of difference. Let's face it. It's going
to take more than me making a fool of myself to drive a wedge
between Pebbles and the object of her devotion." I did not say,
I've tried that twice now. "Pere Qua is offering her something . . . I
don't know what, but neither one of us can give it to her."

Val looked into the dark spaces between streetlights like he
was trying to decide which way to go. I thought I heard the trill
of a clarinet, but it faded like a vapor. "Yeah," he sighed. Like
what I said reminded him of something. "We're losing her."

4.

Pebbles dropped off the radar over the next couple of days, explaining to Val by way of texts, emails, and calls, but never face to face, that she was in retreat with Pere Qua and her new friends, whom she would not refer to as a Death Wish Cult, even though that's what everyone else called them. She instead referred to them as her "prayer circle" and explained that they were re-drawing their mission in light of recent events. It was obvious she was giddy to be on the inside of so much excitement. It was obvious we were in the way.

Val was disgusted. I was flat out worried.

This regrouping was happening everywhere. It seemed that no one was comfortable with fluidity anymore and steps were taken to consolidate identity whenever possible. The third eye ladies formed unions, convinced that they were ripe for exploitation by commercial and military interests. The Wish Locals established a charter, published a manifesto, and hosted barbecue parties. The Wish Phantoms expanded marauding operations out to the suburbs, complete with shuttle service. And gulf coast shrimpers were beginning to meet and cooperate in ways that made Val very nervous.

Everyone had something to protect. Everyone felt underprotected. I suppose this is how the worst eras in history get their start.

I first saw batwing graffiti spray painted on utility poles throughout Maringy and the side streets of the Quarter. Then the pattern started showing up on T-shirts. I eventually spotted a batwing tattoo on a goth girl's ankle. Val gave in to the trend, and one morning he plopped a box of batwing shirts and cloth patches onto the counter of the shop. "Are these Chinese?" I asked. I picked through them, surprised. He didn't get very involved in shop operations anymore, and certainly not in stock.

"Don't complain. Fad'll die out before the shirts fall apart."

I didn't approve but couldn't be bothered to argue. I was surrounded by the ghosts of fashion. We had elephant pants, skorts, men's bolero jackets, sporrans, and earth shoes gathering dust in every corner. Well made items, unnecessarily well made. Val's Vintage had been easier to restore than anyone guessed possible, perhaps because it had never been a particularly pristine environment in the first place. I had not seen Bobby Rebar again since that day Val sent him away, but every morning when I reopened for business, the shop was a little cleaner, a little more orderly, and a little better stocked than the day before. My guess was Val was having Bobby do night work, acting as our own filthy little cobbler's elf. Eventually the only sign of the skirmish with the Wish Phantoms was the new lock on the door and the misalignment of the iron gate.

Two witchy young women browsed a rack of men's Oxford shirts when Val dumped a stack of the batwing T-shirts on an already overloaded card table. He propped up a hasty sign: "Batwing Tees=3/$10." One of the ladies snorted.

"I think the fad is already over," I said.

The other woman looked up, spied the T-shirts and smiled. Her ivory teeth were edged with violet lipstick that had become gloppy over the bumps and cracks of her lips. The accident looked a little sexy, as if we'd caught her in a moment of voracious fruit eating. "Oh that's too right," she said. To me. About the shirts.

"Is it?" I asked.

Val definitely had an eye for cool.

Both women lost interest in the Oxfords and hustled over to the batwing shirts, discussing how much cash they had between them. Then one shot me a quick, shy look. A flirty smile to go with it. The other gal did the same damned thing. The little look, the little smile. When Val caught this, his smugness turned sour. I could only shrug. Eventually the women had extracted three shirts that pleased them, and pooling their coins and crumpled bills they approached me at the counter.

I said, "Will this be all then?"

Before surrendering their money, the purple lipstick girl asked, "Okay, but will you sign them?"

"The shirts?"

Val shouldered in. "Why would he do that?" But they ignored him and only had eyes for me. For that small triumph I'd sign their mothers' breasts.

Purple Lipstick's companion unfolded one of the shirts and spread it across the new glass countertop. Then she rifled around in a small leopard print clutch made from real fur that was coming off in clumps like mange. Probably nutria. She extracted a violet Sharpie. "This could work, but I wish I had one of my fabric markers. Do you think we should come back?" She asked this of her friend and me.

I looked back to my work area, about to offer the use of a puffy paint pen that she might find amusing, but I thought better of it. "I'm sorry dear. We don't understand." I pointed down at the shirt, the batwing design. "What do these wings signify?"

"You're kidding right? Mister," said the young woman. Her teeth were very purple now. "That's not wings. That's a cape."

So?

"That's you, sir."

And the other girl leaned in to confirm it. "That's you."

"Holy shit, Dad."

The young women fought urges, allowing the moment to fill them up like helium. Exchanging bright glances, fingers twitching. Looking at me as if I were the most adorable baby they had ever seen. Finally one of them said, "I'm so glad you didn't know."

Val rolled his eyes.

I took another look at that design. Not batwings, but a cape. A scalloped, jagged cape. I cleared my throat. "This has to do with that night."

Purple Teeth grinned. "The night you ninja-ed the Phantoms. Makes it more funny is even the Phantoms dig it."

I can't say that I needed a moment to digest this information. I needed a lifetime. I've never been anyone's idea of a hero. As if he could read my mind, Val summed it up best:

"Well. Fuck me."

I reached to touch the silk screened image on the shirt spread out to receive my signature, but then stopped short. The violet Sharpie lay on the counter, a loaded gun as far as I was concerned. So there was an emblem in honor of my one brave night. A night that actually belonged to Bobby Rebar. Was this funny? It didn't feel funny. We had taken insurance money to cover an act of vandalism we'd arranged.

That difficult thought receded, replaced by two very simple realizations. One, I was famous. Two, young women were flirting with me. I grabbed the Sharpie, uncapped it, and signed the shirts with a confident flourish, reinventing my signature on the spot. I made the V in my name the sexiest, most thrilling V that has ever been executed on fabric. Perhaps a fifteen year old, *Twilight*-obsessed girl could have done better, but I doubt it. The young women paid for their garments and insisted on kissing my cheeks before they left the shop. My face burned, and for every possible reason.

Val had several things to say about what had just occurred, but I paid little attention. He tried to get me to pre-sign shirts, but I was not ready to take that step. At which point he began signing the shirts for me. The woman had left her violet marker behind so he continued to use that. I did not stop him.

"I'm taking an early lunch," I announced. I was wildly high, my mind swimming with impossible fantasies of sexual encounters that were as chivalrous as they were orgiastic. I grabbed my pumpkin lined cape and fastened it around my shoulders, even though the day was already impossibly hot. "Watch the store? I'm going to find Martine."

Val gave me a *you must be kidding me* look, but what he said was "Sure, Pop. Go wild."

And in that instant I became one of Val's commodities. A moderate one, to say the least, but a thing of value nevertheless. He returned to forging my signature. Bowing his head over the counter, his black hair fell like a curtain to hide his concentration—not just any old curtain, but fine, beaded curtain from a 1970s era head shop. It fell straight, except for one thick, dry coil of white amongst all that luxuriant, heavy, cat black stuff.

My heart, my heart. Time isn't supposed to run this way.

Martine and I ordered Rumrunners and drank them unironically in the courtyard of the Napoleon. During the course of our liquid lunch, we received three bills, two of which were for other diners.

"Nothing changes," drawled Martine, as he examined an itemized list that included crab bisque, avocado salad, and Bordeaux that we had not had the pleasure of consuming. Our waiter careened by, and though he moved like a figure skater, the signs of a permanent hangover ravaged his otherwise elegant features. Martine tucked the bill into his belt like a dollar into a stripper's thong. "Try again, hon'," he said, and the waiter responded with the most depressed scowl I'd ever seen.

"I disagree," I said. "All these factions are factioning, but one very important and already well established group has fallen utterly apart. The weight program is shut down. Too many third eye ladies distracted by other concerns. Doesn't that cause you grief?" I drew my cape in so that no one would trip on it. It was bunched up on my lap, but that was too warm, so eventually I let the damned thing pile up on the flagstones around my feet. To Martine's credit he did not criticize me for wearing it to lunch. In fact he praised me for my developing sense of panache and flair, citing that the color went well with the new clouds.

He said, "Eh, I'm not bothered. That Tracy was a bitch on wheels but maybe not always wrong. Seems peculiarly narcissistic to be watching one's weight when the clouds have gone orange and Elvis is back."

I shooed a sluggish fly from a bit of desiccated lime rind that had been left on the table by a prior customer. "My dear friend, the only thing you can hope to control is yourself. You give that up, you give up all else."

I expected more of a spirited fight, but Martine merely grunted and said, "Yes, that's true too. Both positions, hell almost any position that comes with a set of guidelines, will work. I'm just having difficulty working up a genuine *belief*." He sucked on the narrow red straw, like a boy. "I mean, you do your thing, all preachy and smart, and I'm with you. But I get ten steps away from your fire and my head is in the clouds again. Wondering what they taste like."

I knew well what he was talking about. If it hadn't been for Rollie and her steely attention, no amount of logic or common sense would have kept me on the plan. At least not in the first months.

Then Martine said, out of nowhere: "You are good looking Victor."

"Pardon?"

"And you know how to attract and conduct attention."

"And where is this going I wonder?"

"Hush it."

He peered over my shoulder. I fought the urge to look back. "What is it?"

Martine affected a bored tone. Talked through his nose to underscore his nonchalance. "There is a man standing in the middle of the restaurant. He looks demented. He is staring at the back of your head, I think. His nose is a tragedy, and the rest of him ain't so hot either."

"Gerald Pollin?" I started to turn.

"I believe so. I also believe he's fixing to attack you. His fists are balled into, well, fists actually."

I had just enough time to appreciate the meat of Martine's analysis before Gerald Pollin launched towards me, red faced with arms raised. You'd think the advantage of coming at a seated fellow from behind would have been enough, but Gerald was just no good at this sort of thing, and all I had to do was stand and twist in time to deflect his attack with my outstretched arm. Like Bela Lagosi, I gripped the edge of my cape so that it formed a curtain in front of my body. Just a theatrical habit, good for business; it's the way you stand when you stand in a cape you hope to sell to someone else. Gerald hit my forearm and lost his footing on the stone floor. His fall may have been aided by a patch of greasy butter or unswept salad greens, but the effect was that he'd slammed into a solid wall of velvet cape, the power of which was impossibly righteous and elegant.

The restaurant erupted in applause.

This time Gerald fell onto the back of his head and there was no blood that I could see. He lay peacefully, possibly thinking, "This again?" Quite conscious, he stared up at the orange clouds that floated over the courtyard. Martine took advantage of the moment to steal the rest of my drink.

"That man does not like you, Victor," he said. Our waiter, carrying a tray of bread rolls and Bloody Marys to a table of low-tipping high school girls, stepped over Gerald Pollin's body as if prone fools were common as dirt at the Napoleon.

Martine still pretended to be bored, but there was a new, tiny edge in his demeanor. A different waiter phoned the police, and I felt that I should stick around to file a complaint. But Martine was agitated, even if only I could detect it.

"Let's get out of here," he said. He dropped thirty dollars on the table. Outrageous generosity, I thought, but impressive enough that I stumbled after him as he exited the restaurant with uncharacteristic efficiency.

Once we hit the steamy banquette I asked, "What is it?"

"That man," said my friend. "There was a knife tucked up his sleeve."

"I really doubt that."

"I saw it Victor. Your friend wanted to do serious damage to you."

Martine walked fast, but he made turns onto blocks that lengthened the journey back to the shop. As if he thought we were being followed.

"But isn't that all the more reason to stick around and file an assault report? We should go back to the restaurant."

Martine stopped. He was a bit flushed, suddenly not so sure. He rubbed his face. "Yes, but," he said. He looked around. He seemed lost. "Yes, but..."

Then he collapsed.

5.

A matched pair of insanely beautiful young men waited in the lobby of the Tulane Medical Center along with old women, ragged children, and fish eyed fathers. Martine's lads stuck out because they were so godly—both tanned and muscled, straining in their tight knit polos and tennis shorts. Visiting hours had just begun, and when I entered the lobby they looked to me with puppy eyes.

"He chucked us out," said one. I could not remember either of their names, but I was guessing that at least one, possibly both, went by Todd. "Said you should go on in soon as you arrived."

"Don't take it badly," I said. "I was with him when he had the attack." I'd brought with me a bouquet of peach colored roses. Waved them at the lads, who smiled through their tears. They seemed happy with this explanation, which was better than the likely truth: that Martine in hospital was a lot like an old, angry woman, hooked up to IVs, dressed in a paper gown, body laid bare under bright light for all to ogle, but nobody seeming to give a damn. The last thing he wanted to see were these models of humanity's excellence. Still, being pretty wasn't their fault. Not entirely. I felt a little sorry for them.

"I'll remind him you really want to see him," I said. "At the very least, I'll give him your best wishes."

Todd 2 appreciated this more than I'd expected, reaching

out to squeeze my hand. The other Todd brightened up with a useful memory. "Miss Pebbles says hello. Asked us to look out for you."

That was good news and from an unexpected quarter. I said, "She's been by the card shop? That's good, I've been missing her." Twice I'd seen her on the street since The Elvis assassination attempt drove her deeper into Pere Qua mania, all got up in her prim Sunday drag. To be honest, we'd pretended not to see each other in order to avoid conversation. So it was sweet that she was asking about me. I made a promise to myself to buy her a beanbag toy from the hospital gift shop before I left.

I thanked the Todds and made my way to Martine's room. A young Cajun nurse was finishing up with him. She was built from square blocks of muscle wrapped fat, so I leaned around her to see Martine accept her attention with weary humiliation. An inspection, a tuck, a jostle. She picked up a plastic pan, sneered at its contents, put it back down again. Bleary eyed, Martine attempted a comic expression of desperation, but not much is funny when you've got tubes running in and out of you. His hand was bruised and taped with a plastic siphon jammed in it, an arrangement that did not look very scientific. When the nurse hustled off, I dropped the roses on a side table.

"Private room," I noted. "Nice."

Martine lifted some fingers. Tested his voice, failed.

I sat in a square pine chair thinly upholstered with yellow carpet, shifting it so that I sat directly in my friend's line of sight. Martine was a lucky, lucky man. He'd had a heart attack of the friendly warning type. If things didn't change, the next time he'd be dead. Plans were underway to re-plumb his chest. He was sedated.

I said, "Todd and Todd want to visit."

Martine coughed. Said something like *baffle*.

"Basil, yes I forgot. Todd and Basil. They want to see you, and you're being cruel to them. Are you enjoying that?"

More finger ruffle. My heart buckled. I reached out to touch his hand, which curled weakly over mine. His lips were the same color as his skin, and his skin was the same color as his hair. He looked like a sand castle version of himself. Paler and weaker than I'd expected, Martine looked worse now than when he was lying in the street, clutching his chest like a bad comedian.

"You look like shit," I said, my eyes starting to smart. I petted his brow.

Loff eh, he said.

"Love you too, my boyo."

We were quiet a long time. I think he was going in and out. I could think of nothing to say that wasn't inane or critical. I went with inane. "Big room."

He did one of those puffs through his nose that in a healthy person signals impatience, but in a sick person means "wait for me to catch up with you." Finally he formed a clear word: "Need."

"You need the nurse?"

"No." Puff and pause. Puff. "Need room," he managed. And then he sort of smiled. "For," and the next word needed a lot of breath. He sucked it in, and the subsequent hang time almost had me reaching for his call button.

But he finally wheezed it out: *El. Fazz.*

It took me a few seconds to figure it out, and when I did, I laughed loud, too loud for a hospital. Which was okay, as the light shimmering in Martine's eyes was a blessing. "Well that's for fucking sure my dear, that's for sure. You need room for elephants. By my count there's up to three of the cunts in this room right now. Except we're not supposed to talk about 'em." I wondered if he was the last man in the world to finally give a damn about dying. Or about wishing and dying.

Martine was too tired to laugh, so I did the job for the both of us, and in no time he slipped into a slack, open-mouthed doze that had me weeping quietly. I stayed a while. Martine woke once and I made up some gossip that was likely to be true when he got out. He drifted off again and the nurse returned with a set of small appliances, swabs, and hoses, the use of which I did not want to discover.

I scooted the chair back and stood, seeking appropriate distance. Martine's nurse was an expert psychologist though. She said, "I'll take care of the roses," without looking at me. Meaning I could scuttle off if I needed to.

"I'll be back tomorrow." But Martine was out and couldn't hear me. It came off like I was making excuses to the nurse.

Back in the lobby Todd and Basil bounced to their feet, ready for news. I said, "He's talking, making jokes. Resting. Looks awful, so maybe it's not a good time for you to visit. You know how vain he is."

Sad smiles on the both of them. Their pair-ness reminded me of the women in the shop who'd wanted my autograph. Todd/Basil clutched a white sack of mini pralines, while Basil/Todd carried the latest issue of *New York* magazine wrapped loosely around a catalog from a naughty wholesale toy distributor. These were get-well gifts that would please Martine to have even if he could not enjoy them yet.

I acquiesced, wondering how I became the mommy in all this. "All right, I said. You can pop in to drop off your trinkets. Tell Nursey she can have the candy after Martine's had a whiff. But then come right on out. Chances are if he sees you he won't remember later, and he won't be pissed at me."

"Yes, we'll only be a moment. Promise," said Todd/Basil.

Basil/Todd smoothed out his shirt front as if that was going to make a difference. Both lads were drenched in fantastic scents. I wasn't sure Martine was ready for such luxury. Whichever one had brought the pralines hustled the other forward, and he said something odd, like: "Won't be long now."

I didn't understand and let it go. On my way out I passed the hospital gift shop. Sure enough, there was a pile of limp tiger kitties and glitter ponies in the window, and I thought: Pebbles. I don't recall entering the shop, but I was there, suddenly, with a baggy toy cat in my grip. As if I'd awoken from a trance. Thing in my hand. A toy. A stupid—

Pebbles. She would never have gone to Martine's shop, not in her current mood. So where had the boys encountered her? Why were they talking about me? *She told us to look out for you.*

"No. Hey!" I yelled to no one in particular, and I was out of there, running back to Martine's room, swerving around limping patients and stranded carts. I passed a desk where Martine's massive nurse was making notes, and I yelled, "Hey!" at her but didn't slow down, couldn't slow down, not even enough to put words to the base fear that drove me onward.

The door to Martine's room was shut. Patient doors are never shut. I pushed and pulled, but it would not open. Behind me, Martine's nurse was coming on, hollering messy French warnings, accompanied by a male nurse in aqua scrubs. I pounded on the door and yelled back to my pursuers: "They're killing him! They're killing him!"

In a movie I'd have to waste time explaining the situation, but in these times of the Death Wish new rules of drama were in play. Took half a sec for Martine's nurse to be convinced. I demanded the key from her, but she assured me that there were no locks on patient rooms. So she and her partner shoved on the door with me, pounding and yelling as well. The door was blocked, but it began to budge from the cooperative pressure of the three of us. When we created a margin wide enough, I reached in and felt the familiar smooth wood of a chair and tried to dislodge it. The bar type door handle prevented Basil/Todd from wedging anything under a knob, so they had resorted to crude obstruction by piling chairs and carts up against the door. Good enough to keep one man out, but not two plus a well trained woman.

As we three shoved, I called out, "You fuckers! You murdering fuckers!" The male nurse made some sort of request via walkie-talkie, so help was on the way, but in general, no significant attention from anyone else on the hall. Cries of murder not so uncommon then?

We made it in, and there was a picture all right: Todd on one side of the bed, Basil on the other, the both of them pinning down the corners of a pillow over Martine's face. Todd bit his lips and Basil fought back his tears, but they had it under control. They were concentrated, calm. Working.

The male nurse launched towards the nearest, Todd, knocking the lad sideways into Maritne's IV. The tube pulled Martine's hand straight out from the bed before it dislodged, and fluid spurted a weak, pissy arc across the room. Basil, with the bed between him and us, pressed harder on the pillow, reaching over and leaning on Todd's side of it as well.

I still had the toy in my grip, which surprised the heck out of me. I whipped the bean bag kitten at Basil's face, and the thick plastic tag snagged him in the eye. He released the pillow and yowled, clutching his face, and I could hear a hospital cop jangling up the hallway, running and huffing. I launched onto Basil, pulled him to the floor and straddled him. He was way stronger than me, so I fought like a girl, grabbing a handful of hair and putting my knee in his groin.

The male nurse had Todd flipped over in some kind of arm

twist hold that appeared very professional. The hospital cop had his gun drawn as he entered the room, and I swear to God he said, "Ever-buddy freeze!"

The whole lot of us obeyed the fool. None of us, by nature, were violent. Martine's nurse, in all this, had made it to his side. Her hands were on him, fat fingers flittering over his body like a black jack dealer.

"Is he alive?" I asked. Beneath me Basil sagged, gave in even though he didn't really have to. He could have pushed me off and rolled out of that room before Officer Wheezy had a chance to flick the safety of his pistol. I let go of Basil's hair. His eye was red and wet. We both breathed like lovers.

With military satisfaction, the nurse replied, "Yes sir."

When Todd spoke, his mouth was all mushy and full of floor: "Shit."

That night, no sleep. I just lay there sticking to the sheets. There was music again, the brief but frequent skirmishes between club jazz and drive-by hip hop, and in the lulls the hoots of drunken tourists tried to keep new mysteries at bay by preserving the old.

Hell kept breaking loose, possibly because we tied it down with civility. I hated to think like that. But after a day of giving statements to the police and learning just how badly the world had degraded while I wasn't watching, it was hard to listen to better angels. It appeared that Pere Qua's group was one of many in a nationwide affiliation that only became apparent in the timing: so far 67 individuals across the country were attacked, twenty-two of whom had died from their injuries. Of the dead, none uttered wishes before they expired.

The mission had changed, but for reasons that were still unclear. The attacks began with one on one violence, perpetrated by serene and dispassionate assassins like Gerald Pollin. Afterward, the teams were set loose. As Todd and Basil mounted the attempt to euthanize Martine, so did sets of partners in other states embark on similar projects.

I'd given statements to no less than three sets of officers. I spilled my guts, seeing no benefit in keeping any of the secrets I held close. Eventually I related the whole Gerald Pollin story, and the deal I'd made with the Wish Phantoms. I even confessed to my passion for Pebbles, but by then no one was listening. The investigators may have been trying to tire me out, but I'd bored them silly first.

I did ask one or two sensible questions of my interrogators. Like, how did Pere Qua pick his targets? Why were Martine and I targeted? The cops had no idea, which I fully believed.

Street-glow seeped through the blinds. I wished I had a woman next to me. Elsewhere in the house, I wondered if Val was able to sleep. I know he'd spent hours on the phone with Brenda. There are always certain things a boy can only discuss with his mother.

Pebbles had vanished, apparently. Along with any and all known members of Pere Qua's cult of Death Wishers, or so we were told. I kept rolling it around in my head. Todd and Basil had joined Pere Qua's group, which was how they knew Pebbles. Why she told them to "look out for me." She meant just that—look out, boys. The very thought of her sweetness turning so sour . . .

I grew more alert and twitchy as the night passed. Eventually, I heard noise coming from the shop. Bobby Rebar putting in his shift? I eased out of bed, and crept downstairs in my under shorts and FEMA (*Find Every Mexican Available*) T-shirt.

Bobby didn't hear me as I came down, which was a little dangerous given that he didn't seem to respond well to surprises.

I coughed politely.

He looked healthy and clean even if he bore the expression of an animated rat, his flashlight eyes ready for any violent eventuality. I caught him mid-task, hauling in a collapsing cardboard box of poorly packed goods. Three child-sized cowboy boots floated on a sea of chartreuse crinoline. God only knew what lay under that mess. I hoped a fourth boot, at least.

It was probably three in the morning. I said, "Evening Robert."

Two short crazy nods.

"You keeping yourself safe?"

He thought that was a funny thing for me to say. He smiled wide. Open mouth, teeth apart, like he was gonna catch a delicious sandwich that way. It was not too long ago that Val had trusted this nutter to pilot one of his shrimpers. I wasn't convinced he should trust him now, even with these minor night shift tasks. Bobby Rebar could as easily burn down the house as he could sort prom dresses by size.

"It's happening," he said, not quite able to look me in the eye.

"Yes," I agreed, suddenly as tired as I was supposed to be after such a day and night. I sat on a low step. "Something is, anyway."

I noticed that Bobby breathed through his mouth, and that his whole body seemed to throb with the rhythm his lungs created. Was that a sign of illness? Bobby took the boots out, placed them in a careful row.

He said, "I heard what happened to you and the queer." Started digging deep past the crini. "Means you're both wishers." He found another boot that didn't seem to match the others at all.

"Means some crazy people think we're wishers," but Bobby

and I knew that difference was no difference at all. He grinned again, as if he could see the neon target on my back.

He mocked me. "You keeping yourself safe?" He pulled the crinoline out. It was a skirt connected to a shimmery elastic bodice that shed sequins on the shop floor. He carefully scooped those up and piled them on a nearby table. Then he extracted several more boots until he ended up with five matched pairs. As he emptied the entire contents of the box, I realized that he had brought us a fairly valuable pile of crap.

But he was panting. No, he wasn't well after all. "If you could see it like ants," he said. "Like you were God and we were ants. You could see it then." The grin faded, replaced by concentration. I dreaded this. He was talking loopy, and loopy talk tended to get scary pretty quickly. He smoothed his hair back with his hands, turning to me. There was a little more meat on his bones than usual, but he seemed to have aged ten years since I'd seen him last. Poor bastard.

He pointed at me, thoughts in the chamber, ready for firing. "We all went out, spread out, then we came back in. Tight, black mobs of ants. And we were like that a while, but now we're breaking loose again. You was God, you could see it."

I nodded. "Mr. Rebar," I whispered. "You stay clear of Pere Qua, yes? You stay clear."

And from behind me, Val. "S'no problem Pops." Val was always creeping up behind me. He stood on the stair above me, and I had an urge to hug his leg that I suppressed. "Bobby knows better. Doncha Bob?"

Val was red eyed from crying and exhaustion. He thought he was done taking care of me, and then all of a sudden this shit. People tried to kill me, people were going to want to kill me. Target, target, target.

Bobby Rebar's face lit up like he was receiving Jesus in skull print pajamas. Val said, "No problem. Bobby knows he's safe here. That he's got a home here."

Bobby's smile peeled years from his face. "Them pricks are always at me, but I told them, fuck off, cause Mister Val is takin' care of me."

"Really?" I asked Val.

"Sure. We gotta take care of each other." My boy was weary. "Come on Dad. Back to bed, okay? Bobby works better on his own." He touched my shoulder.

"Night Bob," Val said, but the crazy man did not reply, having dived back into a shadow to fight with another box of shabby inventory. Val started up, I followed.

"'We gotta take care of each other?' You and your mother must have had quite a talk."

"Yeah, well. It's getting bad out there." He rubbed the back of his neck till it glowed pink. "And besides," he said, "Fuck those fuckers."

CAPES

1.

In an old azalea and hickory choked neighborhood in Vienna, Virginia, retired pharmacy technician Anita Gorrel was hit by her own car inside her own garage, pinned underneath the front end and against the closed garage door. She was seventy-eight years old, but the impact was not deadly. The real trauma came from fear: with the engine running and her immobility, she thought she would succumb to carbon monoxide poisoning before anyone could rescue her. The garage door was open two or three inches at the bottom, but she hadn't a clue about whether that would provide enough ventilation.

Actually it was her late husband's vehicle, a vintage Chrysler that looked like a tank wearing a top hat, and she rarely drove it. In fact, the only reason she had started the damned thing was so she could move it out to the curb and slap a For Sale sign on it.

She tried yelling for help, but the sound of her own voice, amplified within the confines of the garage, upset her even more. When she started to cry, she wondered if her emotions weren't symptomatic of CO poisoning. She resumed yelling and worked an arm free to pound on the garage door. Eventually tiring of that, she stuck her hand through the crack and tried to pull the door up from the bottom edge. She wasn't strong enough, not in this position.

Her neighbor's fifteen year old daughter, Audra, had played

hooky that day so she could commit a full uninterrupted eight hours to writing, in long hand, a novel about immortal beings who were a lot like vampires but really different. From the window over her desk she saw the old woman's fingers wriggling under the garage door. This was a fascinating distraction that the young wordsmith enjoyed for some time before it dawned on her that something serious was going down. It would be a lie to say that she rushed to Anita Gorrel's aid, but she did get there, eventually.

Once on the scene, Audra required a certain amount of instruction and encouragement from the pinned woman, but she finally managed to raise the garage door. Mrs. Gorrel was in a terrible state, but at least she was still alive.

Audra turned off the engine of the Chrysler, and the old woman attempted to get out from under the bumper, but her legs wouldn't cooperate. Audra, her judgment uncompromised by training in first aid, grabbed her old neighbor by the arm and sort of yanked her a ways out until she could get a grip under both shoulders. But Mrs. Gorrel's house dress was tangled in the undercarriage of the vehicle, and Audra lost her grip, dropping the old woman to the asphalt.

Anita Gorrel was humiliated and angry. She and Audra argued about whether it was time to call 911. Audra was disinclined to make the call, given that she was truant. She also wanted to get back to her project as soon as possible. Anita Gorrel had graduated from interesting to inconvenient.

Perhaps it seems unlikely that all this could go on unnoticed in a densely populated community so close to the Capitol city. But it was mid day and not a single car came down the avenue located only blocks away from a busy strip mall anchored by a Vietnamese grocery. Despite this proximity, the neighborhood was arboreal and isolated, almost a ghost town between school bus shifts and rush hours. That's what Anita had always loved about her neighborhood, its non-remote peace. Audra had no opinion, having never known any other way of life.

Except that Audra was now a *decider*. That was a new experience, one that struck them both at once. Anita on her back, scraped, and apparently disabled, was suddenly and acutely aware that she had no power over the child who crouched over her. She'd never feared Audra before, and in fact had babysat her once or twice when Audra was very young.

This is a good time to point out that both Audra and Anita were armed. Everyone in Northern Virginia carried. It only seemed practical in these strange times. Audra carried a Taurus 738 TCP clipped to her waistband in a sleek snap case that also contained her cell phone. Anita made do with her husband's old Ruger Standard, which she generally carried loose, in the big front pocket of her house dress.

Given what happened next, one might conclude that Anita Gorrel was a bit addled by her confinement. Audra sighed a teenager's sigh as she reached for her snap case. Thinking only *gun*, Anita retrieved her own, but to be honest, her fingers had been tickling the thing for some moments now. She shot Audra, sending the girl and her cell phone flying backwards to the end of the driveway.

Anita Gorrel's strength was renewed. She struggled with her dress and discovered that tearing open the neck was easier than yanking the hem free of the undercarriage. Eventually, she was able to peel the cotton shift away like a skin. Clad only in an old bra, loose panties, and deck shoes, she pulled herself out from under the car. Her legs were useless, and she did not have great reserves of upper body strength, but once free, she found she could roll herself along the asphalt. She rolled towards Audra, then past her. The girl was obviously dead, Anita could tell from the big hole in her chest and the absence of light in her staring eyes. Anita rolled to Audra's cell, grabbed it and dialed for help.

By the time Brenda came home, the scene was cordoned off, cops everywhere, and that asshole Rick was sobbing on the stoop, a tidbit of information that irritated the living fuck out of me. How dare he be traumatized by a neighborhood tragedy when it wasn't even his neighborhood? Granted, he lived there now, and had lived there for a few years, but certainly not long enough to be so extravagantly public with emotion. Brenda and I had lived next to Anita Gorrel for twenty years. We'd raised Val there. It was Brenda's house now, and the only claim Rick had was that he was Brenda's consort. I don't recall much about Audra, except that when I knew her she was generally girly, pudgy in pink, always clutching some pony toy. I don't believe I ever saw her with a baby doll, and that possibly was the most distinguishing feature in her short biography.

There would be no admonishment of Anita Gorrel, as she stroked out on the way to the hospital. I think that Brenda was a little pissed at Rick as well, because she called me before she could work up tears about the whole affair. I cried with her, enthusiastically, eager to share this intimacy under the protective cover of grief. We traded memories of Anita, which were not always sweet. She'd always given us her extra tomatoes and zucchinis in the summer, but she also sold Thorazine and Vicodin to Val when he was seventeen. Ah, suburbia. Brenda filled me in on what sort of child Audra was, and at the end of it all, Brenda confessed that she was frightened.

The dark part of me was very near the surface. I would have loved to believe that Brenda was genuinely afraid, but my suspicion kicked in when she said, "Vic, I want to come down for a visit. What do you think?"

"It's not my house, Bren."

"I know. But I want to know if it will be okay with you."

"You mean to tell me that you think New Orleans is safer than Vienna, Virginia?"

"I want to be with my family."

Interesting. I wanted to ask about Rick, but bit my tongue. "I understand," I said. "But I think it's too dangerous. Too dangerous to travel, too dangerous to be a stranger."

"Vic."

"It's also too dangerous to be near me. I've been targeted once already."

"I want to see Val."

I couldn't argue with that. There was no way that Val would leave his business interests to go visit his mother. "You seem to have made up your mind then."

"Yes I have."

"Well, please wait a while," I said. "Let's see if things settle down, okay? This wave of madness, it has to burn itself out. I want you to stay safe."

I got the sense she agreed, but wasn't about to admit it. "Rick doesn't even know I'm thinking about leaving. You know what this feels like, Vic? It feels like a war is going to happen."

"Brenda."

"It feels like wartime, and all the choices I have made up until now—" she took a thoughtful breath. "I don't know. I'm all instinct all of a sudden. You know how the women in movies say things like, 'With every fiber of my being'? That's what I'm feeling, the fibers of my being. Never knew they were real, Vic. And every fiber of my freaking being is telling me to gather my family around me and hunker down."

I could contain the question no longer. "What about Richard?"

"Yeah, well. To hell with him I guess. He doesn't feel it. Thinks I'm being hormonal."

"You are."

Silence. Then, "I'm still coming down."

Over the next two days, the violence continued. More attacks, more murders, perpetrated by amateurs. Ninety-three more deaths to be exact, some small portion of which were cultists who got caught short in their own deadly schemes. We stayed in—with Bobby Rebar, who was once more a resident in the shop. Val and his mother texted each other frequently, making plans for her visit. He eyeballed me like a wary animal from whatever corner of the room we inhabited together.

On the second night of violence Val and I watched the news together, sitting in a dark room staring at our television set. The light flickered off the walls like specters with attention deficit disorder, and Bobby yelled curses down in the shop. We ignored him. The latest report was that of a man who had been pushed under a train and survived. His assailant, a street mime, had been shot dead as he fled the scene. Not by a cop, but by a witness.

"Daddy, you know what they are saying, right?"

I did. "Shush."

"That there haven't been any wishes since the killings started?"

"Stop. That's crazy thinking, not proof."

"It's all crazy thinking."

Big crash in the shop. Bobby was going to destroy the place, eventually. He was definitely on the down slope.

Crazy. We wanted it to be crazy. Somehow crazy was a comfort. But the attacks were orchestrated. There was no passion at work here. This campaign was anything but madness. I knew, because madness lived in my basement. Madness was a disorganized wreck with fire dot eyes. This terrorism was designed—by jailbird prophets who received their orders from higher sources. A franchise structure was in place, like that of the Mafia, the Catholic Church, or Curves. There were instructions, goals, conclusions. The cruelty of it was cold.

"Where's mom going to sleep?"

I shrugged. "What are you going to do with Bobby when she gets here? He seems to need medical attention."

These were good questions. We had plenty to do, plenty to think about. There was no point in ruminating on imponderables. Some ideas will eat you up. The local station was starting to show lists of the dead, like in wartime. Name, age, parish. Pictures.

When Val was four or five he went through a phase where he liked to draw pictures and tell stories of families—not ours, but similar ones with a mommy, a daddy, and a son—being devoured by animals or burning up in a fire or drowning at sea. No monsters and no magic. All possible disasters. The parents in these dramas were consistently ineffective. Val's babysitters and grandparents were alarmed by his fantasies, but Brenda and I were relieved. It was better for little Val to think these ideas through, and to enjoy them, than to be bewildered by the unknown. At least that's what we thought at the time.

Val asked, "If I wanted to go look for Pebbles, how would I start? I'd go over to her apartment, right?" He stood, started looking around for his shoes.

"I suppose so." My natural inclination in times of stress or potential danger was to stay put, and I hadn't raised Val to believe in villains and heroes. Now the time had come for reaching beyond ourselves, and we were without training.

"It's possible that we might not want Pebbles back," I said. "Not after all this."

Val acted like he hadn't heard me.

Then I said, "I'm coming with you."

"You don't have to."

"I have a key."

"No shit?"

"For emergencies," I said. "She trusted me."

Technically, Pebbles was not a missing person, as she told Val she was going and made it clear that "where" was no business of his. Her bills were paid, and at this point for us to go to the authorities for help would have merely implicated her as a cultist. There was no evidence that she was in danger, except for our firm belief that she was in deep with a very dangerous person.

Her apartment, underneath all the pillows and scarves, was a bit of a hole, but at least it was hers and hers alone. I know she was proud of living on her own. Val looked around, trying to figure out *how* to look around. Their love being so new when Pebbles took her turn towards the apocalypse, Val hadn't staked out his own territory yet. Her objects were just that: objects. Things placed in the way of getting to the bedroom. But maybe I was wrong about that.

The freshness surprised me. Rooms didn't smell fresh over at our house. "Where do we start?"

"I have no idea," said Val. And then he looked at me as if to say, *you know her better than I do.*

At first I thought, this is exactly what I expected: her computer and desk were off in a corner, half hidden behind a fake Japanese folding screen. Her bed was a mattress on the floor topped by a tangle of pink tinted sheets that I didn't want to think about. Fuzzy, electric colored pillows held down a half broken couch, and every chair was draped with batik print sarongs. I was disappointed, seeking a revelation after having put in so many hours across the avenue, peering at the mysterious rose colored light from behind her window.

"There isn't anything personal here."

"There's tampons and tweezers in the bathroom," said Val.

"You know that's not what I mean. Is this how the apartment usually looks?"

"Pretty much." Val sat down at her computer. While he waited for it to power up he went through the drawers of the desk. "Here," he said, waving a hot pink post-it pad. The top sheet said *P-word: H1LLeLk1tty*. "That's pretty personal."

A low two-shelf bookcase tilted with the weight of paperback novels by Anita Shreve and Taylor Caldwell with creased spines. A Riverside Shakespeare with a yellow USED sticker lay on its side, anchoring the shelf to the floor. The refrigerator in the kitchenette featured voodoo head and alligator claw magnets holding down coupons alongside a dozen remaining words from a magnetic poetry set. But that was it. "There aren't any pictures," I said. "Or notes, that sort of thing."

"Must be all on here." Val leaned forward. Pebbles' desktop picture was herself in a skimpy tank top, grinning out of the screen as if she could see us from the other side. All cheeks, eyes, bare shoulders, and the sheen of perspiration. "Okay," said Val. "Buncha music files. Some games. She's got photos in here, see?" And he showed me a folder of snaps from the Quarter, mostly of buildings, parades, and sunsets, but once in a while there was the odd picture of me posing in a cape, or Val squinting in the sun.

Three photos of herself with Pere Qua, all taken the same day out in front of Jax Brewery. Pebbles was wearing one of her severe little suits while Qua stood next to her, bowlegged in pencil jeans, boots, and a tucked in Hawaiian shirt. Ex-con formal wear. The chrome Jesus-Head-and-Praying-Hands for a belt buckle was a nice touch. Looked like it weighed about two pounds. Pere Qua's little white bristle beard glowed against his tan skin. He'd clamped a hard arm across her shoulders to pull her in. She smiled, but she was not at all relaxed.

"Looks like he wants to eat her up." Val stood, let me have the seat. I suppose he thought I knew some magic trick to make the computer tell us her whereabouts and whether she was okay. I took a moment to gaze at Pebbles' desktop image; she looked so bubbly and insane—I missed that girl. It was obviously taken well before she'd met Pere Qua. I scanned through the photos again. A quick check told me she'd recently removed and/or compressed several files. But what really intrigued me was the evidence we already had right in front of us.

I said, "So I know it was too much to hope that we might stumble across a diary or a 'Dear Val' letter, but don't you think it's odd that none of her photos go any farther back than a few months?"

Val shrugged and leaned against the dining counter. He seemed to be losing his heart for the adventure. "Are you suggesting that Pebbles has a secret identity? Maybe she's FBI, deep cover. Trying to infiltrate the Death Cults."

"This is your caper, Val. I'm just trying to be observant." But he was right to make fun of me. Conspiracy, traps, and bureaucracy I had long left behind in Virginia, where at any given dinner party there was a good chance that one or more of the guests were CIA, FBI, or (shudder) NSA. And you just didn't talk about it. Down here we were more likely to encounter FEMA, DEA, or KKK, and no one kept his mouth shut about a damned thing.

Val started to bounce around the apartment, leaning into its tiny rooms and pulling out. He wasn't giving up just yet. I sat at Pebbles' computer trying to find my moral center so I could squish it in the name of What Must Be Done, but truth be told, there was probably very little in those trashed and archived files that would help us find her. It was merely personal information—about which I was keenly interested but I had hoped to learn through the conventions of traditional intercourse.

Then Val was in the main room again, his color brightened by the headlight from an oncoming train of thought. He saw the bookshelf, and its beach reader's library. "Her bible," he said. "It's missing."

"She had a bible?" And as soon as I asked the question I knew how stupid it was. Of course she had a bible. "Do you remember what it looked like?"

"Like a bible. One of those black jobs." He shook his finger at a picture in his head and narrowed his eyes as he retrieved the full memory. "And I know she kept a fifty in there that she got as a tip from a drunk city council woman."

"Did she keep anything else in her bible?"

Val shrugged. "I never looked. She just told me about the tip. But she kept the bible right there on the shelf."

"So she's taken it with her then."

"And bought a massive Shakespeare book. Just like the one I had to buy for English 2 in Freshman year."

"She never had that before?"

Val moved across the room and crouched to remove the huge textbook. Several of the paperbacks tilted, and the shelf above sagged. He sat on the floor cross-legged and flipped open the cover carefully. He knew what to expect. And indeed, the pages had been razored out to make a well in the center, just like you see in movies about private schools. Pebbles' black bible was nestled within.

"Yes!" said Val. "You ever notice it was the one book I didn't sell back after Freshman year? It's because I kept a bong in it."

"That was a hundred dollar book. I wrote the check."

"Yeah, sorry about that." He lifted out the bible and began to thumb-flip the pages. The fifty floated out. "Plus, I tested out of English 2 anyway."

Along with the cash a couple of photographs slipped to the floor. And a business envelope. In the envelope a one page letter and a whisper thin necklace with a tiny gold cross—the one I'd seen her wearing when she gave me the watermelon.

The photographs were ancient, and I mean that. They were dusty colored on card stock and easily a hundred years old. Both featured a plump woman with long black braids and a full-length woolen dress seated in the grass with four black puppies. The woman and her dress seemed to be Native American or perhaps Mexican.

The letter was a simpler matter. It was from the Christian college that Pebbles attended for a short while. Apparently she'd made the Dean's list in her first semester. Her second she never finished, having decided to try to make a life in New Orleans instead. Val read aloud: "'Dear Annabeth Lewis'— Annabeth? That's not so bad. Wonder when she picked up 'Pebbles'?"

He really didn't know? She took the name Pebbles when she danced topless on Bourbon Street.

But the necklace. So exceedingly delicate. A woman wouldn't buy such a thing for herself. And a man would not buy it for a woman. No, this was a treasure to be offered to a lovely girl child, something her mother would have to keep safe for her for years: *you, my dear, are this exquisite.*

I felt dirty looking at her things. And not in a good way.

"Val, put all that away. That stuff is precious to her. "

"Stuff she hid in a bible. But now she hides the bible in a Shakespeare book." He sat back on his ankles, considering. "Because the people she's with now, Pere Qua or his followers, they'd flip through a bible."

"But not Shakespeare. Yes, that makes sense. But the items themselves?"

"Don't mean anything." Val reassembled the bible and its treasures and tipped it back into the hidey-hole of the Shakespeare. "Except that it means she's not completely lost. There are some pieces of her life before Pere Qua that she values enough to protect from him."

He lived in hope. I did too. I poked around in her computer files. The trash was full of trash: online shopping receipts, a couple of jpegs that turned out to be pictures of the sidewalk, and dozens of band flyer pdfs. I was about to give it up when I noticed that her last accessed file still sat quietly in a general folder. The one page doc named "GO" was authored by JB and it featured three columns of names. There was no obvious order, but some of them I recognized. In the middle of the first column, *Martine Bernier*. Eight names down from his: *Victor Swaim*. I knew what this was.

The jolt that ran through me didn't show, thank God.

There was probably no way to protect Pebbles much longer. I opened her email program, mercifully auto-filled except for her password: *H1LLeLk1tty*. Nothing in her message history jumped out—most of her messages seemed to be to or from Val, an exchange that dried up days ago. From my wallet I fished out the four different calling cards given to me by the detectives who interviewed me after the attack on Martine. Only two included email addresses, so I sent the GO doc to them as an attachment in an empty message with the Subject: *Pere Qua's list*. I had no idea how sophisticated these blokes were, but the initial impression would be that one Annabeth "Pebbles" Lewis of Arkansas had sent them a very valuable tip.

How long would it take the detectives to act, and what

would they do exactly? Hell, would they do anything at all?

"Whatcha got?" asked Val after I was quiet too long.

"Nothing. I thought I might find something in the email."
I logged off and shut down the machine. "I'm afraid we're
skunked, son. Let's get out of here before one of the neighbors
calls the cops."

2.

Martine was discharged a day later than originally planned, and I collected instructions for his medication schedule and eventual therapy. I planned to stay with him, on and off as needed. He would have a nurse coming around too. He lived in an enormous 1850s era Greek revival style home on Magazine Street, and I was assigned to an airy, cool guest room lined with books and Canadian patriotic decorations. It was the room his family used when they came south for a visit, being the least southern, least gay room in Martine's entire house. Other rooms were more dramatic: some functioned as miniature art galleries while others seemed like chapels for lost religions. There were two gleaming studios he used for dance parties. Yes, he had parties where people danced. I looked forward to the next one, now that I was in shape.

Sadly, Martine wouldn't be partying any time soon. The only good thing about his falling ill was the weight loss. But his shine had faded, his color drained. He didn't look right in his peachy gold bedroom, but he took to his bed gratefully. Though excited to leave the hospital, he was defeated by the drive home. As soon as the nurse left us alone he said, "Love, I need a big whiskey sow-wah."

I didn't bother with an answer. He couldn't have anything he liked, not for a long time, and he knew it. He was just trying to pick a fight in hope that conflict was just as restorative as any of his other vices. "I'll get you a pudding," I said.

"Oh, I guess that's just as nice," he muttered. In seconds his eyes fluttered and he had drifted off to sleep. I knew he'd get better and better every day, but at the moment I was gutted.

I toddled down to his huge, shiny kitchen with its bone colored marble counters and copper pots that looked suspiciously unused. I went through the pantry and the refrigerator ("ice box" in Martine's parlance), and there wasn't much to work with. We'd need to restock with serious intent soon, but in the mean time I could dash down to the grocery deli to pick up a few items.

Martine's security codes safely in-pocket, I ventured out to find the entire sky was a mixture of orange and black. Storm rolling in. I got my umbrella open just before the big drops started plopping down hard, like it was personal this time. The sidewalks of New Orleans are ridiculously dangerous, so broken as to make walking on the streetcar line seem sensible. I think that's why our old people are the most graceful old people you'll ever see on the dance floor. They have to be.

My purple, yellow, and green umbrella didn't handle well. I kept grazing tree limbs as well as other pedestrians, and while most reacted with grace and good humor, one feller seemed down right irritated by my clumsiness. Eyes down, I picked my way over broken chunks of asphalt, tilting the umbrella this way and that, when I connected with a pair of long, narrow cowboy boots and rain splashed jeans.

"So sorry!" I attempted to step back but banged into an iron gate behind me.

"Jesus Chris', will ya watch it?"

"Really, I do apologize." I leaned back, and the umbrella drizzled streams all down the front of me. He was a tall man, drenched and miserable. He looked like he'd been hit in the head by every rain soaked, low hanging branch in Louisiana. A folder full of red paper was jammed under his arm, and he made it clear he didn't have time for this. But we were in a small tangle, me against the gate, him against garbage canisters on the other side. We worked it out, and he got through it with a bit of curse therapy. Just as we broke free of one another, he looked me in the eye. He recognized me, I could see that much. I thought there was something familiar about him as well. His irritation melted away, replaced with a dangerous focus.

And then he ran away. He backed up, turned, and just ran. Like I was Lon Chaney or something. Extraordinary.

By the time I got to the deli, I'd forgotten my purpose. There were a couple of cops and road workers in line to buy po' boys, but all I could do was stare for a while. No one in the grocery seemed to think I was a monster, so that was some small comfort. I bought a few random items, including a beef sandwich with extra gravy that I knew Martine could not eat, but maybe he'd enjoy the smell. When I left the shop, the rain had shifted from vengeance to constancy, and the streets flowed with cigarette butts. And red paper. Just a few sheets, but a little red goes a long way towards being noticed.

Of course. The tall man I'd run into was Boney Maroney. The skinny lad with Pere Qua the morning after Mirella had passed and turned the clouds orange. Now I had an inkling as to why he ran off in such a hurry. Red paper. He'd been posting notices.

There was one quite near, on a light pole, running in the rain. Before I could get close enough to read it, I recognized the black columns. The lists of names.

Now I knew for sure. I had seen Pere Qua's man, and these were his flyers. But he hadn't run because I'd spotted him. He ran because he found *me*.

I'd let the umbrella drop to my side, and I was soaked in a matter of seconds. I tore the list from the pole and put it in my pocket. I turned on the sidewalk, slowly surveying the neighborhood and weighing what few options I had. They were everywhere, it seemed. Red lists with no explanations, no instructions. Perhaps none were needed. I took out my cell phone and tried to figure out whom to call first.

An old ivory-eyed gal wearing rain gear made out of garbage bags pushed an Albertson's cart along the edge of the street close to the curb—not along the sidewalk, that would have been impossible. She paused to inquire: "Honey, you lost?"

"No Ma'am, not really. But I sure don't know what to do."

"You get news?" She cast a glance at the phone in my hands, as if to say, *well there's your problem*.

I nodded. "And I don't think there is anything I can do about it."

"Hm," she said. "Well, what was you on your way to doing? Before you let yourself get caught?"

I focused on a coffee shop, just a block away. Food. Always food with me. "On my way to pick up some pastry," I said. My vision swam, and I let go of just about everything, except those red pieces of paper. They danced forward, detached and floating.

"That's right then," she said. "They still there."

She meant the pastry. A minor point, but true.

"Yes. Yes of course."

"People always thinking they need to change because things change. Get a damn donut. Settle your head."

So I did. I hustled to the café where I purchased a cinnamon scone and an iced latte, and as I consumed them I thought of nothing else. Afterwards, I brushed off the crumbs and called one of the cops to whom I'd emailed the file. I had to be careful not to give too much away, not wanting him to know that I had added home invasion to my hobbies.

He was Detective Danny Collier, and I remembered being abstractly worried by him when we'd first met. He'd had one of those Mississippi dry-county accents, like Foghorn Leghorn contemplating death, unsettling seeing as he was a young African American gentleman. He sighed a lot as if he could read my tiresome thoughts. Now listening to his comedy cracker voice on the phone, it was difficult to picture him speaking.

When I introduced myself, his tone went from polite to strained in an instant. He knew about the notices already, and if my identification of Pere Qua's tall, thin associate was useful news, he did not let on. Nevertheless he assured me that every lead was being thoroughly investigated.

It was clear the detective's nerves were frayed, but I had to ask, "And what can Mr. Bernier and I expect in the way of protection?"

At which point Collier suffered a mild eruption of temper. "There are a hundred and twenty nine names on the list, Mr. Swaim."

"I understand that, but we've been attacked before. I feel as if that makes us more vulnerable. Especially given Mr. Bernier's condition."

Collier took a calming breath. "I would agree sir. I *completely* agree. And do you know what else makes you more vulnerable? Swooping around the Quarter at all hours like you're the Prince of Darkness. Mr. Swaim, you're going to get yourself killed, and it'll be for something stupid."

"Pardon me?"

"We know it's you. And we have enough Phantom shit to clean up, we don't need to be tracking your caped ass as well."

My caped ass. "I swoop around like the Prince of Darkness?"

He swallowed audibly, perhaps pulling on a paper cup of cold, bitter coffee. "Was there anything else I can help you with?"

Well damn. I wished I was more confused, but the picture was embarrassingly clear. "Just off hand, how often do I do this swooping?"

Collier was frustrated, but he listened. "You're saying it isn't you? It's your cape, that big black and orange thing."

"How often, Detective Collier?"

"I don't know. It's a low priority. About four times so far? Always after midnight, rushing like God knows what out of alleyways with the rats, scaring the living shit out of people. Usually couples making out."

Bobby. I thought back to Martine's attack. Of all the confessions relevant and frivolous that I'd made to the detectives that day, there was one thing I held back: that Bobby was the vigilante who'd successfully fought off the Wish Phantoms the night of the break in. Why did I leave that bit out? Vanity? I mean really, I told them about Pebbles for Christ's sake. Why would I humiliate myself as a failed lover but preserve my unearned reputation as an idiot hero?

I did not like what that said about me.

And now Bobby had taken his act to the streets, apparently. Jumping out at people at night. The detective was absolutely right. He was going to get himself killed.

"No," I said to Detective Collier. "It's me, of course it's me. I'm very stressed. I go a little mad."

Collier could smell it over the phone, "Bullshit," he said. "Do you care?"

His anger was gone. "Not if you put a stop to it."

After Collier hung up, I called Val to check on Bobby, but

Brenda's flight was coming in that day so the boy was up to his eyeballs in imaginary concerns. He hardly understood as I described Bobby's midnight rambles. He didn't seem to think there was much to do about it. "He's a night rat, Dad. What difference does it make if he's in some half-assed costume?" And besides Bobby had apparently relocated to St. Anne's Mission, having heard that we would be expecting Val's mother for an extended stay. Bobby had good instincts, if not good sense.

Within hours the lists were famous, and the media started to refer to those of us who were named as "red-listed." The city had attempted to remove as many of the posters as they could, but some of them, like the one I'd torn down, could not be accounted for. Val said a couple of reporters were trying to locate me for a comment, and I noticed I had messages on my cell from numbers I did not recognize.

Martine's home was my elegant refuge, and I imagined myself as a member of court, insulated from the plague-ridden rabble. But Martine dreamed all night. I know because I slept in a chair in his room. It was not uncomfortable, being one of those overstuffed brocade deals with a matching ottoman. I know a number of gentlemen who prefer chair sleep when the engineering and biochemistry is right. I parked my butt next to French doors that led to a small balcony overlooking the riot of colorful slanting rooftops and courtyard gardens of his neighbors. Of course, at three in the morning none of that mattered.

"Hey. What?"

"I'm here Martine. Do you need anything?"

Some fumbling. "Stay put. Just gettin' a sip of water." There was a jug and cup within his reach. I listened to him slurp. He sighed, the way you do when you're parched and then sated. "Not used to the dark," he said.

"I can put on the bathroom light."

"No I like it. But I'm awake. Not used to sleeping through the night, either. The nurses were always waking me up every coupla hours, taking readings, sticking stuff in me and up me."

"Oh. What do you want to do?"

"I want to go back to sleep." Martine chuckled then coughed. His lungs sounded cavernous.

"I could poke you with a letter opener if it'll help you relax."

"You're too good to me."

He sounded old. But then a heart attack followed closely by an attempted murder is bound to put years on one. I reached for the television remote and flicked on the set to the public station. They were showing old episodes of Doctor Who all night. I kept the sound very low. "That a little better?"

"Looks like shit." He meant the 1970s BBC production values on his high definition screen. A Dalek scooted towards a military officer, looking like it would topple over before reaching its destination. Martine closed his eyes. "Why the hell are you here, any way?"

"You were dreaming. I wanted to be close."

"I dream. So what." He opened one eye to watch a Dalek extended its little egg beater thingie at a woman who was probably supposed to be Queen Victoria. Martine sighed. "It isn't over yet, is it?" He wasn't talking about the program.

"Quiet Martine."

"Tell." His mouth was thick.

I leaned over. Perhaps he wouldn't understand or remember. "No, it doesn't seem to be over, but there isn't much we can do about it either." I tugged the silky edge of Martine's quilt top up to his chin. "Whoever is doing this, whoever is promoting the attacks, they still have us in mind. A couple of Wish Phantoms are watching the house, on and off, if that's any comfort."

Martine puffed a puff, his mood undecipherable. The medication he was on meant he was falling off the edge of a cliff, over and over again. I envied him. In this state he had no responsibility, not even to himself. I leaned back and watched the show, listening to the small, unhealthy noises that Martine made through the night. It was always good, spending time with friends.

3.

The first thing Brenda did was make a big deal about my weight loss. At first I liked it, but then it was uncomfortable, like when a teenaged boy is called a heartbreaker by his aunt. Brenda looked fine, a little thicker, a little more permanent in the world. She had cut her dark hair short, and it was coarser, flecked with silver. But we all age.

We met up for breakfast at a restaurant—neutral territory. When she touched Val her fingers flickered over his shoulder, his hands, his hair (to get it out of his eyes), and I could tell she was happy he was still a bachelor. We were the right age for it, but neither of us was ready to be a grandparent yet. But I'd almost forgotten. She reached to pull a Blackberry out of her purse, twisting in her seat. The little eye, there in person. It winked at me. Made my toes and fingers go all hot.

Good coffee, pulpy juice, dry croissants. Brenda was warm, I was polite. Val regressed. "Nothing on the news so far," he said, stirring his milky coffee. "Maybe this list thing is just a hoax. You should come back to the house tonight and I'll make dinner."

"Don't make it sound like I'm hiding out, Val. I'm taking care of a friend."

"Martine has a nurse."

"Guys," said Brenda.

Val looked a little stopped up. When the waiter came around again, I ordered mimosas. Brenda liked this. "You don't have to work today?"

Val said "Yes," and I said "No," simultaneously.

I laughed at the boy in a way I hadn't done for a while. It was slightly poisonous. "Sorry Boss. Taking a personal day."

Val's smile was theatrical.

The day proceeded without unusual violence. And by that I mean those of us who had been listed remained safe. I also mean that Val, Brenda, and I managed a civil day. Brenda wanted to do touristy things which was only natural. She'd never been to the Quarter before. She found Bourbon Street amusing, but more than that she was deeply impressed by Val's popularity with young, pale, eccentrically made up women. I spotted at least two young people wearing T-shirts with capes on them.

There was no talk of Pebbles. No talk of the Wishing either. We tamped down so much, it was like we were a real family again.

We drank a bit. Stood in line for muffalettas at the Central Grocery. Browsed art and antique shops thoroughly buzzed. Despite being accompanied by two men, Brenda was the target of much flirty attention from musicians and jugglers. A dude with neon pink hair convinced her to sit for a Tarot reading in Jackson Square. He muttered to her in deep, slushy tones and touched her outstretched hand with startling intimacy. Her amusement softened, and when she stood to pay him he embraced her. I'm certain that I saw him slip his tongue into her ear, but Brenda swore this never happened.

Fortune tellers operate by reading their marks, and for that reason I think that conferences between seers and patrons should be kept private. Like your dreams, no matter how off the wall they are, they say something about you that can't or shouldn't be said out loud. Brenda wobbled towards us, recovering herself in a way that was familiar to me but not to Val. The boy wanted to know, "So what did he say?"

Her eyes were smoked. "He said he could hook me up with some hash. Oh, and that even though I had restrained my divine spirit, I would succeed in my mission."

"Your mission. Which is?"

"He didn't tell me, so I haven't a clue."

Cold bolt. This last part was a lie.

A piece of red paper skittered across the stones, sailed on an imperceptible breeze, and everyone in the square paused to watch it go. A reminder of mortality. The pink haired Tarot Reader seemed most sanguine about it, choosing to watch me watch the paper. Val lost his cool a little, ran after the scrap and scooped it up, looking embarrassed. He crumpled it up like the child he was, and threw it in a bin. Spell broken.

Val received a call mid-afternoon. We were all a wee bit staggery. He said there was a problem with one of his new boats that he had to deal with. The slight false tinge to Brenda's disappointment sobered me right up. I knew all along she'd been waiting to get me alone.

"But honey," she said to Val. And nothing more. She knew him, oh yes. Nothing he liked more than leaving a clingy woman for the sake of business. Valmont made his handsome, princely regrets and then walked off in the direction of money.

Hairs rose up on the back of my neck. We were on Royal at that point, in the slim shade of a balcony. It was hot and we were drunk. Her suggestion was entirely reasonable. "Take me back to the house, Vic. Think I need a siesta."

When we got back I discovered that Val had cleaned up my room for her use. She insisted I guide her up the narrow stairs. I was eight kinds of panicked, wondering just what Brenda had up her sleeve. The room was free of dust and papers, and there were fresh linens on the bed. The curtains were drawn, but the room was fully illuminated; damn, he'd replaced the bulbs in the shabby chandelier.

Brenda went to the bathroom as soon as we got in. I waited for her at my desk with its neat stacks of stationary and cups of paperclips. I wanted to be pissed, but it was so nice. Brenda emerged, having changed into a sleeveless knit top, her shoulders strong and lovely, but too pale. She was wearing natural cotton Capri pants with those little tie things at the bottom. So, not a negligee, that was a relief. She was barefoot though.

She sat on the edge of the bed, just across from me, her expression neutral. And she got right to it, without any prompting from me:

"Here's what I think, Victor. I think you are going to die." There was pale pink paint on her toenails. She breathed and I caught the perfume of alcohol and whatever lotion she had just coated herself with. The air conditioning kicked up to a panic level. "So what's your plan?"

I had many. I had none. She leveled her gaze at me, and in her eyes I saw an almost wolf-like pragmatism. Where was the love? There was love for Val, I'd seen that and it was genuine. But were there no shreds for me? Not even nostalgia?

"I'm keeping my wish private," I said, trying not to sound wounded.

Apparently that was no problem. She nodded, kept her lips in a soft line. "That's certainly your right, and I'll not trouble you about it."

Her respect caught me off guard. I said, "I'm happy to hear suggestions, of course. I want what's best for Val. And you, I suppose."

Brenda refused to be insulted. That would be trifling under

the circumstances. "When I ask you about your plan, I'm not just talking about the wish. I'm talking about what seems to be an inevitability."

"Since when did you get so—"

"We're no longer in the realm of superstition, Vic. This is happening. Someone tried to kill you. They'll try it again."

I let that hang in the air without response. What was she getting at?

Her eyes filled with tears, but not enough to fall. No other part of her body showed any emotion other than resignation. "You need to control it. I don't want you to suffer. And I don't want Val to see you suffer."

Now I got it. What an evil woman. And in my own damned room. "You want me to kill myself? Here I was worried you wanted to fuck me."

She was never surprised by me. Not ever. She continued as if we were having a perfectly rational discussion. "I don't want you to kill yourself. But I don't want you die badly, either." She reached back on the bed. One of her travel bags rested there, partially unzipped. She rummaged around in it until she found what she was looking for. A plastic baggie full of pills.

"Here," she said, handing it over. "Morphine sulfate. More than enough to kill you, certainly enough to kill the pain should someone get to you first and do a sloppy job."

I held the baggie out, amazed. No response was sane. So, come the next attack I was supposed to fall to the ground, gobbling pills. How dignified. "How do these pair with Pinot Noir?"

"Pretty well I imagine. Vic, don't throw them away in some angry gesture. Please."

She was serious. I pocketed the drugs. Martine was going to get a kick out of this. Someone should. "So now you expect me to think and act like I'm going to die?"

Brenda thought about this. "Yes. At the very least."

I patted my pocket. "And the most is me doing the job myself, quietly and efficiently. Is there a middle choice?"

"Not sure. I guess you should think about your preference. How you want to go."

Actually, she knew me well. I always liked wine and pills.

Brenda turned kind then. She made her own weather. "You want to lay down with me?" She patted the bed. "You look so good. Maybe just a little nap to dream away the booze."

"No thank you, dear." I was chilled to the core, but there was no point in letting her try to warm me up again. "Something about your gifts are off putting." I stood and made my way towards the door, so grateful I had somewhere else to go. The room was icy, made unfamiliar, if not entirely hostile.

"But Brenda," I paused. "How would you want to go, just out of curiosity? You've obviously thought this through."

Brenda wriggled out of her pants and lay down on top of the thin, knotted spread, exposing pink cotton panties to me. Her thighs looked like a national park. I mean that in a good way.

She put her arm over her eyes. "Not sure how to manage it, but I want to die laughing."

What a good choice. "At some horrible dark secret no doubt."

"You know it."

Before I could slip away, she called me back. "Victor?" She looked at me from under her forearm.

"Yes."

"If it's easier for you, we could leave it like this. With you thinking I'm a cold hearted, oversexed witch."

"It does make our conversations simpler."

"Don't be an idiot. I love you. I love Val." She raised up on her elbows and tucked her chin into her collarbone to give me that *look*, full strength. "You think I don't have a bag of pills for myself?"

I hadn't thought about that. And yes, the information complicated my prejudices. "But that's all, right? You don't have any special presents for your son—"

"Oh, good God, Victor. That's disgusting."

"Glad you think so. It never hurts to check."

4.

The Elvis sat next to the President of the United States, touching knee to knee on a red cushioned sofa across from the President of the People's Republic of China and some European dude whose title and country he'd forgotten. They were sitting in brocade chairs, gripping the armrests like twin Captain Kirks. The Elvis had seen a steady stream of dignitaries today, filing in by twos and threes in what he assumed was a ranked order, but now, looking at the European, he wondered if it was by weight or alphabetical or something else.

The Lawyer had wanted him to wear a white suit, but The Elvis thought that was going too far. Like a bride in her thirties, he opted for cream, with honey colored loafers and tie. He'd been summoned to the White House for what was meant to be a consultation with the President. But then the visitors came, world leaders, each with their own terrified concerns. The Elvis contemplated God. He and the Presidents had run out of things to say to one another, perhaps because they were sufficiently embarrassed by what had already been said.

Do you feel real?

The President's staff worried about the music. The power of it, and the future of it—questions that weren't even questions, and so could not be answered. The Elvis drank bottled water. He was completely clean and sober, in small part because they no longer made the stuff he liked. He didn't know what pill did what job any more. A stack of presents had collected in the corner throughout the day—plaques, medals, totems. Tributes from all nations. Humorless gifts from the gravest givers.

Do you have any special powers? Did you miss us?

When The Elvis made his decision, he signaled for the lawyer. Then he stood, happy, not even slightly nervous. At this point anyone else would have wished him luck, but these men seemed submissive, almost embarrassed by what he was about to accomplish.

Damn right, he thought, but what he said was, "I got this."

Please forgive us.

And then, as if to prove the essential goodness of man, The Elvis walked out the front doors of White House. He handed his suit jacket to the sergeant at arms and yanked on his tie until his throat was exposed. He walked all the way out to the front gates and through them. Then he walked down the middle lines of Pennsylvania Avenue until it intersected with Constitution where he veered off to approach a sno ball vendor parked on the side. He ordered a red, white, and blue cone.

He did all this alone. No one dared to interfere.

This time the helicopter above merely photographed him. And that's what we saw next. A man, overdressed for the DC heat, eating a sno ball in the middle of what should have been a busy street. He looked contemplative.

The video ran on the six p.m. news. All stations. It preceded a Special Announcement. The most famous lawyers tend to be ones who lost their cases or who won cases for clients that were obviously guilty. One of those lawyers spoke for The Elvis. On one side of the screen, the Lawyer at a podium. On the other side of the screen, the shaky helicopter-shot video of The Elvis enjoying a frozen treat on Constitution Avenue.

The Lawyer: "The Elvis wants to express his deepest faith in his fellow man. The Elvis wants to echo, in the most human terms possible, the sentiments expressed by the President in last night's address. Death cult participants are not evil. They are lost lambs, and we need to find them and take care of them. In doing so we will preserve ourselves and persevere in these strange, often blessed, times. He calls on you to love and protect with love. Reject fear, reject anger."

We watched The Elvis' tongue turn bluish from the syrup.

"To this end, The Elvis, along with the support of SonyVerse Entertainment and the United States Government, has made a commitment to promote peace. He pledges that upon completion of his current recording he will go on tour, performing only in communities that have contained and eliminated violence associated with the Death Wish phenomenon." The Lawyer stepped down from the podium. He was not going to take questions at this time.

And that was it.

Genius. If we were good little humans, The Elvis was going give us some sugar.

And the video went on. It was fascinating, partly because of the near white suit—so much could happen on a sloppy hot day. It occurred to me that I had never seen an adult finish a sno ball before.

"Hunh," said Martine. He sucked up some brie on melba toast.

"I know what you're thinking," I said. "Party time. Well, forget it."

Martine swung his hand out, put it on mine. It was still yellow bruised from where they'd inserted the tubes. His fingernails looked antique. He said, "I know it's no fun, with me like this." And then he let loose a multi-staged, wet cough that rattled the knick-knacks on the shelves.

"You kidding me? This place is like Disneyworld."

"That's right. Forgot Brenda was in town. You two meet up yet?"

"Oh yes."

Martine shifted up on his elbows. "And?"

"Well, Val had business to take care of and we were alone at the house, and well, nostalgia prevailed. One thing led to another as they say."

Martine grinned. "Get yourself some special pills. Second best aphrodisiac is the fear of death. First best is Elvis."

That joke was not funny. "Don't need 'em," I said. "Not yet any way." Could he hear the hollow in my chuckle? The pills in my pocket took on a heavy aspect.

A family, crappy or not, is a romantic organization. Feeling frisky after The Elvis announcement, Brenda, Val, and I took a midnight, moonlit stroll along the Riverwalk. It was a beautiful, steamy evening, mostly couples and a few vampire kids out there with us taking a break from the evening's festivities to breathe in the vitality of the river and watch the lights flicker on the bridge. We could hear the barges sigh. Brenda was so bold as to loop her arm around mine and rest her hand on my bicep. We pretended I was mighty and leaned together on the rail, looking out at the black, lightless mass that was Algiers.

And Brenda messed it up. "So whatever happened to that Pebbles girl you were seeing?" she asked Val.

I spoke for Val: "She's traveling. It's a sore subject."

Brenda didn't buy it for a second but she shut up anyway. She was a bad wife, but a fine mom.

Val clarified the matter. "Pebble is caught up in the cult

crap. She's in with a guy calls himself Pere Qua."

"One of the Death Cults? Jesus, Val." Then she took a moment. "I'm sorry honey."

I squeezed her hand. I shouldn't have done that.

We went back to the house, drank wine, and then Val went off to wherever he went. I used to not think about it much; he usually went out late and he was always back by morning. Back when things were normal, I just assumed he was at some all night hipster party. And then when he was with Pebbles, I figured I could find him across the street. But now I was worried about his nightly prowls. Was he walking the streets looking for her?

Brenda and I went up to my room and wound up in bed together. She climbed on top, laughing like a moon witch. No way would I last under that situation, so I remembered Brenda from before, half naked, all evil Brenda, the way I'd left her, in her panties on my bed. Wanting me dead. That image calmed me down considerably. I regained control, my fingers sliding along the sweat of her thighs. I rolled her over, slowed it down. She fought me on this decision, but we reached a compromise. It got very good for her. Very good, followed by a pretty good. Then the spoiler: I thought, *this could be the last time I fuck*. I never came so hard in my life. At last, the terror of my imminent demise had found a way to express itself.

We curled around each other like dogs and passed out, and I dreamed that Brenda's solution, my suicide, made perfect sense, and that everyone was completely on board with it. Happy, even.

We slept and dreamed while Bobby Rebar was out there in the night, wrapped in my big black cape, no doubt with sweat rolling down his mania-hardened carapace of a chest. The cape, being the color of night, the color of oblivion, made him invisible inside its drape; all he had to do was step back, stand against a wall or a tree and draw the heavy fabric around himself. People passed so close without seeing him, especially the couples drunkenly chatting on their way back to a poorly chosen hotel. Bobby Rebar, on the lurk! Perhaps inelegantly in stained jeans and heavy work boots, but his beggar's scuttle served him well. If he didn't go too fast or too slow, he looked as if he were floating.

Sometimes they *almost* saw him and wouldn't accept it. Looking straight at him, and him not breathing. Many times he'd taken shortcuts through back gardens of grand homes where a light snapped on in the kitchen or the bedroom, and there'd be some curler-headed figure peering out at the opaque fact of him. In such cases he simply crouched and stared back until the light flicked off.

I'd suspected that Detective Collier's description of Bobby's midnight ambushes were superficial, slanted to conjure up images of crude, frothing madness. And I was right. This prelude during which Bobby stoked uncertainty, house by house, housewife by housewife—this was art.

At one in the morning Bobby was cutting across properties in the Garden District when he spied two vampires sharing a joint on the front porch of an elegant home. He slipped across the street and melted against a shade tree where he could observe his prey head on.

Raggedy little Miriam was almost passed out, so Mick Breglia had settled her into an old wooden rocking chair with a cushion for support, tilting her head just so. The Phantom King prattled on, and Miriam formed a caring shadow. Mick sat sideways on the top step with his back against the rail throwing peace signs at the patrol cars that rolled by.

It was Martine's house, and though popular rumor had it that The Elvis's promise would put an end to wish violence, Mick was unwilling to discard his new vocation as community protector, not when there were still goodies to be claimed. When he showed up for duty at midnight wearing his short white cape like a Century 21 jacket, Martine's big nurse answered the front door and passed a loaf of foccacia and a bottle of table red over the threshold before shutting the house up, locking every lock she could find.

Miriam started to snore, and Mick dropped off as well. Like iguanas, experienced street brats can sleep anywhere it's warm. Bobby figured it was time to strike a little fear into the hearts of men, but when he made it back across the street again, he saw little Esme Fateh climbing the porch. She hadn't spotted him, so Bobby dropped low beside the neighbor's hedge to become an extension of the dark shrub.

Esme hit Mick on the shoulder, and though he threw his arms and legs out to the stars, never was he in danger of falling off that step. The same too with Miriam. Mick yelped, and Miriam rippled from head to foot as if the loa were sneaking out her big toe, but she did not open her eyes.

Esme shook her head.

Mick grinned, did an Elvis: "Hey little momma."

"Shut up fool," the child said. She had trashed her gangsta wear for tights and a short pleated skirt that ruffled up over her bum like a tired carnation. A ribbed T-shirt showed off swelling breast buds that were no match for Miriam's mature, free-swinging sisters. Nevertheless, Mick gave Esme a bright, lazy smile as if she were truly beautiful.

"Let's get outta here," she said, trying to look pleasant under the heavy ghost of jealousy. She picked up Mick's long, skinny arm and tugged, somewhere between urgent and playful.

"I got biz, sweetie." He nodded towards the house.

"Ain't no biz no more. Anyhow, she can cope."

As if she'd heard, Miriam let one rip.

Mick wasn't so sure, but the little girl pulled him up. "I got Daddy's key card," she said. "Means we can get into the school if we wanna." She was referring to her father's department building on the UNO Lakefront campus.

"Woof, we'd need to get somebody to ride us out there."

"Big man."

Mick gathered his cape and considered all the mischief he could get up to at the college that had just informed him he would not be part of their entering class in the Fall. No doubt other deciding factors were the emptiness of the wine bottle and the creeping warmth of his high. He was in no condition to resist anything, much less a force of will like Esme. Soon Mick was being pulled down the porch steps towards the dark, crooked sidewalk. Also towards Bobby the shrub.

The stars were popping and the breeze was sweet and hot. Typically not much of a talker, Esme was going on about something now—The Elvis, the record, the tour. Her peppery voice sounded like it was coming from an old fashioned radio with someone twisting the volume knob back and forth real slow. The air was layered with wide bands of heat, delicate ribbons of chill, and alternating scents of flowers and garbage. It hit Mick hard; he was too high and had gotten up too fast. He laughed and said, "Wait a second."

Little Esme stopped. Her stoned boyfriend panted in the heat. She could wait all night if necessary.

Bobby Rebar was only half as patient as Esme. He felt about to burst.

Mick side-staggered, brushed up against a bloom-heavy bush that surprised him. No way would he make it to UNO, not tonight, not ever. Time for plan B. He grabbed Esme up, bent his long torso over her tiny one, and almost swallowed her face with his. It was a sweaty, sloppy kiss, his tongue shoving past her sharp teeth. She didn't seem to mind. When he pulled off he was dizzy, but Esme was keen as ever.

Mick asked, "How old are you again?"

She said, "Fourteen." An unmistakable lilt to the lie.

Mick laughed. He stumbled back two steps and looked at a distant lamplight like it was the moon. He needed to get back to Miriam before he went too far. Esme was glowing.

And there was one of those noisy, short gusts of warm air, the kind that makes the trees sound like burning paper. Mick's lank hair lifted, and he closed his eyes for a second. He told people he sensed things sometimes, warnings, thrills, brilliance—right in his bones. Said he didn't need a brain. "Back," was the only word he could form.

"What?"

They'd paused in front of Martine's neighbor's mansion and its tiny gated yard. Toys and shadows strewn all over. Shadows that changed. Perhaps they'd stopped here for a reason.

That shadow. Some dark mass close to the hedge, just beyond the edge of what the street light could show them. A changing mass.

Metastasizing. It came, spider slow.

Our Robert was brilliant at being invisible, but not so good at holding his breath. Or breathing in general. Nobody respects an avenger with bronchitis. The first cough was so constrained it sounded like a puppy's bark, providing enough information so that Mick understood what he was peering at. He'd been in this situation before, face to face with a black caped adversary—me, according to legend. Only this time Mick knew better.

Mick said, "You ain't Mr. Victor, are you?"

Bobby was inexperienced with rhetorical questions.

"Nope."

Mick exploded, lunging towards the writhing blot. This was certainly not the way it was supposed to go down. Bobby took off running, cutting across properties and bounding over courtyard walls. He couldn't breathe, but he could run. Just not as fast as a drunk teenager and his sixth grader girlfriend.

Having never met little Esme Fateh before, Bobby was unprepared for her improvisational skills or her capacity for meanness. She was a scrapper. They'd ended up in another yard, and a light flicked on at the top of the house. They'd roused the owner. The light shone down on Bobby, who was flat on his back and for a moment immobile and blessed. Mick staggered, raising his ridiculous cape to cover his face, and Esme was hissing, "*shit-shit-shit.*" The little girl was easily the only one of the three who still had her wits about her.

One thing was for sure. This battle was over, and to the relief of all participants. The passion of violence is fleeting for those who are not regular practitioners. If Bobby could have seen anything other than the cleansing light of discovery, he would have noticed that Mick was sobering up from the adrenalin rush and that Esme was disgusted by the whole encounter. She said, "Run, you dummy!" An instruction for her lover, but Bobby was in one of those psychic places where everything, bad or good or urgent, was about him. He rolled out of the light and was up, perhaps not in a flash but certainly with an athletic grace he'd been training for all his street life. The big kid and the little girl were gone, but he could hear their shoes pounding away.

Bobby jolted when he heard the whine and bark of a cruiser siren. He pursued a trajectory that had him vaulting over garden walls, looking out for the homeowners, their guns, and their koi ponds. He'd learned the hard way that a garden was incomplete without a rock lined, ankle twisting water feature that in darkness presented itself as nothing more than a moonlit glimmer on the lawn.

Eventually running away became running home. Home was a variety of hidey-holes, but what he wished he could do was sneak back into Val's shop where it was cool. He angled towards lights and sounds that were familiar. His pace slowed, and the fear that had propelled him drained away. No one was looking for him. No one ever looked for crazy Bobby Rebar.

Back in the Quarter, he shied away from the bright, noisy bars. The night was young for everyone but him. Bobby strolled up Royal, lit golden by the display windows of closed antique shops teasing lovers with jewelry and paintings and dramatic furniture made precious by time and wine. He was near our shop, but if he came back to us he'd have to return the big black cape, something he wasn't ready to do.

He sulked towards Chartres, passing tourists who giggled at his shabby get up, a poor imitation of the elaborate costumes worn by the vampire and ghost guides who conducted steamy walking tours along these same streets. One such group was moving away from the solid, quiet wall that surrounded the Old Ursuline Convent, which in its own way was like a koi pond at night—a dark surprise in a carefree district. Even if you didn't know its history and its legends, just walking by the place was unnerving. Bobby watched a pod of tourists wobble after a greasy pirate with an absurd feathered hat. But they left someone behind.

Mick Breglia leaned against the stone wall, head back, heaving, staring up at the sky. His Adam's apple worked the length of his sweaty neck, catching starlight. When he saw Bobby crossing towards him he held up his hands and made a face. "I give up man. What the fuck, you know?"

Bobby shrugged. He looked for the little girl. She was the mean one.

"Esme went home. She's just a kid," Mick said, beginning to relax. "You are really fucked up, aren't you?" Next to him the plaque in the wall said: *OLD URSULINE CONVENT HOME OF THE URSULINE NUNS WHO CAME FROM FRANCE "TO RELIEVE THE POOR, SICK AND PROVIDE EDUCATION FOR YOUNG GIRLS"*. Further down the wall there was a large gate for admitting vehicles. It was always closed, and it rattled in the slightest of breezes. Sometimes it just rattled from the vibration of a passing car. Everyone knew that, but it didn't stop Bobby from twitching when it happened again.

Mick laughed. "You wanna see something really cool? Come over here." Mick led Bobby to the guard's door adjacent to the vehicle gate. It was half barred and one of the few places where one could peek inside without paying a fee. "There's vampires in the attic, you know. All the windows and doors on the third floor are fastened shut by 8000 screws blessed by the Pope."

Bobby peered in as instructed. It wasn't a good angle, but he could make out the brick paths and the squared short hedges. Though large and rambling, the convent complex was a plain affair, conservative.

Mick said, "No. That way, by the tree. Do you see her?"

In one of the few corners of the garden where security light did not reflect off the convent façade, Bobby saw a woman in a long white garment, playing the shadow game. At first he thought she was a misplaced statue, but then he saw her move. Her arm raised and the drape of her sleeve created a wing shape as she brought her hand to her face. A soft hood shadowed her eyes, but her red-lipped pout glowed.

"Sister," Bobby breathed. Mick spasmed in excitement giggles. The ghost nun was breathtaking, no doubt about it. She was beatific, in fact, especially as she drank a can of Diet Coke and smoked a roach that could be smelled all the way out into the street.

5.

It was too much to hope for an immediate cessation of madness just because The Elvis had decreed it. There were still bursts— violence, panic, so forth. I was up too early, watching the way the blush of dawn now lingered with the orange clouds. I made coffee.

Brenda was still in my bed. I had no idea whether Val had made it home last night or how he'd react if he figured out that I'd "stayed over." But by six am, those worries were vapors. Detective Danny Collier had dropped by for a surprise visit. When he knocked I was at the door in an instant. I think he was disappointed to find me up.

"Coming to check on you like you asked," he said, stretching his mouth into a wary grin to let me know he was doing no such thing.

I invited the young man in for coffee and immediately remembered the other contradictions that he embodied, besides his ill-fitting accent. He was quite small, but his suit jacket strained across the shoulders, and while his face was soft and calm, his eyes were blinky, darty, over excited. He sat at our kitchen table, his hands carefully embracing a warm mug as if it might run off the table if he weren't diligent about it. I guess that was a cop thing. The mug featured a classic red Community Coffee logo against a bone glaze background, but I'd run out of the good stuff, so I made this morning's pot out of generic grocery grind. I would come to regret that bit of lazy house-keeping.

I sat across from Collier and he got right to it: "There was some trouble last night, up in Mr. Bernier's neighborhood. A skirmish in the front yard of a city judge."

"Is Martine all right?"

"He's dandy. The bother didn't get that far. Three trouble makers, all of them gone into the night. But the judge feels like he got a good look at one of them from his bedroom window. It was Terence Flick."

Apparently I was supposed to make something of that. He waited on my reaction as he sipped at his mug. I asked, "So you think this Mr. Flick was headed for Martine's?"

"No." Collier looked at me funny. "Terence Flick? You don't know that name?"

I did not.

"Homeless fellow, unrepentant self medicator? Been in front of the Judge many a time. I was pretty sure you knew the man, seeing as he worked for your son. And I heard he was a friend of yours in particular."

I realized he was referring to Bobby Rebar. Was Bobby's real name Terence Flick? I'd never known that, and to think I'd gotten into the habit of calling him Robert to give him his dignity. "I see," I said, "I'm sorry for the confusion. We know him as Bobby. He got in a fight? Was he hurt?"

"Given the speed with which he vacated the scene, I'd say not physically. But it seems clear he's not an altogether well man. Judge said he was got up in a big, black cape. Looks like he's our night stalker, our Dracula man. But then you knew that, didn't you?"

I played with my coffee spoon like a guilty man. No reason

to put up a fight. "I had an inkling, yes. When you mentioned it the other day on the phone."

"You might have let me know."

"You'd have put him away."

"Yes. Of course we would have. We would have picked him up on the outstanding warrant—or is the fact he smashed up your son's shrimper just not an issue? And then we would have sent him for a psychiatric evaluation."

I must have made a distressed sound, because Collier practically jumped down my throat: "What the hell? Why is it everyone thinks going to the mental ward is like a being put in a kill shelter? Granted, maybe he shouldn't be in jail, but he sure as hell should be under professional care, don't you think? Or," and here he kind of leveled himself at me, lining me up for the shot: "do you really think he's better off living in your shop with the rats and the mannequins?"

So that was it. Collier knew a lot more than either of us were inclined to admit out loud. Continuing in this vein he said, "Been a lot of stuff we let slide, on account of there being so much serious shit to tend to, Mr. Swaim. But it looks like the cape crap just got amplified. Which is why I'm talking to you at all."

I nodded. "Perhaps you should tell me what happened."

Collier leaned back and tried to look relaxed, all the time watching me with those over active peepers of his. "Judge hears racket in his yard, goes to the window with a flashlight in one hand and a gun in the other, and the first thing he thinks is that carnival Indians are fighting on his lawn. Then his eyes work it out that two of the fellas are in capes, and the little guy seems got up like a leprechaun. So one cape guy is wrassling the other cape guy, and they're getting all tangled up when the leprechaun gets in it. Judge beams the flashlight down just as your Mr. Flick rolls over on his back. Judge said he sort of stared up into the light like a fish. That's when the other two ran off like animals, and a second later Flick was up running after them. Cape all whippy and everything. Judge said it was a dramatic escape with that big black cape and all."

"You said the other one was also wearing a cape."

"Yeah, a Mutt and Jeff team. The big one was wearing one of your white capes."

Mick and Esme. I felt sick. "Mick Breglia," I said. "That's the tall one. I made short white capes for the Wish Phantoms."

"No kidding," Collier drawled. "We're a little more confused by the little one. Sure you don't know who the little dude is?"

I shook my head no, looked at my own coffee. Was that my tell?

"Well you think about it. I bet you come up with something. You still have my card, I know that. And if your friend Flicka makes his way back here, you know what to do, right?" He took a big gulp of coffee, like he was fixing to bolt. As he set the cup down he made a face. Too strong? "Just take it seriously. Take it *all* seriously, okay? This could be a one time problem or it could be the start of a whole new thing. No way to know."

"I understand, sir."

Satisfied for the moment, Collier took another gulp and put his hand on the arm of the chair. But he didn't get up. He had one more quip to deliver, like he'd practiced it and everything: "Cape on cape violence, man. It's a real shame."

He thought that was funny. I didn't. Poor Bobby. Poor Esme. And no room to say Mick should have known better. "I think I know what you mean, Detective. White people in costume? Sometimes we can't contain ourselves. More coffee?"

"No, I'm good, I'm good. Where is it you're from, Mr.

Swaim?"

"Virginia," I cleared my throat. "Northern Virginia, near DC."

"Ah. So not deep south and not even dirty south. More like the shallow south. You all got no need to rise again. All you have to do is hike up on your elbows a little to get a good look around."

Wow, he'd worked up a whole routine, hadn't he? Luckily, he laughed at his own joke so I wouldn't have to. Down the hall, the creak of my bed. Brenda was up. Then the iron squeak of the shower. Collier gave me a hopeful look.

"Val's mother," I said. "From up north as well. She's visiting for an undetermined amount of time, things being the way they are."

The Detective nodded, his grin fading into something just a wee bit more sympathetic. "That's real nice, Mr. Swaim. You all enjoy your family time." He'd made all the leaving noises that were customary, and he'd even leaned forward on his seat a couple of times as if he were about to scoot, but so far Detective Collier wasn't making much progress. He seemed to slip down into a thought as he stared into his coffee mug. Like he was on the verge of a detecting breakthrough.

In an odd tone he said, "You brew a good cup, Mr. Swaim."

"Thank you." It wasn't really rich enough for my preference. I swirled my cup to cool it off. I hadn't made much of a dent.

Collier leaned back, gave me a look. "Go on."

"Is there a problem?"

"Drink your coffee."

"I'm sorry?"

"Drink the damn coffee."

I did as I was told, gulping down nearly half the cup. The

man had a gun after all. Then I put my cup down and stared.

"See."

It was still full.

"Oh my lord."

Collier agreed. "That is seriously screwy."

The world only needs one bottomless cup of coffee, when you come to think of it. And at the moment we had two.

Collier turned thoughtful. He got up and took his mug over to the sink. He emptied it, and much to my relief all that came out was a mug's worth of joe—no endless waterfall of coffee spending the resources of a messed up cosmos. But when he tipped it back up, it filled again. Perfect temperature.

"What if I want to milky it up?" he asked.

I didn't know, but I took a guess. "Get another cup from the cupboard? Start it with the milk and then pour your other in?"

"That might could work," said Collier. He poured out the mug again, but this time kept it tipped over, his finger wrapped around the handle like a trigger. "Maybe I should take this with me."

"Yes," I said. "Please."

His tone was reverent. "This is a new one."

"I believe so."

He meant it was a new wish. Which was significant seeing as one of the strongest rumors to come out of the carnage of Death cult activity was that the attack campaign had stopped the wishing. It's hard to prove a negative, so folks filled in the gaps with sheer belief. But now we could say that was wrong. Someone with a simple idea had slipped though the cracks. In my mind it was a little old lady who died tired of getting up to grab the pot all the time.

Collier left quietly, like he was sneaking out early from church. We were both bemused by this latest fortune. As soon as he left, Brenda came shuffling in, wrapped in a flannel robe with her hair all wet. "Morning, babe," she said, and she moved instinctively towards the counter and the coffee pot.

I stopped her. Pushed my cup across the table. "Already poured you one. *Babe.*"

We anticipated that the coffee wish, as basic as it was, would have a devastating effect on agribusiness in Central and South America, but we didn't realize that it would give a boost to manufacturing industries elsewhere. Because the way to permanently stop your cup from refilling with coffee once you'd filled it was to destroy it. This meant that paper and plastic disposables were in high demand and that there was a run on cheap crockery, especially the sort of novelty mugs sold in souvenir shops and truck stops, prompting a boom in I ❤ slogan pottery production. Val laid in a supply of mugs he had custom printed to read *Die For Milk*. We sold the whole crate in two days. At one point there were at least six full cups of non-premium coffee distributed throughout our kitchen until we learned how to manage the bounty. For example, I figured out that if I poured my coffee into a bowl, I could live a normal life again. For whatever reason bowls did not refill, nor did any receptacle not expressly designed for drinking.

The coffee shop where Pebbles had worked shut down, but within the week it re-opened as a wine bar called It Could Happen. We were getting very good at adapting. Every time I walked past I looked in hoping to see her cleaning off a table or pocketing a tip. But no, and they had a new red head already. She was a bony little thing but appeared to have the same eye straining fashion sense. The day that I saw she was wearing the yellow Valvolene T-shirt that I'd seen Pebbles in at one of her performances, I could resist no longer.

I entered the tiny dark paneled café, still redolent of Arabica beans even though there was a pot of something oniony and spicy steaming away on a cook top behind the counter—the "bottomless gumbo" advertised in the window, no doubt. I was going to have some of that, along with a sturdy red. It was early in the day, and there were only two other customers, both pulling on fishbowls of pink wine (the Rose´ special) as they hunched over their laptops. Wifi and alcohol, a classic combo.

The small flat screen television mounted behind the bar played soundlessly, tuned to a daytime drama where nearly half the male actors were attired in some version of Elvis tribute wear as they performed what appeared to be conventional living room, bedroom, and hospital based arguments with the women in their fake lives. Side burns, beaded jump suits, leather. One of them stomped moodily around in a matador's cape, but not one of mine, thank goodness.

The red headed server came to me, and I was flabbergasted. Miriam. Everyone had forgotten about Miriam, and here she was in Pebbles' hair and Pebbles' clothing. What could she have been thinking? I could see now the red hair was a cheap costume wig, with the strands swinging stiff and getting caught up where real hair wouldn't. But the shirt and the pink denim mini skirt were authentic, skimpy garments that hung loose on Miriam's stick figure body where they barely contained Pebbles' beans and rice fed curves. The only thing Miriam had going for her was a pair of long legs tapering down to whispery ankles. She was easily five inches taller than Pebbles.

I said, "My dear," as she attempted to hand me the wine list and slink away without a word. I don't know that she was trying to slip away from me or whether she was just very bad at service work. I gently took her wrist, and that stopped her. She wasn't upset by my imposition. She stood still, as if it were my right to detain her. Her body had no will, no resistance instinct. "Miriam, do you remember me?"

She blinked at the sound of her name. "Uh huh?"

"Do you?"

"I said already." The door behind the bar opened and an older man with movie star skin and geometrical facial hair came out with a tray of plastic wrapped fruit plates. He made no eye contact with Miriam, but she sort of snapped to, regardless.

"You better order," she said.

"Sure. The Rose´ special and gumbo. Okay?"

The man returned to the back. Miriam frowned. "Gumbo's sorta burnt. Get the cheese," she said quietly.

"Fine. I'll have the cheese plate."

"Cool." She decorated her pad with scribbles and was off.

The soap opera on the television had given way to a newsbreak. There was new video of The Elvis, this time of him rehearsing. He was looking slightly sweaty and harried, but that was appropriate. The man was at work, after all. He was dressed in a loose velour tracksuit with a towel around his neck. The segment lasted all of five seconds because when he caught sight of the videographer he frowned and moved out of the frame. When they cut back, the newscaster looked triumphant; he was utterly unperturbed by what was obviously a document of violation.

Miriam returned with my wine, a bowl of gumbo, and an enormous heel of tough bread. Oh well. She put the stuff in front of me then cocked her hip to one side. She said, "Took you long enough."

I'd never had a waiter or waitress say those words to me before, but then Miriam was no common server. For a moment I considered that she had the basic relationship mechanics wrong, until it dawned on me that there was something much more personal in her criticism. "You have been waiting for me?" I asked.

She spread her bird like arms. "Duh."

She meant I was supposed to have spotted her before now. "I never saw you here before."

"You stare at me everyday," she argued.

"Do I?" Did I? How was that possible? This was an important conversation apparently, and it was already derailed. My panic was rising and I had no idea why. I took a long swallow of my wine, after which I was very firm with Miriam: "Why are you wearing Pebbles' clothing? Those are hers aren't they?"

Miriam smirked, like I was the dimwit in this exchange. "Mr. Bobby said it was the way to get your attention. I was s'posed to wear this clown shit till you noticed. I'm s'posed to tell you: him and Mickie are okay."

The gentleman who'd brought out the fruit plates re-emerged from the back, this time just to scowl at Miriam. There were no new customers to tend to, and everyone's glass was still at least half full. Whereas she was shy and unfocused before, now Mata Hari felt a bit more like herself, and she gave him the Big Eye right back.

"Bernard," she said to me. He moved back into the kitchen. "He's a German who speaks Turkish, or is it a Turk who speaks German? Anyway I call him a *tjerk*. Get it?"

"Your biases are too rarified for my tastes."

"Whatever. He gets pissy because there isn't anything to do around here."

I didn't care about that. And I didn't really care if Mick and Bobby were "okay," not after I'd been baited with this Pebbles lookalike. In fact I was irritated. "What about Esme," I asked, perhaps too sharply.

Miriam was ready enough. "Baby bitch run off home. Things got too hot, you know? 'Sides, the cops are looking for a boy, right?"

"Well that is a small relief, I suppose." I tasted the gumbo that she had warned me against but brought anyway. She was right, it was bitter. "So this elaborate lure. What is it that Bobby wants from me?"

Miriam was scratching at her arm, distracted, her eyes gone blurry. Making red lines in her colorless flesh. Not a good look for a waitress. Pebbles was pale, sure, but there was always a blush of health creeping around her shoulders and cheeks. Nothing creeping around Miriam except ashes. "I dunno," said Miriam. "I was just supposed to show you."

With Bobby giving the orders I should not have expected more.

One of her customers finished and approached the counter. She watched him as if he might do something potentially interesting. He stood there a moment, tapping his wallet against the glass, and suddenly she hollered out: "Bernard!"

Miriam's boss came out of the back and rang up the fellow's bill, obviously annoyed by the necessity of doing this. The customer paid with cash and accepted his change. Before leaving, he approached Miriam and offered her two dollars that she snatched from his fingertips like the money had been hers in the first place. The customer seemed frightened and fascinated, his eyes dropping to her pointy breasts jiggling loose under Pebbles' T-shirt. He smiled at Miriam, but she did not thank him.

I fear she had made a friend for life.

"You like the job," I asked.

"Shit yeah."

"You make it look easy." I collected her non-cash grubbing hand in mine. Her fingers felt fragile, like cheap toys. "Let's go through this again. It seems like there are bits I didn't catch, sweetheart. So Mr. Bobby and Mick are doing well. That's smashing news. But you say Bobby asked you to dress up in Peb-bles' clothes to get my attention?"

Miriam nodded. "Right, right. On account of the cops. He says they're watching your connections, so to speak. We gotta be subtle." Miriam's other customer completed his quiet feast and crept towards the register. He gave her one nervous side-ways glance and she screeched for Bernard again, who scuttled out and dutifully processed the check. This was a card based transaction, and it bothered Miriam that she couldn't see or feel the tip. "Hate that shit."

I was still wrapping my mind around Bobby's exquisite paranoia. Did he really think I, or any of his associates, were being surveilled? Lordy. I stifled a chuckle. Danny Collier had ordered me to take it all very seriously. "Is there a particular message you are supposed to deliver, darling? I mean other than the fact that Mick and Bobby are a-okay."

Miriam looked at me like I was a complete dope. She tugged at the T-shirt with both hands in pinch grips below the collar line, snapping it across her chest. Apparently, I'd missed the *ob-vi-ous*. "Well there's her, I guess."

She meant Pebbles.

6.

Are all cloisters rumored to be haunted? What ridiculousness. The Old Ursuline Convent, constructed in the mid eighteenth century, was the only remaining building from the original French settlement, and the tough sisters within had provided expert medical care and were renowned for their pharmacological expertise. They also founded a girl's school and orphanage, and specialized in training guaranteed virgins sent over from France to become suitable wives for local men. Eventually they moved their act uptown, and the convent was converted to an archive and museum for the Archdiocese, possibly because the sprawling structure had proven impervious against fires, hurricanes, politics, and legends.

So yes, the place had been full of nuns for nearly a century, and those nuns were actively involved in providing "marital training," a concept that provokes wistfulness or anxiety depending on your way of thinking. But did that mean the grounds were thick with rosary belted specters tending the herb garden during the full moon? I doubted it, but still, as I waited in the shrubs for my Pebbles in the dark morning hours, watching tendrils of mist accumulate into wraiths, I was in an uneasy frame of mind.

Miriam had reported the arrangements to me, so already the details were in doubt. I was to crawl over the convent wall to meet Pebbles at three a.m. Getting over the wall was madness, hardly the lusty maneuver depicted in films, but I think I learned something interesting about sneaks; fear of discovery gives way very quickly to practical matters, which is probably why cat burglars and home invaders can do what they do at all. I'd made quite a bit of sweary racket once I started scraping my belly across the cement and smashing up my knees. But at some point my inner bully beat up my inner fat kid, and I hauled my ass over.

I had not told Val because frankly, this was an insane adventure coordinated by Bobby Rebar. Somehow he and Mick Breglia had formed an alliance, the purpose of which was not altogether clear. I blamed myself and the irresistible fancy inspired by the capes. That psychotic Bobby was the ideas man was awfully telling.

So I'd been through a lot, is my point. It was late, I had tested myself physically, and my heart was thumping, both from supernaturally tinged paranoia and the unlikely possibility of seeing Pebbles again. I had hope, but I fully expected to be there for the rest of the night, only to be discovered snoozing in the bushes when security did their rounds at dawn.

And then she came. Just as Miriam promised, all done up in a pale robe like something out of a religious painting. She floated across the grass tentatively, but when I stepped out to catch her attention she ran the rest of the way, into my arms.

I can't be blamed for kissing her the way I did. Propriety, decorum, those were luxuries I'd left at home. Pebbles kissed me back deeply, if only for a short time. She smelled like roses and furniture polish. She broke the kiss, a look of surprise lighting up her eyes, but I wasn't about to let her go from my arms. She was okay with that.

We spoke in whispers. "What the hell. Is this a Snuggie?" I

said. I rubbed the sleeve fabric between my fingertips and gave her an all over friendly pat down of sorts. Nothing dirty, just a quick grope. I could tell she was mostly naked under her garment.

"A staffer gave it to me. I play Mother Cabrini on the tour, and one of the docents lets me sleep upstairs. I think she likes the whole sanctuary angle. Then at night I sneak out and flit around the grounds. Me and the ghost tour fellas have a routine worked up and everything."

I tucked a strand of red hair back behind her ear, careful not to disturb her hood. "So now you are an actress."

She flashed a bright smile. We both knew she was hiding from Pere Qua, but for the moment this flirtation was all that mattered. Rather than risk another kiss from me, she stepped in and laid her head on my chest. I kept my hands as still as I could, flat against her back. I'd done enough wandering. I had a feeling that in the future we would pretend this intimacy never happened.

I still loved her. "You have to tell me where Pere Qua is so I can let the police know."

She pushed back, shook her head. "No Victor. I can't. He's too dangerous and he doesn't care about dying. You know what he's trying to do, right?"

"He's trying to kill wishers."

"Right," she tapped my chest. She'd removed her nail polish. She was serious about this gig. "Because after Mirella he learned he can't make people wish his way. So he decided he needs to stop the wishing altogether. Stop the changes from even happening. You have to be careful, Vic. Mr. Bernier needs to be careful."

I nodded. "Because Boudreau's done with the shakedown phase."

"Exactly. No more extortion and terrorism. He doesn't want anything more from you than your death, plain and simple."

I released the girl. "Which reminds me. Val's mother is in town."

"That's not funny."

No it wasn't. Something shifted in the morning air, and a heavy scent of blossoms floated by. Pebbles shivered. She said, "He's not gonna hurt me, you know. But he'll damn sure use me to get to you. So don't worry about me here. I'm good. Real good." She raised a white draped arm to show me. "In fact, this feels way too natural."

"Sister Pebbles? How very rock and roll."

She smiled. "Don't tell Val, okay?"

"That's a tough request, but I understand. He'd tear these walls down."

Pebbles' smile disappeared. "No, he wouldn't."

Pebbles shooed me away at the first hint of dawn. I'd promised her I would return the next night, but she begged me not to. The point of her seclusion was to keep me safer. That's why we hadn't found much in the way of personal items at her apartment. When she realized what sort of monster her guru was, she sent as many things back home as she could while maintaining the illusion that she was still her devotional self. Pere Qua already knew about me and Val, so there was no need to pretend we weren't in her life, but she didn't want him to know anymore about her loved ones in Arkansas than was absolutely necessary.

"He doesn't even know my real name," she said.

But I did. Sweet Annabeth. Despite her stern caution, I would return. And I would bring her a present, perhaps just a token. If only to reassure her that we did have a future.

The Elvis took a quick, public break from recording to visit Graceland, or rather to visit his mother's grave which had been moved to the property by his father, Vernon. The Elvis may not have been fully prepared though, and while he seemed perfectly sanguine at the prospect, observers reported that his left hand began to tremble as he stood there in the Meditation Garden reading his own name in bronze on the enormous granite slab— one of four fanned out in front of a fountain: his mother, himself, his father, his grandmother. A separate, smaller marker for his twin, Jesse Garon, who was stillborn. The Elvis seemed to speak quiet words to his deceased family members, but over his own grave he was silent and wide-eyed.

Back in the airport, The Elvis moved through the terminals flanked by nearly a dozen skilled protectors, but that failed to stop an attempted assault by a real estate broker on his way home to Athens, Ohio from a conference in Tuscon. The broker had no idea why he snapped, but the slightly paunchy fifty-eight year old just couldn't control himself when he saw the security phalanx cutting through the crowd of weary, frustrated travelers. He tried to launch his body into the space between two of the bodyguards, and was down, pinned, and unconscious inside of a minute. The other guards closed ranks around The Elvis, and they swear to God he was there at that moment.

But in the next he was gone.

The Elvis went missing for nearly twenty hours. It was a global nightmare, and the once joked about concept of an "Elvis Sighting" now took on a grimmer aspect. But he eventually reappeared, wandering into a gift shop in Gatlinburg, Tennessee where he bought a pair of aviator sunglasses and some taffy. By all accounts The Elvis looked like a wreck, as if he hadn't slept all night or worse. The few photographs of his interception by SonyVerse agents showed him to be sullen and sloppy. He wouldn't say where he'd been, but he did say he was eager to "get back to work."

His face bore the shadow of a coyote. It made me think of things that hurt me as a child but were meaningless now. Uncles who made promises. Girls who laughed when I fell off my bike. Dumb stuff you grow out of and forget.

I realized that I was a person who made promises I couldn't keep, so I returned to Martine's to avoid Val, and being away from Brenda's influence was an added bonus. Martine was improving every day, or at least he was giving one hell of a recovery performance. The morning after my rendezvous with Pebbles, I slept in late in his Canadian guest room. When I awoke I found Martine in the drawing room crabbing at a delivery boy with an armload of calla lilies. Lounging in a plush chair like a lesser Barrymore, Martine was back into his own clothes at last: pale silk blend slacks, soft leather loafers, and a billowy pirate style shirt, open enough so you could see his mottled, still bruised torso. His chest hair was growing back, shock white. He had one leg propped on a footstool and a glamorous antique walking stick across his lap. I figured it was for thwacking the hired help because he didn't look like intended on going anywhere soon.

He looked wonderful, even bitching at a florist.

"Now who needs new clothes," I said by way of announcing my presence.

Martine grinned huge, waved me to his side. "Good Morning!" The florist was relieved, leaving the disputed arrangement on a dark wood side table. Martine grabbed up a bit of his own pant leg and gave it a tug. "I'm swimming in these, isn't it marvelous?"

"Myocardial infarction diet. Works wonders, I hear." I gave

him a peck on the top of his curly old head. He smelled expensive, and seeing him healthy and laughing made me want to sing. I looked around. There were linen draped tables, a crate of wine waiting to be unpacked, and of course, fresh flowers. Martine was crazy, feeling good. "Stunning," I pronounced. "But you'd better not be planning a party anytime soon."

"Victor, I don't plan parties. Parties come to my door, unbidden. I just like to be prepared. Think I should Elvis it up?"

"Please don't. Besides, the King's looking a little rough, if you ask me. Like this messiah business is weighing on him."

"I saw the news." At which point he took the opportunity to give me the once over. "You're looking a little rough yourself."

Wheels rumbled down a nearby hallway, and I caught a quick glimpse of a young pony-tailed woman pushing a handcart loaded with more crates. Martine frowned. "She better not be scuffing my floors." He leaned out of his chair a bit to watch as she rolled by.

"She's not. Settle down."

His eyebrows up. "I'm having *fun*."

"And leaving the door open to all kinds of strangers, I see."

"I'm bored of caution."

"Like you've ever given caution a whirl. Look, don't ask me questions, but we're not out of the woods yet."

Martine stuck out his tongue at me, then grinned like I was the biggest idiot he ever met. "You know what I decided, laying there in that hospital? That I ain't never gonna die. Solves the problem right there."

"I guess that's a plan. But have you considered, especially given your recent experiences, that you don't need to die to be seriously inconvenienced?"

There was a slight click in his throat. He wasn't one-hundred percent yet. "Your coyness isn't intriguing as it should be,

Victor. I'm a gay man who lived through the last thirty years rather robustly. If you have something to tell me, then do so."

"It's just that Pere Qua is out there, and he's close. And he still has intentions." I moved next to him and squatted so I could speak low: "I saw Pebbles last night. She's in hiding. From him."

Martine nodded. "Well that is sort of exciting. You don't lead a glamorous life, but you do what you can, don't you?"

He didn't know the half of it.

He asked, "You gonna see her again?"

"I'm going to try. Val doesn't know."

Martine smirked as if he'd expected as much. "It's always been you and her, hasn't it?"

"Meaning?"

"Your affair of the heart."

I felt defensive. "She asked me not to tell."

Martine closed his eyes as if he were suddenly tired. He took my arm and leaned sideways in his chair. With only inches between us, his breath transmitted an elegant, herbal aroma. I imagined he had a boy come in to polish each and every one of his teeth with a cloth, like pieces of silver. He said, "Miss Pebbles is a child. You should not leave it to her. I know you ache to have something between you two that is wholly your own, but now is the time for you to be a father not a lover."

I said, "Val's doing fine."

"That's not what I mean. You didn't ask for it, but you have a responsibility to the girl. She's in your life because she put herself there. You and Val were never competing for her, not the way you think. She attached herself to you all because she wanted to be part of a family. And despite the fact that you play Daddy on odd days and he plays Daddy on evens, that's what you and Val are, a half assed family. You even have Brenda back. How the hell did you swing that, Victor? You all don't even seem to like each other most of the time."

The delivery girl rolled back by, cart empty, followed close-ly by the lady who tidies Martine's house. He took a breather as they passed out of earshot, but he wasn't done with his speech. "That's what we're all looking for, aren't we? Us fools pouring into the Quarter and spilling over the edges like ex-pats inside our own country? Well, *your* country, but you get my drift. We want easiness, openness. Plain old street love. When you first came all those years ago, before the storm, remember what you found? Remember what you came back for?"

He stopped short of waving a handful of dirt and turnips in my face, but only barely. "That common embrace, like when you were a child. You didn't have to be special or necessary or even particularly good. You just had to be there to get love. Pebbles is a child like that. She just wants to hang around and be a part of Krewe de Swaim. Or a part of something really strong."

I did not like where this was going, and I tried to pull away, but Martine's fingers were clamped down. I'd have to hear him out, all the way.

"And for that she'll let you kiss her. She'll let Val do what ever he wants. That's how a girl gets on in the world, Victor. Hell, that's how some of us boys get on, too." He chuckled, but there wasn't anything funny in what he was saying as far as I could tell.

"You're saying we took advantage of her?" My feathers were ruffled.

Martine sighed. "I'm saying your imagination is too nar-row. But that's the bachelor's curse. And when neither you nor Val could let her settle into a safe place in your lives—didn't matter where—she ran towards a stronger embrace."

"We drove her to Pere Qua?"

"You didn't take care of her. You came on to her when she needed someone to help her make sense of things, and Val took her for granted. That bastard Boudreau? All he had to do was wait."

I was too angry to say much of anything. Pebbles and I were friends, more than friends. I loved her. I saw all of her shows, didn't that count? I was the one she reached out to. We were together when Gerald Pollin changed our lives, and she gave me a watermelon. I'd do anything for her. So what if there was a horny edge to it all? She wasn't my daughter.

And I made that point clear: "She's not my daughter."

Martine leaned back and breathed in, fully inflating his chest. Then he let that go, slowly. He was thinking. His pronouncement: "Technicality."

7.

I left Martine's around noon, already late for opening the shop, but my brain was rolling. What Martine was getting at was the need for me to end it all. Not my life, as Brenda had suggested, but my life as a child, my life in suspended romance. He had watched me progress and improve during my time in New Orleans, but that was mostly a physical transformation. Emotionally, I was still arrested. Hence my unshakeable attraction to Pebbles. Well, I hardly needed him to tell me—I could go to any woman on the street to get that specific analysis. But the other part of it of course was the danger. My mid life crisis was not purely my own. The girl was in trouble. She couldn't hide in that convent forever. Regardless of whether I felt more like a lover or a father, I'd have to make her safe again, and that meant flushing out Pere Qua to remove him from our lives.

I put in a couple of halfhearted, distracted hours at Val's Vintage, trying to formulate a sane plan. It occurred to me that this was how Bobby had spent his hours as well, before he settled on his new career as The Vague Avenger. He too sat in the dark surrounded by silent human shapes of clothes, listening to the skitter of unseen claws. Maybe the madman was right.

I closed the shop and rifled through the stock. I selected a preposterous yellow cape with purple and green lamé fleur de lis appliqués dripping down like combat insignia from the carnival wars. I fastened it around my neck and emerged into the hot glare of the afternoon sun, marching several blocks to the Café Du Monde. The Café had made few changes in light of the coffee wish, with the only external sign that operations had been affected being that the cup was delivered upside down and dry over the saucer. Everything else, including the cheap prices, remained the same, and the open-air patio was as popular as ever.

Is there any condition more unfairly maligned than normal life? At the metal tables customers were having the same heated conversations they always did, about money, about the babysitter, about the correct way to drive a stick shift. And then the servers brought out cups, and already diner reactions appeared thoroughly acculturated: that careful retrieval, the tipping up, and waiting. It was all a habit now, like something that had always been. Amazement was overrated. Adventure was not even possible.

I collected the edges of my cape, holding one side out and the other to my shoulder as I sashayed an unnecessarily snake-like route through the tables. Always prepared, a few patrons snapped cell phone pictures, and by the time I claimed a table at the other end of the café, the buzz of discussion ratcheted up. I had been noticed and recorded. I ordered coffee and two plates of beignets, which arrived quickly from an uncharmed waiter. I turned my cup and watched it fill with a perfect café au lait. Steam rose from the sugared buns. As I dropped the first delectable puff into my mouth and jammed it in whole, I heard a giggle or two. Good.

I knew people on the plan who hadn't eaten a single donut in years. The cost was too high. This one released some kind of dope through my system. My blood was singing. When the waiter came by I said to him, "I'm not going to live in fear any more. I'm tired of hiding from the crazies."

The waiter's white paper hat bobbed. Yes, he approved of that sentiment.

Of course I hadn't been hiding, not really. Anyone could have found me at Martine's or at the shop. I ate the next beignet like a workman. The only hiding I had been doing was from Brenda, and look how that turned out.

Alone and without conversation to slow my consumption, I quickly had my fill, both of beignets and attention. I left a wad of cash on the table and made quite a bit of fuss as I skidded the iron chair across the concrete. I stood and inspected myself for sugar and crumbs, shaking out my cape. Then finally, I did something I'd never done as a sober adult. I belched in public. Very loudly, with a smile on my face, in fact. I made my exit to the music of moans and murmured complaints, as well as a smattering of applause.

I took the long way back, circling the shops near the casino, grabbing a pint at the Crescent Brewery, and skipping down Bourbon. The sweat poured into my eyes, but I larked on like a street performer, deliberately cutting through groups of tourists and grinning like a lunatic. Like Bobby, come to think of it. At one point I found myself caught up in an impromptu second line, but I managed to dance my way out of it, nearly backing into one of those silver statue men who are supposed to stay quieter than the Queen's Guard, but this bloke whispered at me, "Fuck off."

A couple more beers later I was back on Esplanade feeling rather ragged. Being a one man parade was exhausting, but I still had work to do. I made sure that I was seen entering Pebbles' building and then stomped on up to her apartment. I entered using the key she gave me, and proceeded to lift all the shades and turn on all the lights. I walked from room to room, hoping that I was noteworthy from the street. The sun began to set, and I knew there was no lovelier light than the rosy glow emanating from Pebbles' rooms, especially as the scent of stewed suppers permeated the humid evening air.

I should not have been surprised, but Brenda appeared at my window across the street. I saluted her. She crossed her arms, but she was smiling. *Okay, now what?* She had no idea of the romantic history that had transpired between these portals. I wasn't even sure she knew that I was in Pebbles' apartment.

It was the busiest time of day traffic wise with cars sailing back and forth, radios pumping. And there were neighbors on the sidewalks making their way home, many carrying sacks of take-out or groceries. Val appeared next to his mother, and he opened the window. Brenda stepped back a little. It was none of her business, but she would be damned if she missed a single word.

"Dad. What's up?" He was working hard not to lose his cool in front of, or rather over, the neighborhood. "Why'd you leave the shop so early?"

I opened Pebbles' window a crack and said, "Oh just fine, thank you!"

And then Val got his first good look at my attire. His eyes went wide. He mouthed something I couldn't quite see, but I'm pretty sure it was a message along the lines of *"Are you drunk?"* Passersby slowed their pace, and I saw shutters and drapes parting all up and down the block. I opened the window fully to allow the grand tackiness of my cape to be revealed. Cowered in the filthy gates of a long closed wig shop were a couple of scrawny goth kids sharing a cigarette over a beat up guitar. One was wearing a cape print T-shirt. They looked up at me, and I waved. They waved back.

"Come home," Val ordered. His civility was wearing thin.

At which point, Brenda thought to intercede. She still had no idea. "Victor," she said, adopting a casual pose to show off her bare arms. "You having a good time?"

"Oh yes. Oh yes. 'Live each day as if it were your last' I always say."

"Whose apartment is that?" she asked, but Val pulled her back away from the window.

"Dad, what's going on?"

Perfect. Perfect, perfect. "Been going through Miss Pebbles things," I said. I was a little out of breath. The thrill of such looniness. No wonder Bobby was a dancer. "And I think I know where she is."

Val was still. Then he was gone.

"I said I know where Pebbles is, and I'm going to meet her tonight!" This I shouted to the air. If my guess was right, Val was running barefoot down the steps of our house. Back in my room, Brenda and soon her shadow, receded. She was no longer interested in my apparent breakdown.

Val burst out from the side of the building looking like a streak of ink in a comic book. He dodged cars as he trotted over the avenue, barefoot. I had only moments to get what I'd come for.

They sobered me up. I didn't see the point, but Val and Brenda fed me heavy food to soak up the alcohol I must have consumed to excess. I told Val that I thought Pebbles was hiding out in the old convent, but he didn't believe me. Perhaps I lacked credibility when I explained, "because that's where a heavenly creature would hide."

He and his mother discussed the possibility of heat stroke or sun poisoning between themselves, as if I weren't even there. I had been placed in front of the television set like a demented grandmother.

When Val stepped away to answer a phone call, Brenda seized the opportunity to hiss into my ear, "I didn't give you those pills for recreation, Vic. Take them all or don't take any."

"You know me too well. Or not at all."

She looked nervous. "Let's go for well. You're not drunk, so what is all this nonsense about?"

"I'm trying to be a good father," I said.

She passed up every smart retort that crossed her mind. I was impressed. I touched her newly tanned arm, breathed in her familiar/unfamiliar scent. "What if I said you still have a chance to see me killed?"

"Oh yeah?" She smiled crookedly.

"Go out tonight," I urged. "Try every Sazerac in the Quarter. And tell everyone you meet that your crazy ex husband is such a loser that he's gonna hook up at the old convent tonight. That he's hiding some tramp out there in the gardens."

Brenda pulled back, but she was listening.

"I told you," I said. "I found Pebbles. That's true. But you can't tell Val that it's true. It's too dangerous."

Brenda checked her objection when the boy concluded his call and came back into the room. I pretended to be absorbed with the television but was only barely attending to the newscaster pimping fresh Elvis coverage at the top of the hour. Having caught a glimpse of our apparently intimate exchange, Val asked Brenda, "How's he doing?"

Brenda proved herself. "He needs to go to bed," she said with unquestionable authority. "And I need a drink. Just let me put a little color in my cheeks, and I'm gonna see what your town has to offer a cougar on the prowl."

"Mom."

"Just kidding sweetheart. Except for the drink. I'm gonna go get hammered, not nailed."

Ugh. I was squeamish about Brenda's and Val's relationship sometimes. I leaned forward to catch the latest on The Elvis. Apparently the recording sessions had been postponed. No new video, but there was a blurry balcony picture of the man in a white robe. It looked like he was trying to grow a beard and failing. Or trying not to and failing. Either way, he didn't look healthy.

Val was still trying to get a good bicker going, talking some nonsense about safety, etc. In response, Brenda's voice got snappier. Val backed off, but only a little.

I tried to break it up in my passive aggressive way. "Hey," I said, meaning they should look at the television, but I was unsuccessful. The Elvis' spokes-lawyer was saying something unlikely about the King's desire to travel, as evidenced by his recent surprise appearance in Tennessee.

Val dogged his mother from room to room. I could have told him that was a mistake. Voices were raised, a door was slammed. Val came back to the living room and sank onto the sofa.

"She's putting on anger make up," he said.

I nodded, pointed to the set. "The Elvis is coming to New Orleans."

Val sighed. He didn't care about The Elvis. What he cared about was the fact that his family was reunited and settling back into their old habits. His mommy was going out on the town and his daddy was wigging out. Just like old times. He said, "Let's get you to bed, old man," and he walked me to my room, full of his mother's things. Perhaps in his child man's mind he thought we could share.

It was a perfect New Orleans night, hot and moist enough to nurture courtyard bound jungles. I slept little, kept awake by the street sounds and the scent of Brenda's conditioner rising up from the pillowcase. By midnight she had not yet returned, and I slipped out of my bed without Val's notice. I grabbed my cape.

On my way, I stopped into the bar at Le Richelieu Hotel for a quick gin and tonic. I needed to fortify myself for the clamber over the convent wall. There was every chance I'd be better at it the second time, right? The bar was dark and small, overlooking a glowing blue swimming pool that took up most of the courtyard. In the far corner, two lovers groped against the brick wall. An Elvis and a Vampira. Tour guides on a break. I felt in my pocket for the baby gold chain I had taken from Pebbles' apartment.

Within minutes, I was back in the convent garden, security lights and the moon competing to create the most haunting shadows. It hadn't been easier to get over the wall, but at least I was prepared for the burn of concrete that pushed my shirt up over my belly, as well as the feeling that my feet would be driven into the topsoil by the weight of the drop. The phrase "catch your breath" is too apt when you are a middle-aged, amateur stuntman.

Though I'd not specifically arranged to meet Pebbles, I hoped she would intuit my presence and offer a sign. A jumble of combatant emotions and instincts, I justified my least noble impulses by reminding myself of the larger mission. It didn't matter how the information got to Pere Qua, whether it was from Brenda's booze tour or via the multiple routes of neighborhood gossip that I'd opened throughout the day. The important thing was that he would know where I would be.

The hedges of the convent gardens were severely trimmed. Low and rectangular, they intersected to form angles. I'd never seen an aerial view of the grounds, but I wondered whether the hedges formed some kind of symbol or spelled out a warning. More likely, they kept you on the brick paths. At the present they made a startling image look even more terrifying; a dark cloaked figure traveled in my direction, and with its feet hidden by the hedge, it looked as if it were gliding above the ground. I'd expected danger, but I hadn't expected weird. Silly me.

The figure stopped. It was on the small side and then I realized—*Pebbles*. Only this time she was got up like a ghost monk or something, her hands and arms hidden in the sleeves and her pretty face entirely obscured by the hood. I hadn't seen a tour group in the vicinity, but no doubt she was expecting an audience. Seemed a little late in the evening for it, even by New Orleans' standards.

I waved her off, not sure what sense she'd make of my gesture. She didn't go away, but she didn't come any closer. After a second's hesitation she turned and moved back to the building from which she'd emerged. Then she was gone again.

Now what? No one left in the garden but me and the praying statues of saints. I announced to the night, "I am here."

And the night said, "I can see that, fool."

Jamie Boudreau, aka Pere Qua, stepped out from behind a statue of a nun we'd nicknamed "Happy," because of her Disney smile and the fact that she seemed to be wearing a bow tie along with the traditional habit and wimple. An odd choice if you wanted to make a threatening entrance.

Boudreau was dressed for it. All in black, everything skin tight, and even his hair was pulled back and shellacked down. If you were to see him on the street, you'd make one of three assumptions—that he was a criminal, a twelve stepper, or an administrator for a local charity. He was clean and mean.

I suddenly felt ridiculous in my yellow cape. This would have been an excellent time for the police to come pouring over the garden wall, as had been my hope. I'd left several phone and email messages for Detective Collier explaining to him how I planned to flush out Pere Qua for immediate capture. But the night was all jazz and crickets and car engines.

"I was looking for Pebbles," I lied.

Boudreau folded his arms, looked me up and down. His little beard was extra pointy and frankly, it looked like it was the brains of the operation.

I said, "I'm unarmed." That was completely true. I had considered carrying a weapon to this occasion, but in my heart I knew I'd do something awful with it as a result of hesitation and ineptitude. The only thing I had with me was my wits. Oh shit.

"Little girl is doing her thing," said Qua, nodding towards impenetrable shadows. "And she does it well." He grinned, showing his teeth like he liked to do. Whatever treatment he took gave them an unearthly glow. But his message was clear.

"I think it's presumptuous of you to claim credit for setting me up," I said. "This is so transparent, any other fool would have stayed away."

"Except a fool in love."

"My meaning exactly. I've trapped myself."

Qua let his tongue slip through his teeth. "That make you feel better about it all, thinking you're gonna die for love?" And then his head snapped up, as if he'd caught a whiff of something on the air. "We expecting company, *Monsieur Swaim*?"

"Guess not." I cleared my throat, stalling, hoping for some flash of insight. "Looks like you're mostly on your own these days as well. Where'd your skinny boyfriend go? Or is he an Elvis fan?"

Pere Qua stepped forward.

"So how does this happen?" I asked.

This was a question he respected. "Easy," he promised.

"And is she watching?"

Qua wasn't willing to answer that. "You need to shut your mouth." He had something heavy in his hand, held low by his hip.

"Because I have something of hers." I wrenched my cape around so I could get to my pants pocket, and as I started digging for that fragile little cross I had a brief panic that I'd lost it or crushed it or something. But Pere Qua interpreted my actions differently.

He snarled and then he leapt, like the man-dog he was, bringing us both to the ground. I really did expect to have been rescued at this point, but seeing as that wasn't happening, I reverted to infantilism, pulling my cape over like a blankie to keep out the monsters. And it worked a little. At least I couldn't see the blows coming.

Pere Qua was waling on me with a short club, but he couldn't quite figure out where to aim. I missed my cushion of fat. But by the time he straddled my back and got a good grip on my arm, bending it sharply behind, he finally got it sorted out. My knees gave way and I sprawled out beneath him, well positioned for a quick, bloody death by truncheon. Pere Qua's breathing was fast but under control. He held me down with one iron strong arm while he jammed a wad of cloth like a linen table napkin into my mouth. I presume to keep me from expressing any final words.

I gave up, released the tension in my body and just laid out limp, half across bricks, half across grass. Pere Qua was amused by that. At least it sounded like he gave out a little chuckle. Before I shut my eyes on the world for the last time, I heard the faint but showy groan of a tenor saxophone coming out of one of the clubs down the street.

And that would have been a splendid way to go. But I am, at heart, a cheater. I peeked. I opened one eye just a slit, perhaps sensing an unexpected hesitation from the man who would deliver me from all my earthly woes. And then I saw what he must have seen as well: Friar Pebbles floating our way. This dying business was strange indeed.

8.

When The Elvis came to New Orleans, he made a point of dining in the kitchens of the finest restaurants and sleeping off his meals in the best rooms his handlers could rent, usually a sun drenched suite overlooking brick streets that echoed with music, tourists, and rattling carriages. He could, lying on those wrecked white sheets, imagine he was not himself out of time, but rather himself in a time long gone—a more flexible way of thinking. The time of preference was elegant, fancy, and filthy, populated by rogues, gentlemen, and sweet young things who needed his help. He'd been reading a lot of Sherlock Holmes stories lately, spending time inside the palace of his head and refusing to sing when he didn't feel like it. Nothing in the studios was familiar. Nothing he used to know was worth knowing now.

So time was the thing. After New Orleans he thought he'd go to Poland and the Ukraine. That would be like traveling into the past, with all those cemeteries and cathedrals and bunkers. He just wanted to get back far enough to catch up. He did like orange clouds though, they were sweet. And these folks knew how to keep a secret, wearing their knowing smiles like precious jewelry. The King was impressed. He wondered if he might just stay put for a while.

His waistline was expanding, and he was concerned about his lack of libido. He didn't really feel juiced about anything except the next plate. The last medical doctor who'd checked him out asked him about depression, whether he wanted to try any of the new medications. The Elvis had emphatically rejected the notion, citing his experiences the last time around. Being sad was something he could and would shake off.

Which is why he let the night security man at The Cardinal take him by the hand at two in the morning when he was wandering the halls. The Cardinal was a six room hotel in a century old building on Dauphine, and it was very elegant, very exclusive. The night man was from the Philippines, and he did not speak English very well yet, but he could tell that the legendary performer was out of sorts, unable to rest, and looking for a distraction. The Elvis followed willingly, even as they moved out of the public portions of the building into hallways and rooms that were obviously off limits.

The basement was filled with hotel stuff—decommissioned furniture, crates of paper goods, jugs of industrial cleaner, etc. There were several lines of water damage obvious on the walls as well as scrub marks from where they'd tried to remove the stains. But the night man was moving through the room, waving The Elvis to keep up. At the back was another door that opened out into a short concrete vestibule and another set of stairs. The night man flicked on the security light, and The Elvis saw that these steps led up a half level to a secret courtyard filled with absolute junk.

This was what the night man had wanted him to see. They walked out and up.

At the back of the tiny junkyard, stacked in a sloppy pyramid against the bricks were a half dozen large television sets. Big, luxury models with deep tubes and the brand Goldstar printed on their fake wood cabinets. The Elvis had never heard of Goldstar, but this was a shocking number of television sets just dumped in a pile. It looked like bad art.

"This shit," explained the night man. He gestured back to the hotel, indicating the upper floors where the guest suites were. "Flatscreen. All new."

The Elvis nodded. Okay.

The night man tucked back into the basement and emerged with a slim, black rifle that he held by the barrel like a broom. He handed it to The Evis and said, "You go."

"I see," said the King. He took the gun, and hefted it. Semi-auto, but he didn't recognize the manufacturer. The piece was banged up but not that old, and it was certainly lighter and easier to handle than he'd expected.

The Elvis shot two television sets and he didn't enjoy it. He managed to convey his concern for disturbing the peace as his reason for not continuing. He did not try to explain to the night man what the real problem was: that shooting a television was only fun when the damned thing was on, and when there was some smug, smiling, never-shutting-up face gabbling away at him. Shooting a dead TV was no more fun than shooting a can. But he appreciated the thought.

The combination of having been beaten imprecisely, the pressure of Pere Qua's knee into my spine, and my general exhaustion made me weak in the head. Pebbles, in her brown cloak that absorbed the night, appeared to be moving towards us with supernatural grace, holding out from her deep sleeve a glinting, magical object that stayed Pere Qua's hand. What talisman worked on werewolves? I couldn't remember.

I hung between worlds. I'd like to think I warned her off, screaming past my cloth gag, but I'm pretty sure that was just me in a failing dream: tall me, young me, thin me. Smart me. Pebbles' fingers around the object were as dark as her cloak.

Pere Qua let go of me and stood up. He'd decided doing something to her was more important than doing something to me. . For the time being.

And the last thing I *really* saw, before it all blinked out? Insanity. Captain Insanity, actually, with Dum-Dum Boy. Bobby Rebar coming over the wall in my big black cape, followed by Mick in his short white cape. They were flying towards us, fast and mad.

Goddamn.

The night man insisted that The Elvis keep the rifle, and even though he rejected the gift, the damned thing was in his room the next day when he returned from Gallatoire's, bloated from Sautéed Soft Shell Crabs Meunière and Shrimp Clemenceau. He lay on the bed, gassing out, humming along to the obnoxious calliope music that was blasting from the Creole Queen, a riverboat docked blocks away. He'd enjoyed a lot of sweet wine with his banana bread pudding, and for the first time in a long time he thought he was beginning to feel like himself again. Housekeeping had drawn his curtains to keep the room cool, but he'd yanked them wide so he could watch the orange clouds curling beyond the balcony he hadn't worked up the courage to use yet. Too public. The rifle leaned against the writing desk, as innocuous as a guitar. The man felt very good. He ordered a Plantation Punch from room service, and this was delivered with an assortment of nuts and butter cookies. He sent information that when he was ready for supper, which would not be for some time, he'd like to try a stuffed mirliton or roast duck, whatever came most recommended. And then he passed a quiet afternoon.

But as the sun started to drop lower in the sky, the French doors of the most expensive suite in The Cardinal opened out onto the balcony, a wide platform that stretched the length of the building, contained by a beautiful iron rail of coils, bird sculptures, and finials made to look like pine cones. There was a filigreed iron table with two pretty chairs under an awning, a chaise for a mad man to sun himself, and a portable bar that could be stocked with liquor, ice, and a barman at a moment's notice. There was also a panel of buttons for summoning service. The sky was still mostly blue, but there was that encroaching pink around the edges of things warning that the day was sliding away and probably quite quickly. The clouds were enormous, low, and from the balcony's vantage point, almost in reach. The moon was already out, impatient to get on with the night.

Those who loitered on the banquettes below saw him right away because, to be honest, they were looking for something special. And there he was, coming out to the railing, shirtless and barefoot in black pajama bottoms with yellow Tweety Birds all over them. His chest was pale, perspiring, and his ever-growing tummy sort of poked out, but he still had the strong, triangular frame of a young man. His hair was bed-wrecked, and he was squinting. The Elvis was not immediately recognizable in this condition, partly because he appeared lonesome and foggy. And serious. He gripped the rail, looked down.

A schoolgirl stopped as if she sensed his presence. She tilted her face up, shaded her brow. She was probably only fifteen or so. He waved at her, and that's when the hubbub started. His smile was unmistakable, and pretty soon people started calling his name from the street. At first he was friendly, responding to each shout out as sweetly as he could manage, pretending to relax with his hands folded over the rail. But as a crowd gathered, getting louder and rowdier, The Elvis lost his guts.

"You all go home now," he said.

They laughed. They weren't going anywhere. Even if he meant it.

And just like that, New Orleans was spoiled for him. The spell shattered. He'd have to leave and very soon. He went back into the room and sat on the bed. The sensible thing was to call the handler and zoom outta there pronto. The crowd outside started a little "come out, come out" chant that went strong for a while, and then faded before it transformed into a song. They sang "Heartbreak Hotel."

Well damn. He kind of liked that. Or maybe not. He felt good one second, shitty the next. And his head was hurting like hell. The migraines were back. He'd not had one since he'd returned, and now they were back? He didn't think he could live through migraines again.

The crowd adjusted to his suffering. They sang "Love Me Tender" next.

Moments later he reappeared to cheers. The crowd had tripled in size and cars were trapped on either end of the block. He trailed the rifle behind him like a toy, and no one saw it until he raised it up and took aim.

At the clouds.

One of the hallmarks of a true hero is that he is never confused. Bobby and Mick had quickly assessed the situation and decided that without a doubt the bad guy here was the ghostly Friar. As they tackled the robed figure the cloak's hood fell back to reveal Detective Danny Collier and not my sweet Pebbles underneath. Pere Qua seemed especially confused; he had been ready to give up on his evening's mission, and I imagine he'd planned to make some show of surrender to stall the cop before bolting from the gardens. The Detective was only one man, after all. But when these tattered, misguided super heroes arrived and attacked Collier, Qua realized he had time to be more thoughtful about the situation.

Collier was swearing, but all I could see was a pile of capes in a ball of violence. Since Qua was distracted by the live action cartoon, I rolled away from him and managed to spit out the rag. This was my rescue?

"Jesus Christ!" I shouted. "He's a cop!"

Pere Qua pivoted on his boot heel and smiled at me like he had all the time in the world. Well, like he had just enough time for a quick murder before the third set began at Café Brasil.

But what he did not know was that behind him Wish Phantoms were coming over the wall, dropping not at all like white winged angels, but like gargoyles, spoiling for nasty fun.

One huge, deep cloud looked like a savaged blood orange. The Elvis aimed, fired. Hit. There were some in the crowd who screamed, but they shut up quick to listen to an impossible creak coming from the sky. It started out metallic but finished like a whale song. The Elvis sobered and took another shot. The next creak was supremely extended. The agony was unmistakable.

Someone said, "Is it alive?"

Barges cruise the Port of New Orleans, and they come from all over, carrying oil, soybeans, you name it. They move slowly, deliberately, as if they are there to remind us that there are other places in the world, other frames of mind. But the damned things crash all the time. Crash into each other, into the Riverwalk, into bridges. One took out a 200 foot chunk of bridge at rush hour. Forty cars went right in the water. The sound of a barge grazing what it shouldn't, that's a horrible thing. Terrifying, because you know it can't stop. Not till it's done.

That's what this sounded like. Like terror, like the breaking heart of Leviathan. "Again," said someone else.

And The Elvis gave the people what they wanted. He always did, you know.

Finding that I was no longer the center of anyone's immediate concern, I reassessed. Here I was in the middle of a legendarily sacred location, the celebrated gardens of The Old Ursuline Convent, after midnight, somewhat beaten up, and wearing an ugly yellow cape.

Mick's Phantoms, all five who had come to our spook party, were a democratic lot. Three came for Pere Qua, and the other two joined Mick and Bobby in their thuggish beat down of Detective Collier, who was still trying to brandish his badge and ID. It was good for him they were poor at this, like schoolchildren, but still I thought he'd do better to draw his weapon soon.

I, on the other hand, just hobbled away. At least until I got to the wall and realized that there was no way I could get over again, not with the several points of pain now radiating throughout my body—my chest and back especially, where most of the blows had struck true. I leaned against the bars next to the vehicle gate. Two young ladies, dressed in the tightest of skirts and the tallest of heels, walked by and squealed when they saw me there.

"Evening," I said, rummaging around for my cell. "My dears, I'm about to call the police, but if you could be troubled, perhaps you might give a call as well?"

One girl, The Brave One I could tell, looked into the garden. Detective Collier had indeed gotten the upper hand and was straddling a wheezing Bobby Rebar as Mick stood back, unsure of what to do next. The Detective appeared to be speaking very firmly, and yes his gun was officially brandished.

"Whoa. Thought you was a ghost, sir," said the girl. The other was searching through her purse. The Obedient, Responsible One. Together they would go far.

"Thank you, love." I punched in the numbers and was

relieved to see that the full compliment of Wish Phantoms, Mick included, had regrouped to concentrate their efforts on containment of Pere Qua. Assuming that Collier had already requested some sort of back-up either before or during the adventure, and also assuming that his request was rendered a medium priority at best, I tried another tack with the 911 operator.

"The convent archive is on fire," I said. And I hung up.

Collier stepped off of Bobby to approach the prone and ornately swearing Jamie Boudreau, who seemed unhappy to be restrained by a gang of skate punks reeking of Axe Bodywash. Cuffing Qua's wrists behind his back, Collier instructed Mick to stand watch over the prisoner. The rest of the Phantoms he dismissed. That seemed sensible. In addition to reducing confusion, Collier could enhance his reputation by making it seem as if he needed only minimal help to subdue one of the last and most persistent of the Death Cultists.

The boys scrambled over the wall. Mick looked wistful, like he wanted to go with them. Bobby lay still under the stars and slivered moon with that "Uncle" look on his face. My ladies had wandered off in a fit of giggles, clattering to the next jazz club as if it were the 1920s. Collier wiped the sweat from his brow and came to me. "You don't look that good, Mr. Swaim."

I guess I didn't. My adrenaline ebbing, I slumped against the gate, letting my cape drag in the grass. "I'm a little tired," I said. "Where's Pebbles?"

I recognized instinct in Collier's eyes, and my body took that as permission to collapse. Collier caught me under my arms before I fell. "Miss Lewis is safe. She's at a hotel uptown," he said, easing me down. "She called me, you know. Saying you were gonna do something stupid." He laughed softly, and sat in the grass beside me as we listened for the sirens.

"Stay awake," Collier said. "You might have a concussion."

"I don't care," I said. My eyes were already closed. I thought, *I'm ready, aren't I?*

The cloud came down to rest on Louisa Street, like a fat lady's foot in a skinny shoe. It moaned softly as it descended, and before it hit the tar and chip, everyone watching was in tears.

For the first time ever, The Elvis was on a stage and no one cared. He lowered the rifle and prayed.

The orange cloud touched the ground, and its weeping ceased. At first it began to contract like cotton candy, but then it stopped moving altogether. As the neighborhood and its visitors held their breath, the cloud commenced the most natural of processes. It began to dissipate, to burn off. It was only fog, after all.

9.

I love spirits but I'm not good with pharmacologicals. And believe me I've given them a good shot. But they make me dream repetitive dreams. This time the thing that kept rolling through my head was the sentence, "He killed a cloud"—news delivered to me by Detective Collier, one of my many visitors while I was still in the hospital. You'd think I'd remember the people I loved most sharply, but no. Val and Martine were blurs. Brenda was a blur as well, except that I noticed she was wearing one of my bowling shirts, a sure sign she'd settled in. Later, Martine would tease me for calling him "Canada" in my druggy haze, but I think I was probably trying to ask him if I could move into his guest room on a permanent basis.

Collier's active, dancing eyes. A bandage along the side of his brow, attractively cocked like a theatrical injury. He was there to tell me what, again? I know he said a lot. I know he was in golf clothes. "Fucking Elvis. He killed a cloud."

But then I woke up in my own room in Val's house, my face being stroked by soft fingers. Pebbles. I shut my eyes tight. Could be Brenda. Was probably Brenda.

Pebbles giggled, and I opened my eyes. I've never seen a sweeter smile. She was in my desk chair and had somehow ridden its three good wheels to my bedside. My mouth was all dry cotton and salt, and if I'd any moisture left in me I would have been squeezing out tears. A quick look around the room. Brenda's stuff was nowhere in sight.

"She's gone?"

"Ladies and gentlemen, his first words back on earth, and he's still worried about his ex." Pebbles put her cool lips on my forehead. She was wearing a v-neck something or other, and her lovely bosom floated over me. As did a tiny gold cross on an impossibly delicate chain. I made a grab. She pulled back and laughed, putting her hand where my hand was going to go.

"Thank you Victor. This cheap little trinket means the world to me."

Ah well. "Good luck charm," I croaked. The strange grin on her face said, *I don't think Jesus would agree.* But she let it go. I was, after all, a broken up old man.

"Qua," I said.

Pebbles shook her head. "Collier says we're to let it go, Vic. He talked to you about it already. Boudreau ain't going through the usual system. None of them are." She shuddered. "I wish I didn't know that, but I guess Collier thought telling me would make me feel safer. It doesn't. Now I just think dark thoughts about the powers that be, you know?"

I didn't remember Collier telling me anything like that. But there were definitely fragments floating around my brain, sometimes turning and catching the light like flakes of glitter. I knew it would come back to me as I got stronger.

"Anyways, Val's momma moved down to the TV room. She doesn't look like she plans on leaving any time soon." Pebbles handed me a tepid cup of water. I hadn't noticed it waiting for me. I gulped greedily, and she added, "And he sure likes having her here." She sighed like that was a difficult fact of life. "This whole thing." She made a sweeping gesture to include my infirmity. "It's kinda like Hamlet, right?"

I tried to imagine what she meant by that. Though my throat really didn't want me making any lengthy speeches, I could not let this pass. "It's not. Hamlet and his mother don't see eye to eye, and his father is dead before the play starts. You'd know that if you'd read the Shakespeare instead of cutting out the pages."

"Really?" Pebbles looked honestly surprised. "Well don't get snotty about it. Book was like that when I bought it. So what happens to Hamlet's girlfriend?"

Now she had to be teasing me. But if she wasn't I hadn't the heart to clue her in. Suddenly I recalled Martine's jabber about Pebbles, about her fierce desire to be a part of our family. Well, there was even less room now than there had been before. I swear I was still mulling over the possibility of making the sacrifice and putting her needs above mine when the words came out of my mouth on their own accord: "She goes back to Arkansas."

Pebbles didn't protest. I could see she'd already come to that conclusion on her own, and that this conversation was just a test drive of the idea. I wasn't surprised. New Orleans, for Pebbles, had amounted to a failed experiment. She took the cup back and placed it on the bedside table. A prescription bottle tilted against the reading lamp. "Yeah, you're a good guesser. My Dad thinks I should go back to school. I did pretty good for a while there."

I recalled the Dean's letter. I tried to imagine what her father was like. Like me? Like Jamie Boudreau? No, probably a good deal nicer. And younger, no doubt. "I love you," I said.

Pebbles just smiled. It occurred to me that she had heard those words so many more times in her life than I had in mine. Her grace was breathtaking. I didn't feel embarrassed at all. She said, "You should take another pain pill, it's way past time."

"No," I said. I took her hand and put it on my face. She let me. I wanted to stay like that forever. Miss Annabeth Lewis of Arkansas, aka Pebbles, the love of my life. By the time I awoke I didn't even look for her. I knew she was gone. For good this time.

Over the following weeks, as I recovered from my wounds, something very ordinary happened. The clouds over New Orleans faded slowly until they turned white again. It was impossible not to take that as a sign.

There were other signs as well. The buttershrimp suddenly stopped reproducing, and they were over fished in a heartbeat. Poor Val, he was already a wreck. Pebbles had gone, and now he was back to the small time. At least he still had his mother and the clothing shop. And Bobby Rebar to help him out every once in a while. We were trying our darnedest to remember to call him Terry. The use of his given name seemed to calm him, but I wasn't at all sure that he'd ceased his midnight capers.

Brenda spent a lot of time on the phone, and it seemed to me that she was talking with professionals. Lawyers? If she divorced Rick how did she think she was going to support herself? It's not like they needed more under-published Cultural Studies professors in New Orleans. But I didn't ask, and she didn't tell. She tended to me, dressed my wounds, kept me on my schedule. I healed at a reasonable pace, and the pain I felt was mostly good. Like blues pain.

We went out sometimes, to cafes mostly. She called it social therapy. I missed Pebbles very much, but unlike Val I had to keep the nature of my grief suppressed. Once, Brenda held my hand under the table at The Court of Two Sisters while we enjoyed a jazz brunch. Her touch was neither pleasant nor unpleasant, but it opened a portal to the future. She'd have me again, and I'd probably be grateful. But not just yet.

My first non-Brenda outing was at the behest of Martine, who seemed perfectly healthy but unwilling to abandon recuperation as a lifestyle. I tried to tell him that this condition of full time leisure and socializing was called "retirement." He even favored an elegant walking stick as part of his whole get up. But one day he decided it was time for me to get in on the inaction, and when he called he said, "Victor, get dressed. We're going to a memorial service. One of NOPD's finest is being laid to rest."

I thought the worst. "No. Detective Collier?"

"Don't be ridiculous. It's Butchy the dope dog. You remember him? German Shepherd with displaysia."

"I can't say as I've met the poor thing."

"Brave bastard was gunned down by a cornered meth head. They're remembering him with a service at the Moon Walk in an hour."

I saw where this was going. "And a wake, no doubt."

"Yes sir, Tallulah's. All the Abita you can suck down. The pup favored Purple Haze, I'm told."

"You get invited to all the best parties," I said.

"One of the many benefits of being a member of the Chamber of Commerce, my son."

By late morning the heat was intense, and the officers in their dress blues were sweating like hippos. We'd enjoyed a prayer breakfast along with moving tributes to Butchy's heroism, but Tallulah's air conditioning was on the fritz. Even free beer wasn't worth the discomfort. Time to call it a morning. Martine and I strolled the length of the Riverwalk, in the direction of Governor Nicholls, towards another bar we knew, a little less swanky than Tallulah's but hell, it was icy, without windows or tourists. We went in, drank charmless mixed drinks and watched some mysterious European sport on the silent television set above the bar. That early on a weekday, no one else but hardcore alkies in there with us. It was a comfort, if only because we knew where the hell we stood.

It seemed inevitable. Martine was the most patient man alive, I decided. Waiting for me to get back to myself. To shake off the girl and remember how to enjoy life. I was starting to regain my weight, and I wasn't all that concerned about it.

I checked my watch. "I promised Val I'd watch the shop this afternoon. He's taking Brenda to high tea at the Ritz."

Martine smiled. "You're kidding me."

"Nope. You ready to go?"

"I'm gonna have another." He nodded to the set. "And learn the rules for cricket or whatever the hell this is."

"Suit yourself." I left some cash next to my empty glass and walked out of the icy bar into the profound humid heat of a New Orleans afternoon, which is a little like stumbling into the cleavage of a planet sized working gal. A nice, clear sky, the kind that was so happily abusive. On my own, for the first time in a long time, I realized. I could do anything I wanted to. If I wanted to do anything.

I wondered if cancer was due for a comeback. So many things had reverted to their pre-wish status. We still had The Elvis, but he'd lost quite a bit of his charm and novelty. Losing him again would be perfectly acceptable if that meant cats were coming back.

This is what I was musing on as I took my first unaccompanied walk since that night in the convent garden.

I hadn't gotten very far when a young black kid in a school uniform stepped out from behind a grimy, life sized plaster lion that guarded the entrance to Breaux Lo Mein Hot Noodles. He had a long, narrow fish knife in his hand. He was shaky, sweaty, and sick colored around his lips and eyes.

Well, well. Well damn.

The fish knife was for me, I knew that. His shirt front was stained dark with cooked, dried blood.

I asked, "What do you want?" But I knew. The boy was going to do me.

I tossed him my wallet. He didn't want it.

Gently, gently, Victor. "Where the hell you been, boy? The wishing is over. The Elvis saw to that." I tried to keep the panic out of my voice. "And these wish killings, they don't work. Have you ever heard of one working?"

But reason didn't have a chance. There was no telling if this boy was an evangelist or just a street punk out of the loop. He placed his other hand on the knife and held it forward as if it were a broad sword. He tilted his head down a little and glared at me with sick eyes. He'd taken a ceremonial stance.

"Praise Jesus," I said. Try anything, is my advice.

"Yes, Sir. Thank you, Sir."

Polite boy. Violent boy. Probably fast as a whippet dog.

I couldn't run away, that'd be a great way to get stabbed in the back. So I ran at him. He squealed, "Oh no, Sir, please!" and that thin little blade just slipped right up under my ribs. *Wow*. Not really what I had planned. I'd been betting on less inertia and a duller blade. The boy and I went down to the banquette, hard. It reeked of beer and ash, and I felt like I'd been shot with a searing diamond bullet. I'd wondered how the psychological toll of all that had happened was going to manifest, and now I knew. I'd become the sort who ran towards boys with knives. Interesting.

The boy cracked his head, I heard that much. Me, I was flopped over him like a stinking whale. Blood poured from us both. The next thing I remember was the bartender, Martine, and some hooker with black shoes, all of them crowding around, yelling at us to stay awake. My thoughts were weary. *This again.* They rolled me off the boy and I think I heard him groan. I hoped I did.

The knife was in me all the way. I heard somebody say that. Didn't see it, myself. Couldn't. Didn't feel it much either. I grew cold. Cold in July in New Orleans.

In and out. More out than in. Bless me all to fuck. Brenda was right all those years ago; I hung out with the wrong crowd. Not a single one of these bar flies knew how to keep a dying man from dying so fast. That didn't mean they were indifferent. Martine knelt next to me, his voice real close: "Kid's dead, Vic. Kid's gone. You hear the sirens?" He stroked me, touched me everywhere like he didn't know what else he could do.

Death wishes were over. None of them happening any more.

That didn't seem to matter.

I wasn't sure how was I gonna go with this thing. Artsy or profound? Did I really believe in small wishes? I did not.

The black shod lady said, "Wish us some money, baby."

"Shut up," Martine said, real hysteria in his voice. He leaned down, "Hon' it's gonna be okay. You hear me?"

It wasn't going to be okay. I was born to die.

Then there was some kind of struggle, Martine going after someone. He was in no condition for a fight. I think the bartender wanted to quiet me before I could utter a damned thing. I guess the hooker helped Martine because the skirmish grew faint, and I was allowed to concentrate on what I had done with my life and what it had all led up to. My family was a most tentative thing. I had never done good, never done bad. I had only done things weak and strong. I had never invented anything and never spoke an original line. I was top to bottom, unremarkable. I had made no mark.

Now was my chance.

I really believed that. Which meant I was an idiot. Grasping at straws. My last breath . . . I waited on it like an old professor waiting for his new girlfriend. Seemed like days. Finally I said my wish, and I hope it took: "Remember me."

ACKNOWLEDGEMENTS

Sections of *Death Wishing* were previously published elsewhere as short stories. "That What" appeared in *Pank*. "Do You know What It Means" appeared in *Juked*. "Wish Tank" appeared in *Barrelhouse*. "The Elvis" appeared in *>killauthor*. "Karaoke People Are Happy People" appeared in *Storyglossia*. I thank the editors of those fine journals as well as Steve Himmer, Erin Fitzgerald, Danny Collier, and Meg Pokrass for their advice and patience. And to Robert Lasner and Elizabeth Clementson of Ig Publishing, a special thank you for standing by this book.